EVERY TRICK
IN THE BOOK

T0352940

EVERY TRICK IN THE BOOK

Bernard O'Keeffe

MUSWELL
PRESS

First published by Muswell Press in 2024
Typeset in Bembo by M Rules
Copyright © Bernard O'Keeffe 2024

Bernard O'Keeffe has asserted his right to be identified
as the author of this work in accordance with under the
Copyright, Designs and Patents Act, 1988

A CIP catalogue record for this book
is available from the British Library

ISBN: 9781739471606
eISBN: 9781739471613

Muswell Press
London N6 5HQ
www.muswell-press.co.uk

For Rory

Prologue

During his long teaching career Alex Ballantyne liked to point out to his pupils that 'ironic' was one of the most misused words in the English language.

He would play them the Alanis Morissette song of the same name, give them the lyrics, and show how the word was being incorrectly applied throughout. Rain on your wedding day wasn't ironic – it was just bad luck. Likewise ten thousand spoons when you need a knife. Or a traffic jam when you're already late.

The Canadian singer, Mr Ballantyne would say, just didn't get it and, being a learned man who valued knowledge and truth and who was keen that all he taught should do likewise, he would go on to give precise definitions of the way 'ironic' could properly be used. Had his pupils been paying careful attention they would have left his classroom with a clear grasp of irony in all its manifestations – verbal, dramatic, situational, historical, even Socratic.

And had Alex Ballantyne still been able to speak he would have been able to tell any St Jude's pupils who happened to be passing in the early hours of that July morning what, if any, kind of irony could be applied to his current situation – whether being found dead in the reeds of Barnes Pond only hours after his farewell party, an occasion marked by so many wishes for a happy, healthy and long retirement, could correctly be described as 'ironic'.

Everyone who heard the news, both at the school where he had taught and in the community in which he had lived, was appalled. That the newly retired English teacher should be found dead was shocking. That his death should be regarded as suspicious, and possibly murder, was unimaginable.

On this, the first day of the summer holidays, St Jude's School would usually be a place of peace and tranquillity, but today it was bustling with activity. Detectives were questioning the head and members of his senior management team, gathering information about the man who had so recently been a member of staff. Journalists and news crews hovered outside the gates. And phones were busy. Everyone connected to the school – teachers, parents and pupils – was in excited discussion, trying to work out exactly what had happened to Alex Ballantyne and, more significantly, why.

The community of Barnes was equally traumatised. To see police cars parked on the green next to the pond and a forensic tent erected in the heart of the village came as a huge shock to all who had chosen to live here because it was such a quiet area, but particularly to those who had regarded the deceased as a friend and neighbour and could think of no possible reason why anyone should want to kill him.

But it would be untrue to say that there was universal dismay at the demise of Alex Ballantyne. Though none would say so in public, where the only sentiments expressed were those of sadness at the loss of a good man, there were some who were pleased he was no longer alive, hoping that with him had died secrets they would like to stay forever hidden.

(from *Schooled in Murder* by Ben Joseph)

1

Garibaldi looked forward to three things on a Saturday night – a takeaway curry, *Match of the Day* and sex. Not always in that order, and with the third not always guaranteed.

Although he loved reading and never went anywhere without a book, he'd never been one for literary talks. He'd been to a few in the past but had been so disappointed that those who had written books he loved could talk about them so badly that he had for a long time steered clear of them.

So it came as a surprise to find himself, on this particular Saturday evening, sitting in the audience at the OSO listening to a writer talking about his latest book.

It came as even more of a surprise to find himself enjoying it.

'Thank you so much for coming along this evening,' said the man on stage, drawing things to a conclusion. He was wearing chinos, a blue jacket, a striped button-down shirt and a grey scarf. It was the scarf, Garibaldi decided, that made him look like a writer. 'And thanks in particular to the wonderful organisers of the Barnes Book Festival. I'm thrilled and humbled by the way the book has been received – and, of course, by the way it's sold – and I'm particularly pleased to have been able to talk in the area in which it is set. And what a delight it is to see so many familiar faces in the audience.'

Garibaldi looked round the room. He too saw many familiar faces. Not of people he knew, but of people he felt he knew from having walked past them so many times at local haunts – the Farmers' Market, the Bull's Head, the Red Lion, the Olympic Cinema, the tables outside Feast, the independent coffee shops, the benches by the pond and here, the Old Sorting Office Arts Centre. All radiating the Barnes self-confidence that bordered on smugness.

A woman stepped forward on the stage. Garibaldi recognised her as the owner of the local bookshop.

'Well, wasn't that great! A particularly fitting way to round off the Barnes Book Festival because not only is the author local but so is his book. Ben will be signing copies in the foyer, all provided by the Barnes Bookshop, so do get yourself a copy if you haven't already got one. And if you already do have one then get one for a friend! And, once again, a big thank you to Ben Joseph.'

The audience broke into applause.

Rachel turned to Garibaldi. 'What do you reckon, then?'

Garibaldi smiled and gave a nod of approval. 'Not as bad as I feared.'

'So you might get round to reading it then?' Rachel held up her copy of *Schooled in Murder*.

Garibaldi reached out for it. 'You know what? I might even start it tonight.'

Rachel snatched her hand away. 'OK. I'll just get it signed.'

'Signed?'

'Why not? It's nice to have signed copies.'

4

Garibaldi smiled, unconvinced. 'OK,' he said, getting up from his chair. 'I'll get some drinks.'

When he came back from the bar Rachel was standing by the window, book in hand, looking out onto Barnes Green.

'So what did the great man have to say?' said Garibaldi.

Rachel opened the book at the title page and held it up in front of him. 'I told him I was a teacher and he wrote this.'

Garibaldi looked at the inscription –

To Rachel - one of the noblest profession.

'Bit rude, isn't it?'

'What do you mean?'

Garibaldi peered closer at the writing. 'One of the oldest profession?'

Rachel pulled the book back and checked the inscription. 'Very funny.'

Garibaldi handed her the wine and held up his whisky. 'Cheers!' he said, clinking her glass.

'Cheers! Glad you came?'

'I had my doubts.'

'Tell me about it. It was like I'd suggested a visit to the dentist.'

'Well, you know how it is, there's something about Saturday night ...' He checked his watch. 'And it's still pretty early, so ...'

He trailed off and sipped his whisky, encouraged by Rachel's slight nod.

He took her hand as they left the OSO and led her to a bench by the pond where they sat for a few moments, saying nothing, looking at the ducks on the still, dark water. Then they walked along the High Street in the direction of the river and turned off for Rutland Court,

5

Garibaldi's mind very much on the third of his Saturday night pleasures.

When he reached for his key at the front door to the flat he heard a voice behind him.

'Dad?'

At first he thought he had imagined it.

'Dad?'

There it was again – louder this time and definitely real. He turned towards it. 'Alfie! What—?'

'Something's happened.'

'Are you OK?'

'Yeah, I'm fine, but—'

'What is it?'

'Can I stay here tonight?'

Garibaldi looked at Rachel. 'Of course you can. But what . . . why?'

He pushed the door open and followed Rachel and Alfie inside. Alfie threw his rucksack on the couch, took off his coat and sat down with a heavy sigh.

'Why don't I make up the spare bed?' said Rachel, heading to the tiny second bedroom.

'Sure,' said Garibaldi. He waited for Rachel to shut the door behind her and turned to Alfie. 'Drink?'

'Yeah,' said Alfie. 'Anything.'

Garibaldi went to the kitchen and came back with two whiskies.

'Take your time,' he said. 'Whatever you want to tell me.'

Alfie took a big slug of his whisky. 'OK. I've had a row. A big row.'

A big row? Who with? Alicia? Kay?

'I mean, what a prick!'

Or Dom?

Was this the moment Garibaldi had been longing for?

Had Alfie at last reached the conclusion he himself had come to many years ago about the man his wife had left him for?

'Look, Alfie,' he said. 'Remember one thing. You're always welcome here. And you can stay for as long as you want.'

As he said the words Rachel emerged from the second bedroom. 'All sorted,' she said, giving Alfie a smile.

One of the many things Garibaldi loved about Rachel was the way she got on so well with Alfie. He knew she would have no problem with him staying.

Why, then, did he feel so uneasy at the prospect?

Maybe it was the uncertainty. He had yet to find out what the row was about and, suddenly conscious that a flat comfortable for two could sometimes seem crowded for three, he had no idea how long Alfie would be staying.

2

Those locals who like to think of Barnes as a cosy community that has more in common with the country than the capital, call the pond that lies at its heart the 'Village Pond' or simply 'The Pond'. Some, in recognition of the creatures most often seen on its waters, call it the 'Duck Pond' while others, mainly outsiders, follow the lead of Transport for London's naming of the nearest bus stop, and call it 'Barnes Pond'.

Recent arrivals (and well-established residents would consider recent to include anyone who had moved to Barnes within the last twenty years) have no idea that the pond as it is today looks nothing like the pond it once was. They have no sense that the original Barnes Pond was simply that – a pond. There were no gravel areas on which parents could stand with their children and feed the ducks. There were no fences and serried steps and there was not much foliage, no clumps of reeds round the edges. Nor was there much wildlife beyond a few ducks. Recent arrivals will have no idea that the original pond mysteriously emptied itself in 2001 and that when it was refilled two years later, reshaped, remodelled and landscaped with advice from the Wildfowl & Wetlands Trust, it was another thing entirely.

This was certainly the case with Tom Murray, who liked to take Pandora to feed the ducks every Sunday morning. It was a well-established ritual, his way of giving his wife a break and of having special time with his daughter. He would get up when Pandora woke, put her in front of some kids' cartoons, give her breakfast and then take her out, allowing Tilly a lie-in.

He'd take Pandora in the pushchair to Gail's, pick up coffee and a pastry and head back to the pond to his favourite bench. Not one of those by the gravel area facing the Sun Inn but one of those to the side of Barnes Green Day Centre looking across the pond to Essex House, the location of the Saturday Farmers' Market. He would turn the pushchair so that Pandora could look out onto the water between the clumps of tall reeds, sit down on the bench, sip his coffee and tuck into his pastry.

Pandora was happy to sit in her pushchair and look out for the ducks, who, sensing that food was in the offing, would start to drift over. And Tom was happy to sit there for a few minutes, enjoying the peace. This side of the pond was not as public as the gravel area and there was less chance here of being disturbed by other early morning baby walkers. Whenever any of them met up together, particularly other early-morning dads like himself, the conversation was unbearable.

When he had finished his pastry Tom got off the bench, lifted Pandora out of her pushchair and held her hand as he led her down the steps to the water's edge. He opened the bag of food and threw some towards the ducks that had gathered in anticipation. Pandora gave a delighted laugh as the ducks darted towards the bread. Tom handed her some and she threw it in herself, leaning close to the water as he held her arm tightly, a smile beaming on her face as she saw the ducks eating what she had given them.

Tom marvelled at how much pleasure could be derived from something he had done himself when he was young, something his parents and their parents had probably done before him. Despite laptops, phones, screens and technology, this simple bond with nature remained as strong as ever. Nothing had diminished the pleasure that could be gleaned from something as simple as feeding ducks on the village pond.

He crouched down beside his daughter, and as he did, something caught his eye in the clump of tall reeds to his right. At first he couldn't work out what it was. It looked like an item of clothing – a jacket or a coat perhaps. He leaned closer, keeping a firm grip on Pandora and tried to get a better look. Yes, it was definitely clothing. Maybe someone had thrown it into the pond last night. He knew that these benches were popular with late night drinkers, particularly teenagers, and he had often, on these Sunday morning duck-feeds, found evidence of their Saturday night revelry – empty cans, discarded pizza boxes, cigarette ends. He sometimes didn't look too closely at what had been left on the ground for fear of what he might discover.

When the food had gone and Pandora had seen enough of the ducks Tom turned back to the pushchair, looking to the left to get a better view of what had been thrown into the reeds.

He was right. It was a jacket.

But as he peered closer he realised it wasn't just a jacket.

He put Pandora in the pushchair, secured her straps and walked back to the pond's edge to check he'd seen correctly.

He stood by the reeds to look down, and his suspicions were confirmed.

It wasn't just a jacket.

It was a body.

Tom looked back at Pandora and then turned again to look at the body, face down in the reeds.

'Let's get you home,' he said to Pandora as he took hold of the pushchair and walked away from the pond. As he passed the other parents on duck-feed duty he heard nothing of their conversation. His mind was set on getting his daughter home safely, telling his wife what he had found and working out whether there was any way of avoiding phoning the police.

'Hello, I'm Johnny Cash.'

Garibaldi sat in the audience looking at the great American country singer. The BookFest had really pulled off a coup this year. How on earth did they get Johnny Cash to come to Barnes?

'I'd like to sing you a new song,' said the Man in Black. 'It's called, "You left me for that asshole". And it goes like this . . .'

He started to pick at his guitar and over the steady rhythm began to sing:

When I was down, when I was blue.
When nothing in the world seemed true
You walked right out and took my son
To live with that asshole.

Johnny Cash looked out at the OSO audience. They were on their feet, clapping in time and singing along as he broke into the chorus:

That asshole. That asshole.
You left me for that asshole.

Garibaldi stood up and joined in the clapping and singing, swaying from side to side and punching the air on each syllable of 'asshole'.

He felt something in his side. Was it an elbow? He turned to the woman next to him. It couldn't have been her. Both her arms were raised above her head as she clapped along.

There it was again. Definitely an elbow.

He turned again. The woman didn't respond. She was lost in Johnny Cash.

Another poke in the ribs. This time with words.

'Jim?'

He turned again to the woman. She was still singing along.

'Jim?'

He recognised the voice now.

'Rachel?'

'Wake up, Jim.'

He opened his eyes and turned to the voice. Rachel was looking at him, her head propped up by an elbow on her pillow.

Garibaldi yawned and rubbed his eyes.

'You were singing,' said Rachel.

'Singing?'

'Yeah. In your sleep. Your eyes were shut but you were singing. Well, when I say singing it was more of a wail.'

'What was I—?'

'Nothing I recognised. All I could make out was the word "asshole".'

It came back to him. Johnny Cash. The OSO. Barnes BookFest. Alfie.

'It was a dream.'

'Sounds like an interesting one.'

'Yeah. I—'

'Your phone's been ringing.'

'My phone?'

'Yeah. In the living room.'

What was his phone doing in the living room? He always kept it by his bed.

'Alfie,' he said. 'Alfie was here, wasn't he?'

'I turned in to let you talk. I don't know when you got to bed but I guess it was late. What happened? Is everything OK?'

'He had a row with Dom.'

'I see.'

Garibaldi lifted himself up on his elbows. 'And he wants to stay here for a while.'

'OK.'

'I'm sorry.'

'You don't have to apologise . . .'

'I mean, I'm glad he came here, that he felt he could—'

'It's OK. Really.'

'This isn't exactly a big flat, is it?'

'Look. He can stay here as long as he needs to. It's fine.'

'But—'

'What was the row about?'

Garibaldi hauled himself up and sat back against the headboard.

'He hasn't been specific, but something Dom said clearly got to him.'

'And Kay?'

'Alfie didn't mention her.'

Rachel pointed at the door. 'Maybe that was her on the phone.'

Garibaldi threw on a dressing gown and went into the living room, wondering what kind of state he must have been in to leave his phone there. He glanced at the closed door of the spare room and thought of Alfie behind it. He'd slept there many times before, but not often since Rachel moved in.

His phone rang as he reached for it. He picked it up, thinking Rachel was probably right and it would be Kay. His ex-wife always rang him (and blamed him) whenever anything went wrong with Alfie.

It was another name on the screen.

'Hi boss.'

'Jim,' said DCI Deighton.' Where are you? I've been ringing all morning.'

'I'm at home.'

'Why didn't you pick up?'

'I was in the bath.'

'Pretty long bath.'

'I was pretty dirty.'

'We've got a body.'

'Where?'

'A stone's throw from where you're speaking. The pond.'

'The pond?'

'Barnes Pond. Isn't that just round the corner from you?'

'Yes, but—'

'We need you there.'

'OK.'

'You don't even need to cycle. You can walk. So let's get on it.'

Garibaldi looked at the phone in his hand, wondering whether he'd heard correctly. A body in Barnes Pond?

It was like hearing that the ravens had left the castle or that the sun hadn't risen.

*

Garibaldi took a back route, going down Grove Road and cutting through Essex Court. As soon as he reached the pavement of Station Road he could see the police cars and vans and the forensic tent erected on the other side of the pond.

People stood in huddles, looking in the direction of the tent, pointing, turning, speculating. Curious children were being shepherded away from the scene by concerned parents wanting to protect them from whatever atrocity had been committed.

DS Gardner walked towards Garibaldi in a forensic suit. 'Where've you been?'

'I missed a few calls.'

Gardner shook her head. 'Sod's Law. A murder literally on your doorstep and you turn up late.'

'What is it?'

'Male. Sixties. Found by a bloke this morning feeding the ducks with his daughter.'

'ID?'

'Called Tom Murray. Comes here every Sunday morning.'

Garibaldi rolled his eyes. Did she do it deliberately?

'I meant the body.'

'Right.' Gardner flicked open her notebook. ' Liam Allerton. Lives locally. Cambridge Road.'

'What happened to him?'

'Difficult to tell. Doc Stevenson's looking at him. He was found in the water so could be he drowned. Looks very shallow but apparently it doesn't take much, and if he'd been drinking . . .'

'Next of kin?'

'Wife. She's been informed. And a daughter.'

'Anything on his movements last night?'

15

'His wife says he was drinking with friends in there.' Gardner pointed across the pond at the Sun Inn. 'Maybe he was drunk and—'

'OK.' Garibaldi started to put on his forensic suit, cap and shoes.

'Is the bloke who found him here?'

Gardner pointed at a man standing with a uniform. 'Over there.'

'Do we know anything else about him? Allerton, that is.'

'Not much yet.'

Garibaldi slipped on a forensic suit, over-shoes and gloves and moved towards the tent. Gardner followed him as he pushed open the flap.

Martin Stevenson was bent over a body on the gravel at the water's edge.

Garibaldi stood behind him. 'Morning doc.'

'What kept you?' said Stevenson, without turning.

'It's complicated.'

'Do you know that over a quarter of deaths by drowning occur in less than three feet of water?'

'So he drowned, then?'

'Difficult to tell. There are bruises on the side of his neck consistent with strangulation, but I won't be able to say until we open him up whether that's the cause of death. As I said, it could be drowning. Interestingly, it doesn't look as though he put up much resistance. I can tell you one thing, though.'

'What's that?'

'I've never seen such traumatised ducks. I mean – a body in Barnes Pond? Never thought I'd see the day.'

Stevenson stood up and stepped back. Garibaldi moved forward and looked down at the body.

It was the clothes he recognised first. The chinos. The

striped button-down shirt. The blue jacket. The grey scarf round the neck. The face, pale, puffed and bloated, was not how he remembered it, but Garibaldi was in no doubt whose it was.

Ben Joseph.

Liam Allerton must have written under a pseudonym.

3

Felicity Allerton's face wore the waxwork glaze of the recently bereaved. Her words were distant and muffled, as if they were coming from the other side of a closed window, and every time she moved it was with the slowness of someone wading through water. Her eyes, dull with disbelief, moved between Garibaldi and Gardner and the man who sat beside her on the sofa.

'I should have stayed with him,' she said.

'You mustn't blame yourself,' said Garibaldi with a sympathetic smile.

'But I do,' said Felicity. 'I do blame myself. If only I'd . . .'

The man reached out a hand and placed it on Felicity's arm. 'I came round as soon as she called. I'm Ollie.'

'Best man at our wedding,' said Felicity, addressing a space in the middle of the room. 'Ollie was best man at our wedding.'

'I know it's difficult to answer questions at a time like this,' said Garibaldi, ' but we need to find out as much as we can about what happened to your husband.'

'How could he end up there, like that? He couldn't have slipped, it's only a pond. You don't think—?'

'We need to find out about Liam's movements last night,

18

Felicity. The more we know the more chance we have of finding out what happened to him.'

Felicity wrung her hands. 'My daughter's on her way round.' She looked towards the hall as if expecting her to walk in.

She turned back to them, sighed and bowed her head, eyes closed, as if in prayer. She kept her head down as she started to speak.

'I was with Liam for most of the evening. He was giving a talk at the OSO, the Old Sorting Office on the green. It was part of the book festival.' She lifted her head. 'He was a writer. I mean, he hadn't always been, he took it up when he retired, but he'd written this book and he was asked to talk at the festival.'

Garibaldi leaned forward. 'I know, Felicity. I was there.'

'You were there?' Felicity looked at him, her eyes sparking with delight, as if Garibaldi's presence at her husband's talk compensated in some small way for her loss. 'What did you think?'

'I was impressed.'

'Really? I was worried for him.'

Garibaldi leaned forward. 'Why was that?'

'I had no idea how it would go. I always worry he might say the wrong thing or upset people. Liam has ... had a habit of saying things, of speaking his mind.' She turned to Ollie. 'Didn't he?'

Ollie nodded.

'Hardly matters now, does it?' said Felicity. 'Had I known ... I should have stayed with him.'

'Stayed with him where?'

'In the pub. I left early. You see, after the talk he signed some books and he told some friends he'd be going to the Sun afterwards. So there was a group of us there. I should

19

have stayed, shouldn't I? If I had maybe it wouldn't have happened.'

'Who was in this group?'

'Some teachers from St Mark's. You see, he retired from there three years ago and some of his old colleagues came to the talk. And there were some others he knew locally.'

Garibaldi turned to Ollie. 'Were you there?'

'I'd love to have been, but I couldn't make it, unfortunately. I was at my brother's in Winchester.'

'So, Felicity,' said Garibaldi, 'did you know this group of people at the pub?'

'Not all of them, no. I knew the teachers. Or at least I knew them to say hello to. I'd seen them at school events often enough, and Liam spoke about them a lot. Too much, I sometimes thought. He'd get in from school and he'd let rip about them. He'd . . .'

Felicity gazed ahead, as if her husband were letting rip in front of her.

'Can you remember their names?' said Gardner.

'What? Their names. I don't know. I—'

'She's a bit confused,' said Ollie. 'She might need—'

'Of course,' said Garibaldi. 'I understand. 'Take your time, Felicity. Whatever you can remember will be very helpful, but whenever you're ready. I know this must be very difficult for you.'

'Maybe he was drunk?' said Felicity. 'I mean, he liked a drink and he'd already had a few at the OSO and if he had a few more at the Sun and then walked round the pond and slipped . . .'

'It's so difficult to take in,' said Ollie. 'This whole thing is so absolutely unbelievable. It's crazy! And do you know the craziest thing about it? What's really crazy is that—'

'Why would he walk that way round the pond?' said

Felicity, cutting in. 'Why would he walk round the pond at all? That wasn't his way home, so what was he doing there? The pond! There of all places! That's the thing that … I can't tell you how much that—' She looked from Garibaldi to Gardner and then back to Garibaldi, her eyes wide with wonder and disbelief. 'If only I'd stayed with him. If only I'd been with him.'

'Why did you leave the pub?' said Garibaldi.

'Exactly! Why? If only—'

'Did you come home?' said Gardner.

'I had this terrible headache. Splitting. It came on during his talk and I mean there he was with all his friends and it was getting late, so I had a quiet word with him and asked if he'd mind if I went home because I had this terrible headache and he said that was fine and that he wouldn't be long. So if only …'

'You mustn't blame yourself, Felicity,' said Ollie. 'You really mustn't. And you need to tell them. '

'Tell them? Tell them what?'

'You need to tell them what's so weird about it.' Ollie pointed to the table.

'Of course. I must tell them!' said Felicity, getting up from the sofa. She stood still for a moment, trying to find her balance, then walked, as if in a daze, to the table. She reached for a book and picked it up.

'This!' she said, pointing at the cover of *Schooled in Murder*.

She held the book up in front of them as if she was doing a show-and-tell, and pointed at the author's name. 'Ben Joseph. He wrote under a pseudonym.'

She opened the book, leafed through the first few pages, bent back the cover, and smoothed the page with her palm. 'Read this.'

'It's incredible,' said Ollie. 'Unbelievable.'

Felicity handed the book to Garibaldi. She pointed at the place on the page where he should begin.

Garibaldi took it and read. When he reached the lines – *'whether being found dead in the reeds of Barnes Pond only hours after his farewell party'* – he looked up.

He had no idea what to say.

Open-mouthed, with his finger pointing at the phrase he had just read, he passed Ben Joseph's novel to Gardner.

4

DCI Deighton pointed at the picture on the board behind her.

'Barnes Pond,' she said, addressing the team. 'The heart of what the locals, I believe, like to call the village. Is that right, Garibaldi?'

'Not this particular local,' said Garibaldi, giving a wry smile, 'but yes, a lovely place.'

'Wasn't too lovely this morning though,' said Deighton. She pointed at the photo in the middle of the board. 'A body in the reeds. Liam Allerton, local author writing under the name Ben Joseph, who only the evening before had been giving a talk in the OSO as part of the Barnes Book Festival. And as luck would have it our very own local happened to be in the audience.'

Deighton nodded in Garibaldi's direction.

Garibaldi held up his hand, half in acknowledgement, half in apology. He knew everyone thought he was a bit of a smart arse, but he wanted them to know there were limits to his smart-arsery.

'Not my usual Saturday night entertainment,' he said, 'but, yes, I was there.'

'We don't yet know exactly how Liam Allerton died,'

said Deighton, 'but early signs are that he was strangled. He may have been dead before he ended up in Barnes Pond or he may have drowned once he was in it. It's not a deep pond, but you can drown in shallow water. Obviously we'll know more when we get the post-mortem. Any questions?'

Garibaldi looked at Gardner. She'd recently been trying not to be the first to ask a question, aiming for what she had called a more 'reflective' approach. She managed to stop her arm going up, but only just.

'Allerton was last seen at the Sun Inn,' said Deighton. 'He went there with his wife and a group of friends, including old colleagues from St Mark's where Allerton taught for many years before retiring three years ago. His wife, Felicity, left early but Allerton stayed on drinking. We've spoken to Felicity, but first I think we need a report from our literary correspondent.'

She nodded at Garibaldi again.

'So yes,' said Garibaldi, 'I was at the OSO on Saturday night for the talk that was part of the Barnes BookFest. It was Ben Joseph, aka Liam Allerton, talking about this.'

He paused, reached into his jacket pocket, pulled out his copy of the novel and held it up.

'*Schooled in Murder*. Haven't read it yet but, in the light of something Felicity Allerton has pointed out, looks like I might need to read it sooner than intended. And here's why. Now there's a chance that this is nothing other than a bizarre coincidence, but we do need to be aware of it . . .'

Garibaldi paused and looked round the room. He loved moments like this, when he had an audience in his hands. Was this what Rachel felt when she had the full attention of a class?

'OK, so *Schooled in Murder* is a crime novel and, as is

24

generally the case with crime fiction – though not always, of course – the crime in question is murder. In Allerton's book the murder victim is a teacher, Alex Ballantyne. His body is found the morning after his retirement party, but the really interesting thing is where it's discovered . . .'

Another pause and a quick glance round the room.

'The body of Alex Ballantyne is found in Barnes, where the novel is set. And it's found in what we have already heard described as the heart of the village. Barnes Pond.'

He heard a few intakes of breath and saw raised eyebrows.

'That's right. Barnes Pond. More specifically, Ballantyne's body is found in the tall reeds at the edge of Barnes Pond, on the side next to the Barnes Green Day Centre looking across to Essex House. And this, as we know, is exactly where Liam Allerton's body was found this morning. More than that, Ballantyne's body is found the morning after his retirement drinks at the Sun Inn, next to the pond. Where had Liam Allerton been the night before he was found floating in the reeds? The Sun Inn. As I say, these could all be extraordinary coincidences. But it's certainly freaked out Felicity Allerton and I have to say it's freaked me out a bit as well. If it's coincidence it is, let's say, some coincidence. Whatever it is, we need to be aware of it.'

A confused silence fell on the room.

'What happens in the rest of the book?' said DC McLean.

'As I said,' said Garibaldi, 'I haven't read it yet, but I can give you the blurb.' He looked at the back cover. 'Here we go. "*When the body of Alex Ballantyne is found in Barnes Pond the police are baffled. Who could want to kill the newly retired teacher?*

Investigations bring them to St Jude's, the prestigious private school where Ballantyne taught and to the discovery that Ballantyne had been blackmailing several of his colleagues.

25

Sex. Money. Drugs. It seems that Ballantyne knew all about his victims' secrets and they were prepared to pay to buy his silence.

Is one of the St Jude's staff the killer? And, if so, which one?

DI Moriarty's on the case and he's soon discovering that nothing is quite as it seems."'

'So one of those teachers kills him, right?' said DC Hodson.

Garibaldi shrugged. 'No idea. As I said, I haven't read it. Ben Joseph – that is Liam Allerton – didn't reveal the killer in his talk. You don't do that kind of thing with a crime novel. Ruins it. What's known as a spoiler.'

'But Allerton was a teacher, right?' said DC Hodson.

'That's right,' said Garibaldi. 'At St Mark's.'

'So this teacher in his book,' said Gardner. 'It could be him, could it?'

'I don't think we can reach any conclusions.'

'Exactly,' said Deighton from the front. 'I'm not sure what we do with this information at the moment, but, as Garibaldi says, we definitely need to be aware of it. It may well be merely coincidence. At the moment our priority is to find out as much as we can about Liam Allerton, and in particular his movements from the time of his talk at the OSO to the discovery of his body this morning. We also need to know who was in the Sun Inn with him. Chances are they would have all been at his talk, so we should find out from the book festival the names of everyone who bought tickets.'

'This book,' said Gardner. 'Do we need to read it?'

'Given what we've just been told, I think it would be a good idea if we did,' said Deighton. 'We're not in a book club, we're investigating what looks like murder, but given the extraordinary similarity ...'

'It has to be more than coincidence, doesn't it?' said Gardner. 'I mean, what are the chances?'

'I agree,' said Deighton, 'it's strange, but we're in the business of facts. We can speculate, yes, but what we need are facts, and we need to look at Liam Allerton's book in the same way that we need to look at everything going on in his life.'

Garibaldi looked at his boss. She seemed irritated, as if something had got beneath her usually impenetrable skin. Maybe something to do with her home life, the one she had surprisingly revealed to him when they went out for a drink together about a year ago. He'd felt strangely protective of her ever since – a different kind of protectiveness from the one he felt towards Gardner, but there nonetheless. He'd even found himself not only refraining from joining in colleagues' banter and speculation about the DCI, but also disapproving of it.

'So,' said Deighton, pointing at Ben Joseph's author photo in the middle of the board behind her. 'Liam Allerton. Who was he? What was he up to? And why would anyone want to kill him? Find out how the victim lived . . .'

And you'll find out how he died.

Garibaldi finished the line in his head.

5

The Barnes Bookshop was at the heart of Barnes literary life. For over thirty years the independent bookshop, nestling between the post office and a shoe repair shop at the eastern end of Church Road, had served the bookish needs of Barnes and had become an important landmark on the local map. It played an active role in the community, supporting the thriving local literary society, furnishing local primary schools and promoting local authors, of whom Barnes was proud to boast many.

Araminta Warburton, the owner, loved her job. Books were important to her and so were independent shops such as this, not only as beacons of admirable resilience in the face of rampantly powerful tech firms and global digitalisation, but also as a meeting place for like-minded people, those for whom books mattered and who were prepared to pay that little extra to keep such places going. Araminta read widely herself and took great pleasure in sharing her enthusiasm with customers, trading judgements and opinions and providing what she hoped were interesting and stimulating suggestions.

The Barnes Book Festival had been Araminta's

brainchild. Her instincts told her there was an appetite for such a thing and her instincts proved to be correct. After huge effort and commitment, and with the backing of the Literary Society, a few local celebrities and a range of eager volunteers, Barnes BookFest had become an established part of the local calendar.

Now, the morning after the last festival event, she was exhausted, but she was also in a state of shock. First the phone call from Paula and then the string of customers, all with the same tale to tell.

A body in Barnes Pond.

Araminta was horrified, but she was embarrassed to find herself also feeling a little resentful. She couldn't help but feel that, had it not been for the body in the pond, everyone who came into the shop would have been talking about the festival and congratulating her on its success. As it was, all they could do was speculate about the body in the pond. It seemed the festival's success had been eclipsed by the morning's sensational discovery.

According to Paula, the green was full of police and onlookers and a tent had been erected on the side of the pond where the body had been found. The body, apparently, was a man's and it was widely believed, or at least believed by the customers she had seen so far this morning, that the man in question had been murdered.

Quite why the police wanted to see her Araminta couldn't fathom. They had said on the phone that they had a few questions concerning the book festival, but they hadn't told her what they were or why they needed to ask them and she could only draw one conclusion – that the questions they needed to ask about the festival were in some way connected to that morning's discovery. The fact that the body had been found only yards from where the final festival event took place only added to this sense and, as she waited for the police's arrival, she felt increasingly guilty, as if she might in some way be linked to, or even responsible for, what had happened.

When the detectives arrived she thought she recognised the shortish one with greying hair.

'DI Garibaldi,' he said as he showed his card.

'I'm sure I've seen you before,' said Araminta, conscious that her hands were shaking as she went to lock the door and flip round the 'closed' sign.

'You may very well have done,' he said. ' I pop in whenever I can. I've even been known to buy a book. I like to think of each purchase as one in the eye for Amazon.'

Araminta now recognised him more clearly. She had often seen him browsing the shelves.

'I expect you're recovering from the book festival. Looks like it was a great success.'

'I think it was,' said Araminta. 'Completely exhausting, but worth it. There's so much to catch up on I was tempted not to open today, but it's normally quiet on a Sunday, so I thought it would be OK. But now . . .'

'We won't keep you long, Mrs Warburton.'

'I'm assuming this is about . . . the pond.'

'It is. A body was found in Barnes Pond this morning.'

'I can't tell you how shocked I am. I – but I don't see how I can help you. I mean—'

'The body has been identified as Liam Allerton. Writes under the name Ben Joseph.'

The room started to spin. Araminta's eyes tried to fix on something to stop the movement but the room kept turning, the books on the shelves dissolving into a kaleidoscopic swirl.

'Are you OK?'

The voice sounded muffled, as if it were coming from under a pillow.

'Mrs Warburton?'

The room stopped. Araminta stared, open-mouthed, at the two detectives. She steadied herself and took several deep breaths. 'Did you say Ben Joseph?'

'Yes,' said the man. 'Liam Allerton. Writes under the name Ben Joseph.'

'But he was speaking at the fest ... only last night. I mean—'

'I know he was, Mrs Warburton. I was there.'

Araminta looked at the detective more closely. Not only did he come into the shop to buy books, he also came to Barnes BookFest. Part of her brain, still struggling to process the devastating news, was now readjusting her stereotype of the average police detective.

'You were there? Did you enjoy it?'

What was she doing? She had just been told that Ben Joseph had been found dead in the pond and this was the first question she asked.

'I did. Very much so. But, tell me, did you notice anything at the event?'

'Like what?'

'Anything unusual, anything different.'

'I can't remember anything. I certainly didn't see anything that made me think ...'

Araminta broke off. She was in such a state of shock that she found it difficult to recall details.

'How did Ben Joseph seem?'

'It was a great talk. Quite a witty speaker is Liam. I mean, he *was* ...' Araminta shuddered. 'But, yes, a great talk, lively questions and answers and we sold a lot of books.'

'He didn't seem worried or anxious?'

'No more than any writer about to talk. In fact, I'd probably say considerably less. He was quietly confident.'

'And nothing happened during his book signing? No strange or awkward encounters?'

'No more than usual. I can't believe for one moment that anyone . . .'

'And what about the audience? Did you notice anyone behaving strangely?'

Araminta gave a weak laugh. 'No more than usual for a Barnes event. A lot of local faces. But no, I can't say I noticed anyone.'

'Do you have a record of all those who bought tickets for the event?'

'You don't think someone in the audience might have—?'

'We're trying to find out as much as we can about Liam Allerton's movements last night and we're particularly interested to know who was with him after the event. There's a chance they would have attended it.'

'So you need to know who bought tickets. Yes, I should be able to get that for you. '

'That would be very helpful, Mrs Warburton. And, tell me, did tickets all have to be bought in advance or were some available on the door?'

'No. It was sold out. Very popular. A lot of people wanted to go, even though it was a Saturday night.'

'So how many do you think were there?'

'I reckon about a hundred.'

'Well that list would be very helpful.'

Araminta looked from one detective to the other. They said nothing.

'Oh, you mean right now? I see . . .'

'That would be great,' said the man.

Araminta turned and went into the tiny office at the back

of the shop, hoping she could give the detectives what they wanted. Their presence made her feel very uneasy and she was keen for them to go.

Garibaldi browsed the bookshelves while he waited. The shop was one of his favourite places and what he had told its owner was the truth – he derived more pleasure buying from an independent than he did from pressing the Amazon button.

He wandered over to a table where the books of the festival writers were on display and picked up a copy of *Schooled in Murder*. Gardner did the same, and they were both several pages into it when Araminta came out of her office brandishing a sheet of paper.

'Here it is. I hope I've ...' She broke off when she saw the two of them reading the Ben Joseph novel. 'Couldn't resist, I see.'

Garibaldi looked up and nodded. Reading the opening for the second time had not diminished its shock, and he knew he had to read the whole thing as soon as he could – tonight, perhaps, if he was home early enough.

He closed the book and glanced at the overblown quotes on the back cover from names he didn't recognise. He looked at the front – the school buildings with Hammersmith Bridge in the background at the top, the reeds of Barnes Pond at the bottom and the white lettering of the title – and held the book out towards Araminta.

'Tell you what,' he said. 'In exchange for this list of names, I'll buy it.'

'Don't feel you have to.'

'I don't feel that at all. I would very much like to.'

Araminta handed the sheet to Garibaldi and went to the till.

'Do you have a loyalty card?'

Garibaldi felt in his pockets and took out his wallet. 'This may come as a surprise to you but, yes, I do.' He handed it over to Araminta.

'I'll give you two stamps. One for the book and one for coming along to the festival.'

'You don't need to do that. I'll be accused of taking bribes. I can see the headline now. Met cop in loyalty card stamp probe.'

Araminta laughed, and then stopped herself. 'I don't know why I'm laughing. To think of poor Liam. I mean, who ... why ... what?'

'Exactly the questions we're asking ourselves, Mrs Warburton, and we'll do our very best to find out.'

Garibaldi took the book from Araminta. 'You've read it, have you?'

'Oh, yes. So have all the staff. We loved it.'

'Right,' said Garibaldi, turning to Gardner. 'We'll be off.'

'You will let me know of any further developments, won't you?'

'If we have any further questions for you we'll be in touch. I think it unlikely we'll be able to pop in to give you an update.'

'Of course.'

Outside the shop Garibaldi's phone rang. Deighton.

'Jim, I've just been on the phone to the head of St Mark's, Harry Reed. He hadn't heard the news about Allerton. Said he'll get his secretary to send through a list of current and recent teaching staff. If we check that against the ticket sales for his talk we'll know who was there and who might have gone with Allerton to the Sun.'

'Did he say anything about the book?'

'The book? Didn't mention it. He's at home and the

school's broken up for the summer but he's in school tomorrow so we can talk to him there.'

'OK.' Garibaldi hung up and handed the sheet of ticketbuyers to Gardner.

Garibaldi nodded. 'Fancy a walk?'

'Where to?'

'How about the pond? Maybe a pastry from Gail's on the way.'

'Done.'

A Gail's pastry. Just like crossing Hammersmith Bridge heading south, it always made the world seem a little better.

6

Rachel's face was a mixture of shock and disbelief.

'The man we both saw talking at the OSO, the man who signed his book for me is found dead and you didn't tell me?'

'I've been busy,' said Garibaldi.

'Busy? How long does a call take? A text even.'

'I'm sorry—'

'And murdered?'

'Looks like it.'

Rachel turned down the corners of her mouth in a frown of disapproval. Garibaldi couldn't work out what she disapproved of more – Liam Allerton's murder or his failure to tell her about it.

'Where was he found?'

'Barnes Pond. In the reeds.'

'Say that again.'

'Say what again?'

'Where he was found.'

'In the reeds of Barnes Pond.'

'But that's where—'

'I know.'

'That's where the body's found in his novel!'

Rachel walked over to the table and picked up her copy of *Schooled in Murder*. She opened it, flicked past the first few pages and read.

She held the open book towards Garibaldi, turning it round so he could read it. 'Look at this!'

'Yeah, I know. I've been trying to tell you.'

'I thought you hadn't read it.'

'I've read the beginning. Liam Allerton's wife showed me.'

'I don't believe it. He's found in exactly the same place as the victim in his novel. Ironic or what?'

'Exactly.'

'And you didn't tell me! I don't believe it.'

'I was going to, but—'

'How was he killed?'

'Looks like he was strangled.'

'Strangled? That's what happens in the book!'

'Really?'

'Yeah. He's strangled. And he ends up in Barnes Pond.'

'I had no idea.'

'What about Rohypnol?' said Rachel.

'Rohypnol?'

'Yeah. Turns out his drink was spiked with Rohypnol.'

Garibaldi reached for a bag and took out his copy of *Schooled in Murder*. 'I need to read this, don't I?'

'Where did you get that from?'

'I bought it.'

Rachel brandished her own copy. 'But we've already got it.'

'I thought I might need my own copy.'

Rachel looked at the book in her hand. 'Do you want me to tell you what else happens in it?'

'I'll read it tonight.' Garibaldi looked towards the spare bedroom door. 'Is Alfie in?'

'He's with Alicia.'

'Did you talk to him?'

'A bit. But nothing about the row.'

'Look—' Garibaldi raised his eyebrows. 'You're OK with him staying here, aren't you?'

'I'm fine with it.'

'I mean, I'm sure it won't be for long, and—'

'I'm fine. Really.'

'But this place is pretty small and three of us . . .'

'It's OK, honestly.'

Rachel moved towards him and took both his hands in hers. It was a gesture Garibaldi loved, full of warmth and reassurance. Maybe she really *was* OK with Alfie staying and he was the one with the problem.

Rachel gave him a peck on the lips. 'We should go out soon,' she said.

'Good idea.'

'Why don't I check the Half Moon, see who's on.'

'Sure,' said Garibaldi. 'And, talking of music, can I put some on?'

'No problem.'

He had got used to never having to ask. One of the pleasures he discovered after his split with Kay was playing whatever music he wanted to whenever he liked and at any volume. Now he had someone else to consider. Someone who shared most of his musical taste, but who often had work to do or who would rather watch TV. Headphones were an obvious solution and he sometimes used them, but there was nothing like filling a room with sound.

He poured himself a whisky and flicked through the CDs, picking out an album of covers by Shelby Lynne and Allison Moorer. Just what he needed. Dylan, Nick Cave, Townes Van Zandt, Jason Isbell and the kind of harmonies only siblings can provide. What was it about sisters singing together? Kate and Anna McGarrigle. First Aid Kit.

He selected 'Not Dark Yet', sat back in his chair and sipped his whisky. Not dark yet, they sang, but it's getting there. Too right. He shut his eyes and toyed again with his dream. There he was – out of the force, a mature student, doing at this late stage what he didn't do all those years ago. Was it ridiculous? Or now that Alfie was through the system, was this the right time? Could he afford it? Probably not, especially if he carried on buying copies of books they already had. More to the point, what would it do to his relationship with Rachel?

He opened his eyes. First things first. Deal with Alfie's unexpected return. More immediately than that, read *Schooled in Murder.*

He turned to the first page.

He was on page five when the phone rang.

Kay. His heart sank as he read the screen, but he knew he had to take the call.

'He is with you, isn't he?'

'Not at the moment – he's out.'

'But he is staying with you?'

'Yeah, he's staying with me.'

'I was expecting you to call.'

'Yeah, well I was expecting you to call me.'

'What did he tell you?'

'He said there was some kind of row.' He paused. No response. 'Is that right?'

'There was a row, yes.'

'What about?'

'It was nothing.'

'Alfie walked out and came to stay the night with me. It doesn't sound like nothing.'

39

'What matters is that Alfie was incredibly rude.'

Garibaldi sighed. 'Look, Kay, don't play games. Just tell me what happened.'

'It was a perfectly civilised discussion and then all of a sudden—'

'Was it about jobs?'

'No, it wasn't. It was—'

'I thought we'd decided to lay off him for a while.'

'We were laying off him. It was just a discussion. He's graduated from one of the best universities in the world and—'

'I thought we'd decided to let him find his feet, give him time—'

'I am giving him time!'

Garibaldi snapped. 'Look, Kay, I'm busy. And I really don't want to talk about this now. I'll talk to Alfie and—'

'He's an adult, and he's capable of making his own decisions, but we need to know his plans.'

'When you say we, you mean—'

'If he intends to move in with you and . . .' She paused, giving extra weight to the name she was about to utter while also giving the impression that she might have forgotten it. '. . . and Rachel, that's fine, but we'd like to know.'

'I'll call you when I've spoken to him.'

Garibaldi hung up and went back to the book, but the call had unsettled him and he found it difficult to concentrate.

He was only a few pages further on when the phone rang again.

This time it was Alfie.

'Hi Dad. Look, I'm staying at Alicia's tonight. Thought I'd let you know. But if it's OK, I'll be back tomorrow.'

'That's fine. No problem. You can stay here whenever you want, OK?'

'OK, but it won't be for long. Once I've sorted myself out, I'll . . .'

'Take your time, Alfie. Talk soon.'

Hoping for no further distractions, Garibaldi turned off the music and picked up *Schooled in Murder*.

He finished it at three in the morning.

7

https://www.bbc.co.uk/news

BODY FOUND IN BARNES POND

Police are treating as suspicious the death of a man whose body was found in Barnes Pond on Sunday morning. The discovery of the body, as yet unidentified, has come as a great shock to local residents who regard the pond as a focal point of community life in this peaceful leafy area of South West London.

Sheena Lanigan, who has lived in the area for twenty-five years, said, 'It's quite unbelievable. The pond is at the heart of the village and to have it violated in this way is very disturbing.'

Harsal Singh, who owns the local news-agents, said, 'The whole community is in a state of shock. The place is buzzing with rumours and gossip. It's such a popular place for families with children and for people to sit on the benches and it's so sad to think that someone has been found dead there. I hope it's all explained soon and that there is nothing sinister about it.'

DCI Deighton, in charge of the investigation, said, 'We are pursuing our investigations and would urge anyone who has any information they think might be of any relevance to call the police on 101 or contact us via Twitter @MetCC. To give information anonymously contact Crimestoppers on 0800 555 111 or online at crimestoppers-uk.org. We also urge anyone who drove past Barnes Pond on Saturday night after 10.30 pm who has dashcam footage to come forward.'

Barnes is well known for the many celebrities who live there and for its village feel. It is best known to many as being on the route of the annual University Boat Race which takes place each year from Putney to Mortlake. Both crews pass through the central arch of Barnes Railway Bridge.

DCI Deighton turned from the whiteboard to face the team.

'Once the identity of the body is released it'll go crazy. A crime writer murdered. You can imagine the headlines. Whodunnit. Murder Mystery. Need I go on? But we need to be prepared for more than that. Now I have not yet had the pleasure of reading *Schooled in Murder* but we do have here in the room someone who has.'

She nodded to Garibaldi, who got up and walked to the front.

He held up his copy of the novel. 'I started this last night and I finished it in the early hours of this morning. So if I nod off while I'm talking that's why.' A few chuckles. 'The boss is absolutely right. As soon as the media get hold of this, and it won't take them very long, they'll absolutely love it. And they'll be looking very closely at this book. Why? Because, as you already know, the body of Liam Allerton, aka Ben Joseph, was found in exactly the same place as Alex Ballantyne, the murder victim in his novel. But that's not all. It seems that Liam Allerton may have been murdered in exactly the same way. In the novel Alex Ballantyne is drugged with Rohypnol and strangled. That's right. Strangled.'

Garibaldi paused and looked round the room. He saw surprise in the faces.

'Coincidence? It looks unlikely, doesn't it? These are remarkable similarities. And remember that the night before Alex Ballantyne is found in the pond in the novel, he was at the Sun Inn for his retirement drinks party. And where had Liam Allerton been on Saturday night? At the Sun Inn. What's more, both were retired teachers. Alex retires the day before his body is found. Liam Allerton retired three years ago.'

Garibaldi pointed at the book he held in his hand.

'Now all of that,' he said, ' is going to generate a fair bit of interest in this. In an ideal world we should all read it—' He held up his hand in acknowledgement of the groans. 'But, given that we're not in an ideal world and some of you might not get round to it, I'm going to tell you a few more things about it that I think we need to be aware of. Any questions so far?'

Garibaldi looked in Gardner's direction. She kept her hand down.

'OK. So in the book Alex Ballantyne is a teacher and he's found dead in Barnes Pond the morning after his retirement drinks at the Sun Inn. The post-mortem shows that his drink has been spiked with Rohypnol and death was caused by strangulation. In the course of the investigation it is discovered that Alex Ballantyne has been blackmailing several of his colleagues at the school where he works. And where's that? St Jude's School, a posh private school near Hammersmith Bridge. You'll already see another parallel. Where did Liam Allerton teach? St Mark's, a posh private school near Hammersmith Bridge. So Ballantyne has been demanding money from his colleagues in return for his silence. If they don't pay up he'll reveal their secrets, and it seems there are quite a few St Jude's teachers who are keen to keep theirs hidden. One had a sexual relationship with a pupil at a previous school. One has been embezzling from the school charity fund. One has a serious drug habit. And one has been working as an escort. Four blackmail victims and four people who would seem to have a motive for wanting Ballantyne dead. The police are on the case and DI Moriarty investigates. He looks at what was going on in Ballantyne's life, paying particular attention to the teachers who were his blackmail victims.'

Garibaldi paused and looked round the room, checking he had everyone's attention.

'So the question is – are there, and will anyone be look-ing for, any other connections between this book and, for want of a better word, real life? I have no doubt that once the media get hold of the similarities between the death in the book and the death in real life they'll be looking for more connections. So we need to get onto this before they do. How much of this book is a very thinly disguised reality? Are there real-life counterparts to those teachers threatened with exposure of their dark secrets? The answer is I don't know, but I can already see a lot of people fasci-nated by the possibility.'

He raised his eyebrows. 'Any questions?'

He looked in Gardner's direction. This time she couldn't stop herself.

'So you're saying that Allerton based his novel on things that were actually going on, that this stuff was really happening at St Mark's?'

'I'm not saying that at all, but given that there are already some striking similarities we need to look at it. We need to look at everything. We need to talk to the St Mark's head to find out more about Allerton. We need to speak to those who were at his talk and with him at the pub. The OSO and the Sun Inn both have CCTV. We need to look at that. And we need to talk to Allerton's family again. And the usual stuff on bank details, phone records, car. Anything.'

'House to house enquiries are ongoing,' said Deighton, 'in residential properties that look onto Barnes Green and the Pond – Church Road, Station Road and The Crescent. There's always a chance that someone living close might have seen Allerton after he left the pub, but nothing so far. Many of those properties have security cameras – given the location of the body and given the distance of those properties from the crime scene we're not holding out much hope, but there's a chance one might have picked up Allerton walking past at some stage.'

'How about that Day Centre right next to the pond?' said DC Hodson.

'We've checked with the manager,' said Gardner. 'No cameras, and obviously no one there at that time on a Saturday night.'

'OK,' said Garibaldi. 'I'm leaving this here, if anyone wants a read. It has its flaws but it's actually pretty good. At times when I was reading it last night I couldn't work out whether I was doing it for work or pleasure. Shame he won't have the chance to write any more.'

'There's one thing you haven't told us,' said DC Hodson.

'What's that?'

'Who did it? In the book who killed Alex Ballantyne?'

'Read it and find out.'

Garibaldi looked at the confused faces.

'I think,' said Deighton, 'that given the circumstances—'

Garibaldi held up his hand to stop her. 'Only joking. Right, it turns out to be none of the blackmailed teachers, or at least none of the blackmailed teachers DI Moriarty is aware of for most of the novel. It turns out to be the head-master's wife. Moriarty discovers late on that she's been having an affair and that Ballantyne started to blackmail her as well. So the head's wife decided to kill him on the night of his retirement party.'

'Bit unlikely, isn't it?' said Gardner.

'Which bit in particular?'

'First of all, that there would be so many potential blackmail victims in one place, particularly a school like that, and—'

'Maybe that's the point,' said Garibaldi. 'The places that look the least likely are often the most corrupt. Have a look at history.'

'Not just that,' said Gardner. 'There's also the question about how he finds out about all these secrets. I mean if they're secrets how does he get to know them?'

'Good point,' said Garibaldi. 'It seems this Ballantyne teacher was the school gossip. People confided in him. People told him things. Might sound implausible but it works in the novel. He's just one of those blokes people open up to and he decides to use it to his advantage. And if—'

Garibaldi was interrupted by a phone ringing on Deighton's desk. She reached for it, looked at the caller ID and held up her hand. 'I need to take this,' she said.

She looked down at her desk as she listened, nodding but saying nothing apart from a couple of OKs.

When the call had ended she put down her phone and looked up. 'That was from the post-mortem. Cause of death was not asphyxiation from strangulation but drowning. Evidence of alcohol in the blood. And, although this won't be confirmed until the full toxicology report, indications from a screening test suggest . . .'

She broke off, looked round the room and raised her eyebrows.

'Indications from a screening test suggest there was also evidence of Rohypnol.'

8

St Jude's School is one of the most prestigious schools in the country. At first glance, the mish-mash of modern buildings situated next to the Thames on the south side of Hammersmith Bridge, the oldest dating from the sixties, seems so far removed from the traditional image of the English public school that it is difficult to believe that this is one of the very best. But however you choose to calibrate success and construct tables – exam results, numbers to Oxbridge, sporting achievements – there is no doubt that St Jude's is one of the handful of elite institutions always to be found nestling at the top of the Premier League. It may not look much like Eton, Winchester or Westminster but it's very much up there with them.

That such a prestigious, revered institution should have on its teaching staff so many with secrets to hide might not come as a surprise to those familiar with other similarly revered institutions at the heart of the establishment, but it would to those who forked out ridiculous fees to send their children there.

(from *Schooled in Murder* by Ben Joseph)

'We'd like to ask you a few questions about Liam Allerton,' said Garibaldi.

'Of course. If there's any way I can be of help, any way at all.'

Harry Reed, the head of St Mark's, spoke with the kind of exaggerated RP most people, even royalty, had given up on years ago. There was something absurdly formal and pompous about him.

'How much do you know about his death?' said Garibaldi.

'I know he was found in Barnes Pond on Sunday morning,' said Reed. 'Look, I don't know much more, but that doesn't mean I haven't heard a lot of rumour and speculation.'

'What you might not have heard, Mr Reed, and what we can now confirm, is that we are now treating Liam Allerton's death as murder.'

'I see.' Reed sat reflectively for a few moments, taking it in. 'I see,' he repeated. 'Well, as I said, if I can help in any way at all. I'm very concerned that this whole thing doesn't get out of hand.'

'Out of hand?'

'The press and the media have already been sniffing round. I have the school's reputation to think of.'

'And we have a killer to find, so maybe the school's reputation is—'

'I understand, Inspector. It's a difficult time for everyone. All I'm saying is there's been a lot of interest since it happened.'

'Tell me, when did Liam Allerton retire?'

'Three years ago.'

'And how might the murder of a man who retired from St Mark's three years ago affect the school's reputation?'

Reed got up from his chair and walked to a bookcase. He picked a copy of *Schooled in Murder* off the shelves and brought it back to his desk, holding its front cover up to Garibaldi and Gardner.

'You know all about this, I presume?'

'We do,' said Garibaldi. 'Liam Allerton writing under the pseudonym Ben Joseph.'

'Exactly,' said Reed. 'And have you read it?'

Garibaldi felt he was back at school in every sense.

'I have,' he said. 'And I also heard him talk about it the night before his body was found.'

Reed seemed surprised. 'I see. Well, if you've read it you will already be familiar with the rumour and speculation I've already heard about how his body was found in exactly the same place as the novel's murder victim.'

'We are familiar with that, yes.'

'And is it true?'

Garibaldi nodded. 'Yes it is. In the reeds of Barnes Pond. On the same side in the same location.'

'And if you've read the book you also might have some idea of why I'm worried about the possible impact of his death, his ... murder ...' He paused, allowing a silence to give his last word emphasis. '... on the school community.'

Garibaldi paused, unsure whether he'd been asked a question he was expected to answer. He really was back at school.

'A lot of people who read Allerton's book,' continued Reed, 'found it difficult to believe he hadn't based his fictional school on the one he had worked at. This one.'

'I see. And do you think the same?'

'That the school in his book's based on St Mark's?'

'Exactly.'

'There's an obvious similarity in its physical appearance and its location, yes, but that's it.'

'So you don't think other things in the novel – the events, the characters – have a similar basis in, what shall we call it, real life?'

Reed gave a loud laugh. 'Of course not.'

'So you don't think *Schooled in Murder* is some kind of roman à clef?'

'Roman à clef?'

'It means a novel with a key. A kind of—'

'I know what it means,' said Reed.

He looked taken aback – whether surprised by the suggestion itself or by its having come from the mouth of a mere detective Garibaldi couldn't tell.

'You have read the book, haven't you?' said Garibaldi, enjoying the momentary teacher-pupil role reversal.

'Yes, I have read it and I know exactly what you're suggesting. I think it's fair to say that when it was published there was quite a bit of discussion at St Mark's. I know every novel is to some extent based on real life and it's often a mistake to look for parallels. But the problem with this book is that Allerton located his fictional school of St Jude's in exactly the same location as St Mark's. The architecture as he describes it is identical. You don't have to be Einstein to work out what school he has in mind. And the trouble is, once you have in your head the idea that the school he's describing in his novel is this one, you can't stop yourself thinking that the characters he describes, and the events he describes, all have similar parallels.'

'And do they?' said Garibaldi.

Reed made a sound halfway between a derisive snort and a splutter.

'Of course they don't! And that was the worry when it came out – that people would think there are all kind of things going on here.'

'So let's get this straight,' said Garibaldi. 'No teacher at your school has ever blackmailed other members of staff?'

'Of course not. That's preposterous!'

Garibaldi took out his notebook and leafed through a few pages. 'And to your knowledge there is no-one on your staff, now or recently, who has had a sexual relationship with a pupil, who has a serious drug habit, who has embezzled school funds or who has been working as an escort?'

Reed waved his hands in front of him in exasperation. 'You see? As soon as you hear these things you realise how absolutely absurd they are. Completely and totally absurd! That a school like this—'

'A school like what?'

'A prestigious institution, one with a well-established reputation.'

Garibaldi smiled. 'You don't have to delve too far in history, do you Mr Reed, to find many prestigious institutions covering up all kind of things.'

'I'm well aware of that.'

'So you'll understand why I need to ask the question.'

'I understand, yes, and that's my very point. Anyone who's read the novel will ask exactly the same questions. It even says on the back of the book that Allerton taught for many years at a London school. Of course they're going to wonder.'

'I see.' Garibaldi consulted his notebook. 'When you say there's no correspondence between any of Allerton's characters and teachers at your school, does that include the book's murder victim?' Garibaldi turned over a page of his notebook. 'That's Alex Ballantyne.'

Reed nodded, as if he had been expecting the question and had his answer prepared.

'When I said a teacher at St Mark's I meant a current teacher. You must remember that Allerton had retired when his book was published. But, yes, everyone was quick to detect similarities between Liam Allerton and the teacher murdered in his book.'

'And what were those similarities?'

Reed looked to one side and gave a wry smile. 'Liam may have had his victim teach a different subject – Liam taught Maths and he made Alex Ballantyne an English teacher – but he gave him the same, what's the word? Cynicism. Maybe that's it. He made Ballantyne cynical – and difficult. Difficult in the same way that Liam was.'

'How was Liam difficult?'

'He was a good teacher. Excellent in the classroom. Very popular with the pupils . But he liked to do things his own way.'

'What do you mean "his own way"?'

'He wasn't always one for, let's say, protocol. A bit of a maverick at times. Every school has them.'

'When you say maverick . . .?'

'Didn't always play by the book.'

'I see. And did that ever get him into trouble?'

'Not trouble as such, but close to it.'

'What about his relationship with other members of staff?'

'He had his friends. A lot of the staff room liked him and respected him.'

'A lot of them, but not all of them?'

'I didn't do a straw poll, Inspector.'

'So he had his friends, but he also had his enemies?'

'You mean anyone who might have wanted to kill him?'

'I'm not saying that. I'm just trying to get a sense of how he got on with his colleagues.'

Reed sighed, leaned back in his chair and folded his arms. 'Look, I'll be honest with you. Liam was an excellent teacher. Respected by his students. Great results. All of that. But he wasn't always the easiest of colleagues. He had a habit of speaking his mind, of saying what he thought, admirable qualities in themselves but schools are political places and sometimes you need a bit of tact and diplomacy.'

'I see,' said Garibaldi. 'So what kind of thing was Liam Allerton outspoken about?'

Reed gave a little chuckle.' There was no pattern, no theme. He would just say what he thought about things. It could be anything. A colleague's judgement, a disciplinary decision, a management initiative.' Reed unfolded his arms and leaned forward, resting his elbows on his desk. 'I'll be honest with you, Inspector, he had a habit of coming in to see me – no appointment, no sorting out a time with my secretary – he'd just come in and let me know what he thought about what was going on. It would be nice to think he sometimes did it simply to say how much he agreed with things or how he thought something was a good idea but, alas, I don't remember that ever happening.'

'Can you be more specific?' said Garibaldi. 'Anything in particular you remember?'

'There were a few things about discipline, as I remember. A couple of suspensions that he felt very strongly about.'

'What were they?'

'I think there was a bullying incident and drugs may have been another one. And sometimes he'd sound off about the way a colleague had been treated. I'll be honest with you, Inspector, when his name came up at senior management meetings it tended to be followed by a sigh. He didn't always make things easy for us.'

'I'm sure you can appreciate,' said Garibaldi, 'that when everyone realises that Allerton's body was found in the same place as the teacher in his novel they are going to ask questions. But they are going to ask even more questions when they discover that Liam Allerton was murdered in exactly the same way as his creation, Alex Ballantyne.'

'What do you mean?'

'He died by drowning but he had been strangled. And early indications are that there was Rohypnol in his blood.'

'But that's extraordinary! I don't know what to say. I mean what on earth are we expected to make of that?'

'I'm simply giving you the facts,' said Garibaldi.

'So whoever killed him must have known, must have read—'

'Read the book? In our business we like to assume nothing, but in this case that has to be a strong possibility.'

'I don't understand. Why would anyone do it?'

'That's what we're trying to find out. One thing you might also need to know is that several members of your teaching staff were with Liam in the Sun Inn on Saturday night. They'd gone along to hear him talk and then went for a drink with him afterwards. We're going to need to speak to those teachers. My colleague has their names.'

Garibaldi gave Gardner a nod.

'There were four of them,' she said, reading from the list she held in her hand. 'Ewan Thomas, Sasha Ambrose, Ruth Price and Armit Harwal. If you could give us their contact details . . .'

Reed scanned the sheet, his forehead furrowed with concern.

'Are you saying that one of these might have . . .?'

'We're saying nothing at this stage, Mr Reed. We'd just like to talk to them and given that it's the beginning of the summer holidays we'd like to get to them before they jet off to exotic climes.'

'We don't all jet off you know. It takes most of us several weeks to recover from term, and some of us still have a lot of work to do.'

'Tell me,' said Garibaldi. 'Were you surprised when you heard that Allerton had written a novel?'

'Completely. I had no idea that was what he wanted to do when he retired, no idea that he was even remotely interested in writing. And as soon as I read it I realised there'd be a bit of a fuss.'

Garibaldi flipped through his notebook. It contained nothing of significance, but he always liked to do it, as if he was consulting some higher authority or looking for a killer question. He enjoyed the pause, sensing the unease an extended silence created in whoever he was interviewing.

'When I read the book,' said Garibaldi, looking up, 'it came as a great surprise to discover that the murderer was the headmaster's wife.'

'Good God!' Harry Reed let out a loud guffaw. 'I knew this was coming. Are you really asking whether my wife murdered Liam Allerton?'

'I'm just carrying out my investigation, Mr Reed.'

'So you want to know if my wife was having an affair with a teacher and whether she killed her blackmailer when he threatened to reveal it?'

'You have impressive recall of the novel.'

'Of course I bloody well do! Everybody was banging on about the wretched thing for weeks and now it looks as though it's all about to start again.'

'I'm asking the question, Mr Reed, because I am part of a murder investigation. An ex-member of your staff has been found dead in circumstances that exactly mirror the murder of his own fictional creation. My level of interest is of a different order from prurient speculation.'

'It's the same question, though, isn't it? And I'm telling you the answer is no. The wife in his book is not my wife. The head in his book is not me.'

'You mean the head who himself is having an affair?' Garibaldi flicked through his notebook again. 'What's his name again? Let's see. Rhodri Maine.'

'Absurd!' said Reed. 'Neither I nor my wife is having an affair! There is no similarity at all between us and the couple in Allerton's novel.'

'But, as you say, the school in the book does seem to be this one. Strange, isn't it?'

Garibaldi got up from his chair and motioned for Gardner to do the same. 'Well, we'll leave you to it but if there's anything more you can think of that might be of relevance please do get in touch.'

Garibaldi handed Reed a card. He looked at it closely, as if it might not be what it seemed.

'And,' said Garibaldi, turning as he opened the door, 'I'd be prepared for a high level of media interest. Once they get hold of this, you might find yourself pretty busy.'

Harry Reed tried to force a smile but his face crumpled in the effort. He looked like a man whose summer holidays had been completely ruined.

9

The manager of the Sun Inn, a balding man in his thirties, wore the look of a landlord worried that the discovery of a body so close to his premises might not be good for business.

'We'd like to ask you a few questions, Mr Clancy.'

'No problem.' He led them to a quiet corner. 'Can I get you a drink?'

Garibaldi and Gardner shook their heads.

'We have reason to believe,' said Garibaldi, ' that the man found dead in Barnes Pond had been drinking here on Saturday night. Were you on duty that night?'

'I'm on duty every night,' said Clancy.

Gardner took out a photo of Liam Allerton. 'This is the man. Do you recognise him?'

Clancy looked closely. 'Do you know how many people were in on Saturday night? Nice warm summer evening and the place was packed, so the chances of me remembering someone . . .' Clancy peered even closer. 'He does look vaguely familiar, though. Maybe I've seen him walking around. Was he a local?'

'He was,' said Garibaldi. 'And we understand he was

drinking in here late on Saturday night with a group of friends after he'd given a talk at the OSO.'

'A talk?'

'He was a writer.'

'I see.' Clancy gave a nod as if this revelation helped explain things.

'We think there's a possibility that while Allerton was here on Saturday night someone spiked his drink.'

'Spiked?'

'With Rohypnol.'

'What? Here?'

'We don't know for sure, but it seems a strong possibility. Tell me, Mr Clancy, what CCTV do you have?'

'There's a camera inside on the main bar area and two outside. One on the front and one on the car park area at the side.'

'We'll need to look at that footage.'

'OK. I'll sort it. When you say he was a writer . . .'

'He wrote crime novels. One crime novel, to be more precise. Under the name Ben Joseph.'

'Right.' Clancy nodded again, as if this made things clearer.

Garibaldi looked round the pub. 'Nice place. I should come here more often.'

'Local are you?'

'Just round the corner. Business good?'

'Not bad.'

'Any problems?'

'Problems? What do you mean?'

'Usual stuff. Underage drinking. Drugs.'

Clancy shrugged, as if in his whole career in the trade he'd never come across either. 'No. Nothing like that.'

'Must have changed then,' said Garibaldi. 'Time was

when you could get anything in here. Quick word with someone in the car park . . .'

'That must be a long time ago. It's been a different place since . . .'

'Since you took over?'

'Well, yes.' Clancy's tone was defensive. 'When you say this bloke had his drink spiked, how do you know it happened here?'

'All we know is that he was drinking here on Saturday night, and his body was found in the pond the next morning with traces of Rohypnol in it. Once we've had a look at the CCTV we might have a better idea.'

'You think CCTV will show someone spiking his drink?'

'I won't know what it will show until I've seen it, will I?'

'Sure. I – well, look, if there's anything I can do to help.' Clancy looked anxiously towards the door. 'I don't want bad publicity or anything, but if you find out anything went on here I'd like to know.'

'We'll let you know all right,' said Garibaldi.

He headed for the exit with Gardner, walked through the crowds on the pavement and crossed the road. As he headed for the OSO he glanced across the pond at the tent, where the SOCOs were still at work.

The manager of the OSO was standing outside the building, leaning on the railings, looking at the police activity. Garibaldi and Gardner showed their cards and introduced themselves.

'I still can't believe he was talking in this very room only a few nights ago,' said the manager, leading them into the café.

'Nor can I,' said Garibaldi, 'I was there.'

'Really?'

'I enjoyed it.'

'I couldn't make it unfortunately, but I hear it was good.' The manager turned to them. 'So how can I help you?'

'Do you have CCTV here?'

'One camera outside.'

'Nothing inside?'

'No.'

'We'd very much like to see the outside footage for Saturday night if we could.'

'OK, no problem. Why do you need it? You don't think—'

'We don't think anything at the moment. We're just gathering information.'

Garibaldi looked towards the counter. 'Do you do coffee here?'

'Of course.'

'And pastries?'

The manager nodded.

'What do you reckon?' said Garibaldi, turning to Gardner.

'Silly not to.'

Garibaldi walked to the counter and examined the range.

'Could we have one Americano and a skinny latte please and a cinnamon bun and an almond croissant. We'll be outside.'

'Why would anyone do it?' said Garibaldi as they walked down the steps and found a spare table.

'Do what?' said Gardner.

'Kill Liam Allerton.'

'Who knows? All kinds of reasons. I mean—'

'I mean kill Liam Allerton *like that.*'

'You never know. Could just be coincidence.'

'Really?'

'Yeah. Stranger things have happened.'

'Like what?'

Gardner looked thoughtful. 'You're right. It's crazy. Do you think someone killed him *because* of the book?'

'Difficult to say, but you can't rule it out. You can't rule anything out.'

'This book – I'm going to have to read it, aren't I?'

'You might like it.'

'Did you?'

'I didn't think I would.'

'Why's that?'

'First of all because I've never been a fan of crime novels – when I read I like to take myself somewhere else, not back to work – and secondly because I'm not a great fan of reading stuff about schools.'

'What's the problem with schools?'

'I'm not sure. It just makes me uncomfortable.'

Now wasn't the time to tell her the real reason – that reading about schools brought back difficult memories.

'Maybe it's because you live with a teacher.'

'Yeah, maybe.'

The OSO manager arrived with coffee and pastries.

'You all right with the almond croissant?' said Garibaldi.

'How about we share?'

'OK.' Garibaldi reached for his knife and cut each pastry in two.

'So this book,' said Gardner. 'I know I should read it, but couldn't you just, you know, tell me what I need to know?'

'Read it,' said Garibaldi, tucking into his half of the croissant.

'The thing is ever since I broke up with Tim I've kind of lost the reading habit.'

Memories of Gardner's relationship with Smartypants Tim came back to Garibaldi – her worries that she wasn't clever enough for him, her desperate attempts to impress, her devastation when he dumped her.

He had been treading carefully ever since, trying hard not to make jokes at Gardner's expense. He may not have always succeeded, but he'd definitely felt more guilty when he'd failed.

He gave his sergeant a smile and a sympathetic nod and, as he glanced at the tent on the other side of the pond, an image of Liam Allerton's body in the reeds flashed into his head and refused to leave.

10

Sasha Ambrose, like all teachers, loved the summer holidays. She sometimes came out with the line that it was a much-needed break, one in which hardworking teachers could not only recuperate but also engage in the preparation necessary for the next academic year but, like all teachers, she knew it wasn't true. Seven weeks off in the summer may not have been one of the reasons she went into teaching, but it was certainly one of the reasons she stayed.

Today she was more relieved than usual to have broken up for the summer. Every time she thought of what it would have been like had Liam Allerton's body been discovered during term time she shivered. The murmur of rumour, always audible in a school, would, in the face of something of this magnitude, have been deafening. What the student body (always the most imaginative when it came to speculating about the private lives of teachers), would have come up with she couldn't begin to imagine.

Sasha had been fond of Liam. She would often sit with him in his corner of the staff room, where they would express their dismay at the latest management decisions and initiatives and crack a few clues in the *Guardian* cryptic crossword. She knew there were many who didn't like him but she enjoyed his healthy irreverence for authority. She also liked the way he was prepared to listen, always happy to provide a willing and sympathetic ear. Sasha knew she wasn't the only one to make the long walk to Liam's classroom in the corner of the Maths department where, behind a closed door, they would talk about things it would have been ill-judged to discuss, even in lowered voices, in a staff-room corner.

Maybe that's how he had got to know so much.

And maybe that's why everyone got such a shock when they read his novel. There was no doubt that Liam had modelled the school in his novel on the one he had worked at and most agreed that the novel's murder victim, Alex Ballantyne, shared many characteristics with his creator. So it was inevitable that many were quick to look for other parallels, wondering whether any of the teachers blackmailed by Ballantyne in the novel were based on members of the St Mark's staff.

Many may have had their theories but no-one, or at least no-one in public, claimed to have identified the real-life models for any of Liam's secret-harbouring teachers. And no-one, of course, was foolish enough to own up to being a real-life model themselves.

But Sasha knew everything. She knew exactly what Liam had done.

And that was why she was choosing her words carefully as she faced the two detectives.

'So,' said the man who had introduced himself as DI Garibaldi, 'you worked with Liam Allerton when he taught at St Mark's?'

'That's right,' said Sasha, looking from him to his colleague, who was leafing through her notebook.

'And I understand you went to hear him talk about his book at the OSO?'

'I did, yes. A few of us went along.'

'When you say "us" . . .?'

'Teachers from St Mark's. We thought we'd go along to support him.'

'That's very good of you. Have you read his book?'

'*Schooled in Murder*? Yes, I've read it.'

'What did you make of it ?'

'Make of it in what way?'

'Did you enjoy it?'

'Enjoy it? Yes, I suppose I did.'

'You sound like you weren't expecting to.'

'I was surprised when I heard he'd published a novel. I think everyone at the school was.'

'He wrote under a pseudonym, of course. Why do you think he did that?'

'I have no idea. Maybe he wanted a bit of anonymity.'

'And why would he want that?'

'Again, I have no idea.'

'How did you find out Ben Joseph was Liam Allerton?'

'I can't remember exactly how I found out but it was common knowledge pretty soon. Schools are like that. It's difficult to keep things secret.'

'Though in the school Allerton created, St Jude's, there were characters who were paying money to do just that – keep things secret.'

Sasha gave a nervous laugh. 'Yes, well that's the book, isn't it? There's no reason to believe . . .'

'We'll come back to that, Sasha, but for the moment I'm interested in why Liam Allerton chose to write under a pseudonym.'

'Presumably to protect his identity.'

'Well that didn't work, did it?'

'No, but the gesture suggests he didn't want people to know.'

'Maybe, but the cynic in me thinks he might have done it to create a bit more publicity for himself. You disguise your identity to make people more aware of it. A bit like J. K. Rowling and Robert Galbraith, perhaps.'

'Perhaps, but then J. K. Rowling didn't reveal herself deliberately, did she? She was uncovered.'

'Hmm. Maybe. But the cynic in me . . .'

'Much as I enjoyed Liam's book, Inspector, I don't think we're talking J. K. Rowling, are we?'

'You say you were surprised when you heard he'd written a book. Why was that?'

'He'd never expressed any interest in writing. I know a lot of people keep quiet about it while they secretly work away but I think Liam was the sort of person who'd tell you. I mean if he'd been an English teacher it wouldn't really surprise you – the world's full of English teachers writing novels – but he taught Maths. He was good at crosswords, he had that kind of mind, but from what I saw of his reports he wasn't always good at stringing words together. I remember having to send some of them back because they didn't make sense.'

'He wouldn't be the first writer who didn't make sense. Maybe he had a good editor.'

'Yeah, maybe. And maybe being a Maths teacher helped with that kind of novel. You know – clues, logic, that kind of thing.'

Sasha looked from one detective to the other. Why were they pussyfooting around?

'It seems quite clear,' said the man, 'that the school in Allerton's book – its building, its locations, is modelled on St Mark's. When you read it did you notice any other similarities?'

'You mean was there a member of staff blackmailing other teachers?'

'I suppose that is what I mean, yes.'

Sasha laughed dismissively. 'So let me get this straight. There's a teacher embezzling school funds, one with a serious drug addiction, one who slept with a student and one who supplements their teacher salary by working as a prostitute?'

'That's impressive recall,' said the detective. 'You must have read it very closely.'

'Of course I did. If you know someone who's written a book it's natural to look for yourself. You always wonder whether they might have modelled a character on you.'

'I see. And do you think he did?'

'What? Am I one of those blackmailed teachers with a secret to hide? What do you expect me to say?'

'The truth would be helpful.'

'Well, I'm not. Of course I'm not!'

'And what about the other characters? Do you think Allerton based any of them on teachers he worked with at St Mark's?'

'No, I don't.'

'But you recognised the school?'

'Yes. Everyone who knew the school recognised it, especially those who work in it. And, yes, there was a lot of speculation.'

'When you say speculation you mean that people were trying to identify real-life counterparts?'

'I suppose so, yes.'

'Tell me, Sasha, did you speak to Liam on Saturday night?'

'We had a quick word at the Sun.'

'What did you talk about?'

'I can't remember. We were in a big group so it was all very general.'

'And did anyone ask him about the book?'

'We'd all just heard him talk about it so, yes, people asked him about the book.'

'Did they ask him whether it was based on St Mark's?'

'They may have. I can't remember exactly, but if they did I'm sure he came up with the answer he always gave.'

'And what was that?'

'Same as the one he gave at his talk. About everything being based on some kind of reality but being reshaped, reimagined in the creative process. All bullshit of course.'

'Bullshit? Why?'

'Because it was so obvious. The buildings, the location, the type of school. Everything's recognisable.'

The detective paused and looked at his colleague.

'What time did you leave the Sun, Sasha?'

'Just before eleven I think. I can't remember exactly.'

'And when you left was Liam still there?'

'He was, yes, because I remember saying goodbye to him.'

'And did you come straight home?'

'I got a bus outside the pub down to the Red Lion and then took a 33 down here to Fulwell. Look, Inspector, why don't we get to the point here? There's clearly a similarity between the school in the book and St Mark's. But that's not the most worrying thing about the book, is it? The worrying thing is that Liam's body was found in exactly the same place as the body in the book. In Barnes Pond.'

'Exactly, Sasha, exactly. Very strange. What do you make of it?'

'What do I make of it? I have no idea what I make of it! It's so ... so ... I mean ... look, you're the detective, what do *you* make of it?'

'I'm puzzled. Everyone is. As you rightly say, Liam was

found in the reeds in Barnes Pond on Sunday morning. Exactly like Alex Ballantyne, the teacher in his novel. But that's not all. The post-mortem shows that Liam died from drowning, but it also shows he was strangled before he drowned. Early indications also suggest that there was evidence of Rohypnol in his blood.'

'But that's the same as—'

'Exactly. Liam was killed in exactly the same way as the character in his novel.'

'I don't believe it!'

'It could, of course, be a coincidence—'

'That can't be a coincidence, can it? I mean—'

The detective nodded his agreement. 'Seems unlikely, doesn't it? And it raises a lot of questions. The first question we need to ask is who did it, but then we need to ask why whoever it was chose to do it in that way.'

'I really don't know what to say. I—'

'It also raises the question of when Liam's drink was spiked. He was drinking in two places that evening. The OSO and the Sun Inn. And you were with him in both those places.'

'You're making it sound as though *I* did it! There were lots of other people in both places.'

'We're well aware of that, Sasha. And we'll speak to them all. In the meantime . . .' He got up and signalled to his colleague to do the same. He reached into his pocket and took out a card. 'If you think of anything, anything at all, no matter how small a detail, that you think could be relevant, please do get in touch.' He handed the card to her. 'And have a good summer holiday. How long is it you get?'

Sasha looked at the card in her hand. 'How long?'

'Your holidays? How long do you get in the summer?'

'Oh. Seven weeks.'

'Seven weeks? Very nice.'

Sasha showed the detectives to the door, closed it behind them and leaned back on it, breathing deeply.

She was shocked beyond words. When she first read *Schooled in Murder* she had been terrified that someone would find out and, as the weeks and months passed and attention on the book had dwindled, the growing sense that no-one had had brought her great comfort.

But now, with Liam murdered, and murdered in that very specific way, she knew that there would be even greater interest in his novel, and the thought that it might be read even more closely than it had been when it first appeared filled her with horror.

She had never been less looking forward to the first few weeks of the summer holidays.

11

'Ashley MacDonald knew she should never have done it, but once she started she found it difficult to stop. It may have been the glamour. It may have been the sense of being needed. Or it may simply have been the satisfaction and thrill she derived from having sex with wealthy men. Of one thing she was sure – it was about more than the money. Maybe it was the undeniable thrill of having an alter ego, a completely different personality. A bit like Clark Kent and Superman or Bruce Wayne and Batman. When the holidays came, when late nights out during the week weren't a problem, it was a thrill to become Donna Beaumont.

It was the offer of a ticket for Swan Lake that started it off. Ashley loved the ballet but, given the price of tickets, she didn't get to go too often. So when Callie offered her a ticket for free she was quick to accept. That's not to say she didn't hesitate. It wasn't a simple case of going to the ballet with her old friend – there were strings attached. Callie was going with her husband, a client and his wife, but the wife had dropped out. Could Ashley take her place? Ashley had made jokes about set-ups and blind dates but Callie had reassured her that it was all above board and a great way for Ashley to get to go to the Royal Opera House for free. What's more, the client was good fun and Callie was sure Ashley would have a good time.

Ashley's most recent boyfriend had been a disaster, and she was currently 'resting' when it came to relationships. So, free of commitments or any sense of accountability, there seemed to be nothing stopping her saying yes to Callie's invitation.

And when the ballet was over that night there seemed to be nothing stopping her saying yes when Callie's client invited her back to his hotel, nothing stopping her when he went to kiss her, nothing stopping her when he suggested they had sex.

What took Ashley by complete surprise, though, was the way nothing stopped her accepting when a couple of hours later the client offered her money. At first she thought it was cash for a cab, but when she saw the wad of notes in his hand she realised he was paying her for something else.

That's how it all began . . .

Now, as Ashley headed for her pigeon-hole in the staff room, her Donna Beaumont days seemed some way off. She couldn't wait for the start of the summer holidays and the chance to do it again.

'Open in Private'. The words on the front of the brown envelope made her heart jump. What was this?

She went to her classroom, locked the door and tore the envelope open.

Inside was a white envelope. On the front in lettering cut out from newspapers was her name – Ashley MacDonald. She opened the envelope and pulled out a sheet of paper.

On it, in the same ransom note lettering, was written:

I know all about you and your sideline. If you don't want everyone to know about it do what I say. Instructions to follow.'

Garibaldi closed the book and looked sideways at Gardner, whose eyes were fixed on the road ahead.

'My very own audiobook,' she said. 'And very nicely read if I may say so.'

'Don't think I'm reading the whole thing to you.'

'Of course not. I'm going to read it myself. Just haven't got round to it yet.' She let out a sigh. 'I know the boss said we're not in a book group but it's beginning to feel like we are. You ever been in one?'

Garibaldi snorted. 'A book group? You're joking!'

'I thought it might be your thing.'

'Just because I like books and reading doesn't mean I want to be in a book group. In fact it's *because* I like books and reading that I don't want to be in a book group! Half-baked ideas from half-pissed women.'

'I see. It's a woman thing, is it?'

Garibaldi realised his mistake. 'No, I don't mean that. I mean—'

'You mean it's mostly women in book groups.'

'Yeah. I know it's not exclusively so, but—'

'Hang on. Let's get this straight. You've never been to a book group, right?'

'Right.'

'But you know what they're like.'

'I don't need to go to one to know what they're like.'

'Really?'

'Yeah. Like I don't need to go to the top of Everest to know it's bloody high and bloody cold. You pick up on things. You read about them. You listen to what people say.'

'So much for evidence, then?'

Garibaldi laughed. 'OK. The truth is that Kay was in a book club. So I got it all from her.'

'Sore point is it?'

'Kay going to a book club was the least of our problems.' He turned to Gardner. 'How about you? Ever been to one?'

'I have actually. All part of my programme of self-improvement when I was with Tim.'

'So a sore point for you as well, then?'

'I guess so.'

'And what was it like?'

'What was it like?' Gardner paused, as if giving her response careful consideration. 'Half-baked ideas from half-pissed women.'

They both laughed. No damage done.

'So,' said Gardner, *Schooled in Murder*. Do you think Liam Allerton used characters and events at St Mark's as his models?'

'I have no idea. The only person who could tell us for sure is Liam Allerton. And unless we go through a medium that's not going to happen.'

'But do you think there's some woman on the staff who works as a prostitute?'

'Escort.'

'Is there a difference?'

'I'm not sure we shouldn't be saying "sex worker". Less loaded.'

' And while we're on the subject, it's not actually *illegal* to work as an escort or prostitute or sex worker, is it?'

'Not in itself, no, but soliciting is and so is running a brothel and pimping.'

'So when this character in the book is blackmailed it's not actually over something that's a crime.'

'Not a crime, no, but definitely the kind of thing that would ruin a teaching career.'

'And is it actually illegal to have a relationship with a student?'

' It is. Any student under 18.'

'OK, but having a drug habit and nicking funds. Those *are* illegal, right?'

Garibaldi nodded.

'All a bit unlikely, isn't it? Rich pickings for a blackmailer and all in one place.'

'Unlikely, yes. Impossible, no. When it comes to these things I like to remind myself of one thing.'

'What's that?'

'Something my mate Oscar said.'

'Oscar?'

'Oscar as in Wilde. He said to do this is the sign of a thoroughly modern intellect.'

'To do what?'

'To expect the unexpected.'

'Right.' Gardner nodded, but couldn't hide her bafflement.

'You know that old ABC?' said Garibaldi.

'Deighton's favourite. Assume nothing. Believe nobody. Check everything.'

'That's the one. Well, I'm developing it. I'm working through the whole alphabet.'

'So what's D?'

'D is "don't be surprised".'

'And E . . .?'

Garibaldi turned to Gardner in the driving seat. She cast a quick sideways look and smiled.

'Expect the unexpected!' she said with a laugh.

'Do you want to know what "F" is?'

'I think I can guess.'

Ewan Thomas answered the door of his Lonsdale Road flat in shorts, t-shirt and flip flops. He looked as though he was on his way to the gym or to the beach and Garibaldi noted his toned physique with a touch of envy and a stab of guilt. Recently he'd spent more time in Gail's than he had in his trainers – he hadn't been for his usual run by the Thames for over a week.

Garibaldi and Gardner introduced themselves, showed their warrant cards and followed him into the living room.

'We're investigating the death of Liam Allerton, Ewan, and we'd like to ask you a few questions.'

'I still can't believe it.'

'Could you confirm that you were at Liam's talk in the OSO and that you went with him afterwards to the Sun Inn?'

'That's right.'

'Did you speak to him during the evening?'

'Not at length, no. We were in a group most of the time.'

'I'd like to ask you a few questions about Liam's book, *Schooled in Murder* .'

'Please do.'

'I take it you've read it?'

'I have, yes.'

'So, tell me, did you notice any similarities between St Mark's and the school in his book.– what was it called now?'

'St Jude's.'

'That's right. St Jude's.'

'Did I notice any similarities? Of course I did! I mean there's no question it's the same place.'

'And did you notice any other similarities?'

'Look, just because Liam was found in the same place as the victim in his novel doesn't mean ...'

'Doesn't mean we should look for other similarities between the book and real life?' said Garibaldi. 'I think it might mean exactly that, don't you?'

'What I mean is ... OK, when the book came out of course we all read it at school and of course we speculated about whether he was using us, basing his characters on us—'

'I was at his talk, Ewan, and—'

'Really?'

'And at the talk there was a question about whether he based his characters and stories on real people and events. Do you remember?'

'Yes, I do.'

'And he came up with all that stuff about all writers using their own experience but transforming it into something else in the creative process.'

'I remember, yes. All those examples of people who felt they had been unfairly represented in fiction and how difficult the whole thing was to prove in court. It sounded to me like he'd rehearsed it all, as if he'd answered the question many times before.'

'Tell me, Ewan, what time did you leave the pub on Saturday night?'

'I can't remember exactly, but it was shortly before eleven I think.'

'Was Liam there when you left?'

'I think so, yes. I remember saying goodbye to him.'

'And was there anything at all about that evening that you now think might be relevant to our investigation?'

'Like what?'

'Anyone behaving strangely? Anything anyone said that now seems important?'

'I can't think of anything, no.'

Ewan Thomas took the card Garibaldi offered him.

'If you think of anything,' said Garibaldi, 'get in touch.'

'I will. Look, there's one thing—'

Garibaldi raised his eyebrows.

'It might be nothing but I do remember at one stage Liam was standing with someone, heads down and close to each other. It could be nothing but—'

'Who was the someone?'

'Sasha.'

Garibaldi took out his notebook and flicked through it. 'Sasha Ambrose?'

'That's right.'

'Why do you mention this, Ewan? What do you think they were talking about?'

'I have no idea and, as I said, it may be absolutely nothing, but I do remember thinking at the time that it looked, I don't know, conspiratorial. Maybe that's the word, or maybe it was the look of people exchanging confidences. The rest of the time whenever I saw Liam he was in a group.'

'Thank you,' said Garibaldi. 'That's interesting.'

'Tell me, Inspector, do we know anything more about how he . . .?'

'About how he died? As a matter of fact we do. Liam Allerton drowned, Ewan, but there's something else you might need to know about it. The post-mortem has revealed that he died by drowning but that he had also been strangled. And there was evidence of Rohypnol in his blood.'

'But that's the same as—'

'Exactly, Ewan. The book. It's the same as in the book. We're treating his death as murder. It seems his drink may have been spiked, and the chances are it may well have been spiked at the Sun Inn.'

'But . . . who would do that? Why?'

'We're asking ourselves the very same question, Ewan, but if you think of anything, as I said, do let us know.'

Ewan looked down at the card he held in his hand as Garibaldi and Gardner followed him to the front door.

He was still looking down at it, a puzzled look on his face, when they walked to the car.

12

'Alex Ballantyne was what used to be termed a "character". Before the endearing and sometimes dangerous eccentricities of such teachers had been wiped out by the deep-cleanse detergents of professionalism, accountability and scrutiny, schools were full of them, particularly the revered institutions known as public schools.

Ballantyne had taught for nearly thirty years at St Jude's and had spent most of those thirty years at odds with it. Never short of an opinion and never frightened of voicing it, he had spoken out on many occasions against what he regarded as follies. No-one was exempt from it – pupils, colleagues, parents, senior management and, most of all, headmasters. Some described his criticisms as the voice of truth speaking to power. Others, mainly those on the receiving end, called it being a pain in the arse.

Loved and admired by his students, Ballantyne was a great teacher. Generations of boys (and in his latter years, after the school went co-ed, girls) had benefited from his wisdom, his ability to entertain and (to use a word often applied to the teaching profession's "characters") inspire, blending his academic rigour with a light entertaining touch, engaging both high-fliers and the few strugglers who slipped through the school's rigorous selection procedure. But it was his indiscretion that his students loved most – his willingness to share opinions that more tactful, less characterful colleagues would *choose to keep to themselves and would not in a thousand years reveal to pupils.*

Many of the teaching staff regarded Ballantyne in a similar light to those he taught, admiring his ability to see through cant and hypocrisy, his willingness to stand up for what he believed to be right, and enjoying his indiscretion. It was strange that someone like this should be the confidant of so many but, in his many years at St Jude's, that is what Ballantyne had become. Colleagues went to him for many reasons, some to give and receive juicy morsels of gossip, some for advice. There was something about Ballantyne that made people open up to him.

But affection and admiration for Ballantyne was not universal. Some colleagues held him in disdain, regarding him with fear and suspicion, and as his retirement approached, there would be as many pleased to see him leave St Jude's as there would be sad to lose him as a colleague.'

'This is like *Jackanory*,' said Gardner, her eyes on the road to Kingston.

'You're too young to know about *Jackanory*,' said Garibaldi.

'My grandparents told me about it.'

Garibaldi flicked back through the pages of *Schooled in Murder*. 'Do you know what's written in the front of all novels?'

'Do I have to guess or are you going to tell me?'

Garibaldi smoothed a page with his hand. 'Listen to this: "This book is a work of fiction and, except in the case of historical fact, any resemblance to actual persons, living or dead, is purely coincidental."'

'Is that in every novel?'

'Yeah, it is. And do you know why it's there?'

'Presumably to prevent any trouble.'

'Exactly. Trouble. Literary libel. I looked it up last night. There have been quite a few famous cases.'

'So you can sue if you think some writer had based a character on you?'

'Yeah, but it's difficult to prove. I mean how do you do it?'

'I guess you just list all the similarities and make a case for how obvious it is.'

'Exactly. Which is why the advice I came across for writers last night is so good.'

'Advice about what?'

'About how to avoid an accusation of libel or defamation.'

'Don't use their real name?'

'Better than that. Give them a small penis.'

Gardner turned sideways, taking her eyes off the road and, in her shock, letting the car swerve briefly to one side. 'What?'

'The small penis rule. It applies to men, but I think the principle could be applied to women if you're clever. There was this article in the *New York Times* which explained it. It said that if a fictional portrait of someone were to be something you could take legal action on it has to be so accurate that a reader of the book would have no problem linking the fictional character and the real-life one. So libel lawyers have what they call the "small penis rule". One way authors can protect themselves from libel suits is to say that a character has a tiny penis because no-one is going to come forward and say "that character with a very small penis, that's me!"'

'Are you making this up?'

'I'm absolutely serious. And it makes sense. If you give a character some horrible traits or if you have them doing something illegal, like, I don't know, having sex with

84

underage girls, having a serious drug habit or embezzling funds, you're not going to have anyone start shouting that the character who does the illegal things is modelled on them.'

'So these St Mark's teachers aren't going to say Liam Allerton based the character on them because if they did that they'd be owning up to having done bad things.'

'Exactly. Which is why although everyone acknowledges the similarity between the schools they don't acknowledge any similarity between the people. Or at least they don't publicly.'

'Hang on. Are you saying that you think Allerton *did* base his characters and the events on things that were going on at St Mark's?'

'Assume nothing, remember?'

'But all those secrets in one place?'

'Every place has got secrets, Milly. And if we knew how many they wouldn't be secrets.'

Garibaldi paused, unsure whether what he had just said was profound or utter nonsense.

Ruth Price had the busy efficiency bordering on bossiness that gave teachers a bad name. Even in her holiday gear (jeans, trainers, cardigan) there was something about her firm-set jaw and determined gaze that made Garibaldi feel he was about to be set homework and punished if he failed to deliver it on time. As he sat on the sofa in her Kingston flat he felt grateful that the teacher he was living with was a very different creature.

'We're here to ask some questions about Liam Allerton,' said Garibaldi.

'I was expecting this,' said Ruth. 'I guess I must have been one of the last people to see him alive.'

'Exactly. So—'

'So you're talking to everyone who was with him that night?'

'Yes, we—'

'Imagine him being found there. Just like the character in his novel! Everyone's talking about it. All kinds of stories are flying about.'

'We're treating his death as suspicious and it is now a homicide investigation, and we—'

'And you want to ask whether his novel is based on real life, whether any of those characters in his book are based on teachers at St Mark's?'

Garibaldi's mouth fell open. Did Ruth Price interrupt everyone? Did Ruth Price know everything? He thought of the kids unlucky enough to be in her classes.

'Perhaps,' he said, 'you could let—' He held up his hand as Ruth opened her mouth. 'Perhaps you could let me ask some questions without being interrupted?'

'I'm sorry. When I'm nervous I—'

'As you know, Liam Allerton's body was found in Barnes Pond, in exactly the same place as the murder victim in his novel.'

'I know, I—'

Garibaldi held up his hand again. 'The post-mortem showed that he died by drowning, but that he had also been strangled. Early indications are that Rohypnol was in his system.'

'But that's the same as—'

'Exactly. Maybe we could—'

'His drink was spiked with Rohypnol and he was found in exactly the same place as—'

'Maybe we could ask a few questions.'

'Of course. I . . .'

'Let's start with Saturday night, shall we? What time did you leave the Sun?'

'I can't remember exactly but I think it was about 10.30.'

'So when you left Liam was still there?'

'Yes, definitely. I remember going up to him to say goodbye.'

'Had you spoken to him that evening?'

'We were in a group at a table so there wasn't much chance to talk to him alone.'

'When you left the pub did you come straight home?'

'Yes, I walked to Barnes Bridge station – and got the train.'

'Via Clapham Junction?'

'That's right.'

'How did Liam seem to you throughout the evening?'

'Nothing unusual about him. He seemed pretty relaxed in the pub. I think he was unwinding after the talk. You know, all that adrenaline and then when it's over and you have a few drinks . . .'

'Did he seem drunk to you?'

'I'm not saying that. Just relaxed.'

'Is there anything about that evening, either in the OSO or at the pub, anything about Liam or the people he was with that you thought odd?'

'How do you mean, odd?'

'Anything you noticed, anything unusual that might be relevant?'

'You mean did I see someone spike his drink? Or anyone looking at him with an "I'm going to kill you" look in their eye?'

'Exactly,' said Garibaldi, unconvinced that being nervous was enough to excuse Ruth Price's manner.

'It's pretty odd, isn't it, Inspector, that Liam should be

killed like that? It's the same as the book. Identical. Do you have any theories about it?'

'We're exploring several lines of enquiry,' said Garibaldi, so unconvinced by the line that his smile almost undermined it.

He got up, walked to the door, then turned. 'Do you have any ideas, Ruth?'

'Ideas about what?'

'About why Liam was killed like that?'

Ruth Price lifted her head and looked to both sides, as if she were inspecting the ceiling. 'I have no idea,' she said, returning her gaze to Garibaldi. 'Absolutely none. This has freaked me out. Totally. I mean I was already freaked out, but this spiking . . .'

For the first time in the visit Ruth Price looked unsure of herself. The abrasive certainty and the know-all aggression had gone.

Garibaldi almost felt sorry for her.

Armit Harwal didn't regard himself as an elitist but, being a teacher of Classics at a private school, he often had to defend himself against the charge. The man who had introduced himself as Detective Inspector Garibaldi at the door of his Roehampton flat may not have made the accusation directly but there was something about the way he'd repeated the word 'Classics?' that revealed what he was thinking. And when he'd elaborated by saying, "So that's Latin and Greek, then?' and gave his colleague a wry smile Armit was left in no doubt.

'What do you make of it all?' said the detective.

'Strangled and Rohypnol, you say? And his body found in Barnes Pond? Look, I know people looked for similarities when Liam's book came out, but this is ... I don't know what to say.'

'Talking of similarities, Armit, everyone seems to agree that Liam based the school in his book on St Mark's, but aren't so sure when it comes to the teachers.'

'It's a ridiculous idea! It's obvious he made it up. He based the school on one he knew well and then just made it up. But now, Liam being found there, being killed like that, it's weird. Totally fucking weird. Who would do that? I mean ... why?'

'Exactly. Who and why. We're treating Liam Allerton's death as murder and those are the questions we're asking. We're particularly interested in Liam's movements on that Saturday night and I understand you went to his talk at the OSO and that you were in the group that went to the Sun Inn with him afterwards. Is that correct?'

'Yes, that's correct, but surely you don't think I—?'

'We don't think anything at the moment, Armit, we're just talking to everyone who was with him on Saturday night.'

'This Rohypnol thing. Do you think his drink was spiked?'

'It's a strong possibility.'

'At the Sun?'

'Another strong possibility. What time did you leave the Sun on Saturday?'

'I can't remember exactly. About a quarter to eleven, I guess.'

'Before Liam left?'

'Yeah. He was still there. I said goodbye to him.'

'And did you go straight home?'

'What do you mean? You don't think *I* did it, do you?'

'We're not making any accusation. All we're doing is asking what time you left.'

'I went straight home. Walked up to the Red Lion and got the bus down to Roehampton. Look, Inspector, are you suggesting that one of us did it, that we spiked his drink in the pub and then we – I don't know – took him to Barnes Pond and . . .'

'Do you remember anything anyone said or did that evening that, knowing what happened to Allerton, might be relevant?'

'Nothing I can think of, no. Liam seemed fine – at the talk and in the pub – and everyone else was just being their usual selves. I just don't get it. I don't get it at all. Why would anyone want to kill Liam – that's a big enough question. But why would they want to do it like that – that's an even bigger one.'

'Well if you do think of anything,' said the detective, standing up and offering him a card, 'here's my number.'

Armit looked at the card as the detectives left, wondering whether he should get in touch with the others to see what they made of it all and, more importantly, how they had answered the detectives' questions.

It would be the obvious thing to do, but something was stopping him. Maybe it was the same thing that had stopped them contacting him.

Schooled in Fucking Murder.

It took Ted Fox some time to realise that he had a problem. At first he thought it was just a bit of harmless fun. What was wrong with recreational drugs every now and then? Everyone else was doing it, so why not him? And it wasn't as if he was the only one in a responsible job. In his social circle all kinds were at it. Doctors. Lawyers. Accountants. There was nothing about his own position – a teacher at St Jude's school – that meant he couldn't indulge in a few lines now and then, especially if he confined himself to weekends and holidays.

It was when he found himself doing it in the men's toilets of the staff room that he realised it was no longer harmless fun.

He'd been in a cubicle, but had someone seen him go in and guessed what he was up to? He thought he'd been alone in there. No-one had been using the other cubicle (he'd checked) and no-one had come in to use the urinals.

But could he be absolutely sure? Had he been careful enough? Had he done enough to keep it hidden?

Could his own carelessness be the reason he was looking at the note he now held in his hands (his shaking hands), the cut-out letters dancing in front of his eyes—

I know all about your coke habit. If you don't want anyone else to then do what I say. Instructions to follow.

(from *Schooled in Murder* by Ben Joseph)

13

Garibaldi pointed at the grainy CCTV images on the screen behind DCI Deighton.

'The Sun Inn on Saturday night. As you would expect, it's busy. A nice warm evening, so most people are outside. And here –' he nodded to Gardner, who was working the computer. She freeze-framed the screen. 'Here is the Liam Allerton party at a table in the area in front of the entrance. Some are sitting at the table. Others are standing.' He pointed at a man sitting in the middle of the group. 'This is Liam Allerton. His talk at the OSO finished at 9.00 pm and their cameras show him leaving with his group at 9.30. They arrive at the Sun at 9.40 and Allerton sits down at this table. He was there until he left at 11.05. Between his arrival and departure he got up from the table and went inside twice to go to the loo.'

'Do we know who he's with?' asked DC McLean.

'Ex-colleagues from St Mark's,' said Garibaldi, 'and some friends.' He pointed at the screen. 'We can identify the St Mark's teachers. Ewan Thomas, Sasha Ambrose, Ruth Price, Armit Harwal. We've spoken to each of them and they've given their times of departure. They pretty much correspond to what the CCTV cameras tell us.'

'And the others?' asked DC McLean.

'Nothing on them as yet,' said Gardner, 'but we're work-ing on it.'

'So it could have been any one of them who spiked his drink?' said DC Hodson.

'Could be,' said Garibaldi. 'But it could also be anyone else in the pub. The fact is we're not going to see it on these cameras.'

'OK,' said Deighton. 'And what did those teachers have to say about the murder?'

'All shocked ,' said Garibaldi, 'and all astounded that Allerton should have been killed in the same way as the victim in his novel.'

'Well they're not alone there,' said Deighton. 'Here's the *Mail Online*.' She peered at her computer screen. '*Was writer's murder inspired by his own book?*'. And the *Mirror* has: '*Writer killed in same way as his character*'. But there are loads of them. '*Copycat killer?*' '*Murder by the Book*'. '*Barnes killer inspired by victim's book.*' We've issued a press release saying we're well aware of the similarity and it's one of our many lines of enquiry, but we're going to struggle to keep a lid on this. They're all over this book, so I suggest as a first step we all read the bloody thing. I finished it last night but I've delegated our resident literary expert to give us a heads-up, spoilers and all.'

Garibaldi picked up a marker pen and stood by the board.

'OK.' He wrote a name on the board – *St Jude's*. 'St Jude's, the fictional school in Allerton's novel. Posh private school by Hammersmith Bridge. A mish-mash of modern buildings. He added *St Mark's* to the board. 'St Mark's. The school Brown taught at for thirty years. Posh private school by Hammersmith Bridge. Mish-mash of modern buildings.'

He wrote a name on the board – *Alex Ballantyne*.

'In *Schooled in Murder*. Ballantyne, a teacher at St Jude's, has been blackmailing members of the St Jude's staff. Here's who they are.'

Garibaldi added a name to the board – *Ted Fox*.

'In the book, Ted Fox, a Geography teacher, is black-mailed over his drug habit. Cocaine. Can't stop doing it. Even does it in the staff room toilets.'

He added to the list – *Ashley MacDonald*.

'Ashley MacDonald. History. Ashley works as an escort. Top of the range sex worker. Ballantyne asks for money to keep this quiet.'

He put up another name – *Prisha Bedi*.

'Prisha Bedi teaches Chemistry and she has embezzled large sums of money from the school charity fund. And finally ...'

He added *Harry Antrobus* to the list.

'Harry Antrobus. Maths teacher. Harry had sex with a student.'

Garibaldi stepped back from the board.

'So these are Alex Ballantyne's blackmail victims. Each of them pays Ballantyne money to stop him revealing their secrets to everyone – parents, pupils, governors, the public. And then, the morning after Ballantyne retires from the school his body is found in Barnes Pond. He's been stran-gled and there's Rohypnol in his system. DI Moriarty – a pretty unconvincing representation of a police detective but, hey, people don't read these things for their truthful-ness, do they? If they did we'd have pages and pages of him sitting at his desk reading reports, wouldn't we? Anyway, DI Moriarty's on the case and he's the one who discovers what Ballantyne's been up to.'

He paused. 'Any questions?'

He looked in Gardner's direction. She looked over her shoulder and then turned back with raised arm. 'So this DI Moriarty, how does he find out?'

'He finds out when he searches Ballantyne's house and finds the cut-out lettering he used on his blackmail notes.'

'OK,' said DC Hodson, 'and what happens in the book? I mean, what's the action?'

'Action? It's not that kind of book. Most of it's about DI Moriarty going up to the school and trying to find out who's being blackmailed and why and talking to the head and the teachers.'

'Those characters,' said DC McLean pointing at the board. 'Are there any obvious models for them at St Mark's? Ones in the same positions, ones teaching the same subjects, ones who match the physical descriptions?'

'Good question,' said Garibaldi. 'The truth is no-one's saying. It's impossible to believe that the teachers at St Mark's didn't ask those questions when they read the book, but no-one we've spoken to so far has come out with their suspicions. But you're right, we do need to look at them for parallels. And what we really need to look for are teachers up there with exactly the same secrets as those characters.'

'And how do we do that?' said Gardner. 'Do we interview all of them?'

'We can't do that,' said Deighton, stepping forward in front of the screen. 'Not only would it take forever, it would also be done on the assumption that it was a St Mark's teacher who murdered Liam Allerton and we have no evidence that is the case. We have to investigate them, of course, just like we have to find out as much as we can about Allerton's book and its relevance, but we can't spend our whole investigation immersed in the school and the book.'

'But the way Allerton was killed,' said Gardner. 'Doesn't

that bring us back to the book? Isn't that the biggest clue we've got?'

'We can't interview every teacher,' said Deighton, 'with a copy of Allerton's book in our hand, looking at them to see if they match any of the book's descriptions. We can't treat it as some kind of Bible. As in everything we keep perspective, we don't lose sight of basics. ABC.'

Deighton came out with it so often it needed no spelling out.

'Yeah,' said Gardner, 'but that's what we'd be doing. Checking everything.'

'I'm not saying we *ignore* the book,' said Deighton. 'Of course not. But it can't be our only line of enquiry.'

'So any more questions about it?' said Garibaldi.

'Yeah,' said Gardner. 'You've said that in the book the head's wife's the killer of Alex Ballantyne. How, exactly, does she kill him?'

'Another good question. So, at the retirement party she approaches Ballantyne and says there's something she needs to tell him but it has to be in secret. She flirts with him, makes him think it might be some kind of sexual advance. She tells him she's going to sneak away from the party and be on a bench by the pond in fifteen minutes. He's to meet her there. She's already spiked his drink so fifteen minutes is about the right time. When he loses consciousness she rolls him into the pond.'

'Rolls him into the pond?' said Gardner. 'She's strong enough to do that?'

Garibaldi nodded in agreement. 'Yes, it's one of the novel's many flaws. I'll leave you to discover the rest for yourselves.'

'So do we need to talk to Harry Reed's wife?' said Gardner.

'We could,' said Garibaldi, 'but I can tell you already what she'll say.'

'This is the problem,' said Deighton. 'We do things *by* the book, not *because* of the book. We can't suspect people because of what someone's made up.'

The room nodded, but Garibaldi felt uneasy.

All he could think of were the thousands of people who had been suspected on those very grounds.

Prisha Bedi did not look like a criminal. None of the pupils she taught, none of the colleagues she worked with, none of the parents she saw at parents' meetings, would ever have guessed that she had, since her arrival at St Jude's five years ago, embezzled thousands of pounds from the institution that had employed her, confident in the belief that she would not only be an effective, successful teacher but also broaden the ethnic diversity of a staff room which had so often been accused of being predominantly male and white.

Prisha couldn't remember the precise moment when the idea came to her, but she knew only too well why she had turned to it. It had been a moment of great sadness when she delivered her aged mother to the care home, but that sadness was nothing compared to her shock when she realised the financial implications of the move. Care home fees were extortionate and she faced a real dilemma. She was an only child and her mother had been widowed several years ago, so she was in this alone. One option was to sell the family home, the one she had returned to when she took the job at St Jude's, but it was not something she felt she was ready to do. There had to be other ways to raise the necessary money . . .

She knew that whatever she managed to siphon off would come nowhere near the amount she needed. She knew the whole thing was an act of desperation.

But once she started she had found it very difficult to stop.

Now, as she looked at the note she held in her hand, she wished she had.

I know you've been stealing funds from the school. If you don't want anyone to know do what I say. Instructions to follow.

(from *Schooled in Murder* by Ben Joseph)

14

'Quite a few books have inspired crimes, you know,' Garibaldi said to Gardner as she drove them across Chiswick Bridge. 'I was reading an article about it last night.'

'Did it say anything about someone reading *Schooled in Murder* and then killing the bloke who wrote it?'

'Funnily enough, no, but I did jot a few down.' He took a notebook out of his jacket and opened it. '*Catcher in the Rye*, for example. Did you know that Mark Chapman, the man who killed John Lennon, identified with the book so much that he considered Lennon's murder to be the 27th chapter in the 26-chapter book? He even quoted a line from the novel at his trial and wrote "this is my statement" on the inside cover of the copy recovered from his jacket pocket during his arrest.'

'Sounds like he was just a bit unhinged,' said Gardner.

'And then there's *The Collector* by John Fowles, the guy who wrote *The French Lieutenant's Woman*. The character in his book is a butterfly collector with severe Asperger's Syndrome. He captures Miranda, a girl he has been obsessing over for some time, and adds her to his "collection". Apparently a serial killer captured and killed eight young women in the 1980s and was found to have the book in his possession when he shot himself.'

'That doesn't prove the book was the reason he killed them, does it?'

'No,' said Garibaldi, 'but it's pretty suspicious isn't it? And here's another. Listen. Stephen King's *Rage*. Charlie Decker kills his teacher and takes his classmates hostage in what soon becomes a group therapy situation. In 1989, Dustin Pierce took his algebra class hostage for nine hours after reading the book. In 1997 Michael Carneal killed three and wounded five members of a prayer group at his high school; a copy of the book was found in his locker. After that, Stephen King asked that the novel never be printed again.'

'Are we supposed to believe that someone read *Schooled in Murder* and decided to commit a murder in exactly the same way as the killer in the novel? And that they decided to kill the bloke who *wrote* the novel in exactly the same way?'

'Sounds ridiculous, doesn't it?' laughed Garibaldi. 'But it's no more unbelievable than these examples.'

'This thing, this syndrome, is there a name for it?'

'I don't think so. But there's more … listen to this.' Garibaldi flicked over a page. 'There's Joseph Conrad's *The Secret Agent*. Apparently Ted Kaczynski, the Unabomber, was known to read Conrad's works repeatedly. And as a result of the similarities between Kaczynski's personal life and *The Secret Agent*, the FBI recruited Conrad scholars to help them better understand the Unabomber's campaign and motives for mail-bomb terror. How about that? And then there's *A Clockwork Orange*, of course. In 1973 sixteen-year-old boys, dressed like the characters, the droogs, in Burgess's novel beat up a younger boy and another man dressed the same way assaulted a woman because she was "taking up too much space in the dance floor". But here's my favourite.' He flicked over another page. 'Apparently there's a book called *The Fashionable Adventures of Joshua Craig* published in 1909 by David Graham Phillips. American, it seems. And some bloke called Fitzhugh Coyle Goldsborough shot the author six times when he became suspicious that Phillips had based one of the characters in the book on Goldsborough's sister in an attempt to defame her. He then turned the gun on himself.'

Gardner turned to him briefly. 'And has all of this made anything clearer?'

'Not a bit,' said Garibaldi. He snapped his notebook shut. 'It's like everything. The more I know the less I understand.'

'Who said that?'

'Paul Weller, I think. Or it may have been Socrates – I can't remember.'

Gardner said nothing but gave a nod, as if she too couldn't recall whether the words were those of the Modfather from Woking or the philosopher from Ancient Greece.

'I'm sorry for your loss.'

Experience had taught Garibaldi it was better to say something, anything – even the most tired cliché – than it was to stay silent.

Fran Allerton sat opposite him in the living room of the Cambridge Road family home. Her face wore an expression with which, over the years, Garibaldi had become too familiar – the anguished puzzlement of those whose loved ones have been murdered.

'I'm still trying to take it in,' said Fran, 'to, you know, process it.'

'I understand,' said Garibaldi, 'and I'm sorry to have to ask you questions.'

'No, please, we need to know who did this. We need to find out what happened.'

'So tell me,' said Garibaldi, 'when did you last see your father?'

'When did I last see my father? You mean like the painting?' She shook her head. 'Yeah, when did I last see Dad? I guess it was the weekend before . . . before it happened. I came over for Sunday lunch.'

'And how did he seem to you?'

'Same as ever.'

'And what was that?'

'What was same as ever for Dad? Wow, I don't think I can do that. How do you sum anyone up, let alone your own father? He was intelligent, witty. Could be charming. But, yeah, he could be difficult as well.' Fran broke off and reached for a tissue. 'I'm sorry. This is tough.'

'But he was no different from usual on that Sunday?'

Fran shook her head. 'Just the same.'

'Did he say anything about his talk?'

'Only that he was looking forward to it. He told us what he was going to say, ran a few jokes past us, that kind of thing. He's – he was a bit like that. Ever since the book came out he couldn't stop talking about it. So I think Mum and I did what we always did.'

'What was that?'

'We put a limit on him. We reached a point where we said OK that's enough. No more book stuff. Let's talk about something else. It was a running joke.'

'When you say he liked to talk about his book, what did he like to say about it?'

'All kind of things. How amazed he was that he

102

managed to do it, how pleased he was to get it published and then a whole load of insecurities. How well it was selling. Not enough reviews. Bad reviews. That kind of thing. It might be what all writers worry about but I wouldn't know.'

'And when you say your father could be difficult?'

Fran gave a heavy sigh. 'Look, I loved him to bits, right, and I know Mum did too, but he wasn't always the easiest to live with. He didn't suffer fools. He had a temper. And sometimes—'

Felicity Allerton came in carrying a tray. 'Here we go,' she said as she put it down on the table, as if tea and biscuits might make everything OK.

Fran looked at her mother and then turned back to Garibaldi, raising her eyebrows and nodding in her mother's direction, as if to suggest that their discussion of her father's difficult nature might be better continued in private.

'I was just saying, Mum, about how we had a cut-off point for Dad when he was talking about his book.'

Felicity put down the tea and biscuits. 'Yes, he liked to talk about it. Sometimes you couldn't stop him. And now . . .'

'Was there anything you remember him particularly talking about, Felicity?' said Garibaldi.

Felicity smiled and looked up. 'He was excited about it, full of it. Ollie said it had all gone to his head, that it had changed him, but I don't know.'

'About the book,' said Garibaldi. 'As you both know, the circumstances of the discovery of—'

'Unbelievable!' said Fran. ' It was enough of a coincidence that he was found in the same place as the body in his novel, but to have been murdered in exactly the same way . . . it's ridiculous. I have no idea what to make of it.'

'Tell me,' said Garibaldi, 'were you both surprised that Liam wrote a book?'

Fran and her mother looked at each other, as if uncertain who should speak first.

'Totally,' said Fran. 'I mean, I knew he liked reading and he was fond of crime novels, but he never mentioned anything about wanting to write one. I suppose he was always like that. He liked to get on with things.'

'And you?' Garibaldi turned to Felicity.

'Yes, I was surprised, but looking back on it I'm glad he did. It gave him something to do. To be honest, I was dreading Liam retiring.'

'Dreading it? Why?'

'He didn't have any grand plans like some people have for retirement and I thought he was just going to be hanging round the house getting under my feet. I work from home and I could see it being a huge problem.'

'What work do you do?' said Garibaldi.

'I'm a translator. Freelance. Spanish mostly but a bit of German. The thing is Liam's holidays were long, especially the summer one, so we were used to spending a lot of time together, but there was something about retirement, the idea of him being around with no prospect of another term about to begin and him getting out of the house ...'

'I was concerned as well,' said Fran. 'Dad had always been so active. It was difficult to imagine him doing nothing.'

'That's right,' said Felicity. 'And to be honest it turned out to be less of a problem than I'd anticipated. He took up a few things, kept himself busy.'

'What did he take up?'

'He joined a tennis group and started to learn Spanish. Spanish of all things! He could have chosen something else. And he also joined a choir.'

'I see,' said Garibaldi. 'Tennis. Spanish. Choir. Aren't those things that Alex Ballantyne's involved with in Liam's novel?'

Felicity nodded.

'So how much of himself did your husband put into the character of Alex Ballantyne?'

'It's tempting to think he's a version of himself, isn't it? Liam always denied it, of course. And now he's been killed, murdered like that . . .'

Felicity started to sob. Gardner reached in her pocket for a tissue and handed it to her.

'I'm sorry to distress you,' said Garibaldi, 'but—'

'No,' said Felicity, blowing her nose, 'you have to ask these questions, you have to find out. But, yes, tennis, Spanish, choir. It's an easy road to go down, isn't it, that Ballantyne was my husband.'

'To get back to his novel, and the way it surprised you . . .'

'I noticed he was spending a lot of time in his study – well, when I say study I mean the spare bedroom, it's not as though it had a big leather desk or anything. Anyway he spent a lot of time in there with the door shut listening to his music just like when he was doing his marking or his school work. And he was on his laptop, but then he'd always been on his laptop looking things up, finding things out. He liked football – a big Chelsea fan. He was a season ticket holder, went to all the games – well, all the home games that is.' Felicity turned to her daughter. 'What do we do about that?'

'Don't worry,' said Fran. 'Ollie can sort that out.'

'So much to do,' said Felicity. 'I never imagined there would be so many things to sort out. But yes, he liked football. He liked horse racing as well. I used to worry he might develop a gambling habit but I don't think that interested him. It was studying the form, the patterns, the odds. A bit like his crosswords – he loved those as well. Why am I telling you this? Oh yes, so when he was spending his time upstairs I just assumed he was doing that kind of thing.'

Garibaldi thought of Liam Allerton following Chelsea and learning Spanish. He thought of his own QPR season ticket and his attempts to learn Italian. He felt some kind of connection with the murdered man. The more he heard about him the more he thought he would have liked him. He might even have forgiven him for being a Chelsea fan.

'Anyway,' said Felicity, 'he didn't tell me until he'd done it. One day he came down with this pile of paper in his hand and said, 'Guess what? I've written a novel. And I'd like you to read it.'

Garibaldi turned to Fran. 'And did he give it to you at the same time?'

'I only found out about it when Mum had read it.'

'And when you had read it, Felicity, what did you say to your husband?'

'To be honest even as I was reading it I was in a state of shock. I couldn't believe he'd done it and, yes I suppose I was surprised it was as good as it was. So I told Liam I liked it and that it was great. He said he was going to send it off to agents and asked me if I thought he needed to change anything. And I said it was fine. I knew it could be polished up a bit, that the writing could have been smoother but I wasn't going to say that.'

'What did you think about the school he set it in? St Jude's.'

'It was obviously St Mark's.'

'And the characters – did you notice similarities between the characters in the book and the people Liam worked with?'

Felicity shook her head. 'How would I? I didn't know them. I may have met them over the years at school functions and the like and Liam may have sounded off about his colleagues when he got home and was in a bad mood, but I didn't know any of them well enough to recognise them in the novel.'

'When you say he sounded off about his colleagues, can you remember anything specific that he said?'

'Nothing specific, no. The truth is I used to switch off. It seemed that someone up there had always done something to annoy him. After a while, I didn't take it in.'

'When I spoke to the headmaster, Harry Reed—'

'Oh, yes, Reed. Well he definitely didn't like him.'

'Why do you say that?'

'Liam quite liked the old head, Carswell, but he couldn't stand the new one. As soon as he arrived he started taking all these initiatives – you know the kind of thing all new heads do to make a mark – and Liam used to come home fuming about them.'

'So,' said Garibaldi, 'the head in his novel . . .?'

'It's tempting to think that, isn't it? But I can't believe it for one moment. I think all Liam was doing was having a bit of fun, a bit of impish fun.' Felicity stopped as if struck by a sudden memory. 'Not much fun now, is it?'

Fran stretched her hand out towards her mother and rested it on her arm.

'That was the thing about Liam, though. He always liked to speak his mind.'

'Could you show us his study?' said Garibaldi.

'What are you looking for?'

'We don't know. Often you have no idea what you're looking for until you find it.'

Felicity looked appalled at the prospect. 'But I never

107

went in there. I mean, I just let him get on with things and didn't disturb him. You can tell from the fact I didn't even know he was writing a book. I never . . . I can't imagine what it's going to be like when I have to go through his stuff. It'll be . . .'

'We'll have to take his computer,' said Garibaldi.

'Why? You don't think he was—?'

'Standard procedure. It's not because we suspect him of anything. We won't be long.' Garibaldi got to his feet. 'But if you could . . .'

Felicity sat in her chair, her eyes wide and vacant.

'I'll take you, Inspector,' said Fran. 'Follow me.'

'You show them, Fran,' said Felicity, pouring herself a cup of tea and reaching for a biscuit. 'You show them.'

'She can't face it,' said Fran leading them upstairs. She paused on the landing and pointed at a shut door. 'There it is. Dad's study. I can't really face it myself but—' She leaned towards the door, turned the handle, pushed the door open and gestured for Garibaldi and Gardner to enter. They put on forensic gloves and went in.

The spare room, or box room as Garibaldi remembered such rooms once being described, was clearly Liam Allerton's place of retreat. On a large desk up against one wall sat a closed laptop. Books, CDs and vinyl sat on shelves and in piles on the floor on either side of a CD player and deck. A quick glance at the books and music gave Garibaldi a sense of what Allerton liked. Bob Dylan, Joni Mitchell, Bruce Springsteen, Leonard Cohen, Elvis Costello, Nick Cave – the musical taste of a late baby boomer. Ian Rankin, Lee Child, Val McDermid, Mark Billingham – the literary taste of a retired Maths teacher.

Garibaldi pointed at the laptop. 'We'll need to give that to digital forensics.'

'OK.' Gardner reached for it and placed it in an evidence bag.

Garibaldi opened one of the desk drawers and pulled out a wad of envelopes and papers.

'Seems wrong somehow,' said Gardner. ' A bit of a violation. His wife should be going through this stuff.'

Garibaldi sat at the desk and leafed through the pile, opening envelopes, giving everything a quick scan.

'That's the thing about murder,' he said. 'It seems like it's the ultimate violation, but it turns out that it's only the first of many. So many things follow it that strip the victim of all kinds of things. Dignity is one of them. Privacy's another.'

He picked up a bunch of USB sticks. 'We'll need these as well.'

He opened the second drawer, peered in, and pulled out another bunch of papers.

'Looks like this was his accounting drawer.'

He sifted through the statements, receipts and invoices. 'Reminds me we need to look at his bank details.'

He opened the bottom drawer. 'In my experience the most interesting things are found in the bottom drawer.'

He pulled it open and fished out a pile of diaries and greetings cards, putting them on the desk in front of him.

He reached into the drawer again.

'And most are shoved right to the back.'

He stretched further and his hand found another pile of envelopes, this one tied together with a rubber band.

He put it on the table, undid the band and opened the first envelope.

It contained a single card.

'Well this is interesting,' he said showing it to Gardner.

'What the f—' she said, her mouth dropping open.

Garibaldi looked at it again.

> I know all about you and the
> pupil you slept with. If you
> don't want anyone else to know
> then do what I say. Instructions
> to follow.

A blackmail note. The letters cut from a newspaper in ransom note style.

Garibaldi opened the next envelope. Another card.

> I know you've been stealing
> funds from the school. If you
> don't want anyone to know do
> what I say. Instructions to follow.

The next envelope. Another card:

> I know all about you and your
> sideline. If you don't want
> everyone to know about it do
> what I say. Instructions to follow.

The next:

> I know all about your coke
> habit. If you don't want anyone
> else to then do what I say.
> Instructions to follow.

'I think,' said Garibaldi when Gardner had handed them all back to him, 'that we should take these away too.'

Gardner put them into an evidence bag. 'What's going on, boss?'

Garibaldi shook his head. 'I have no idea but you remember what I said about how DI Moriarty finds out that Alex Ballantyne has been blackmailing?'

'Yeah, he found things when he . . .'

'Exactly,' said Garibaldi. 'He found cut-up letters from newspapers when he searched Alex Ballantyne's house.'

There were many reasons why Harry Antrobus had moved to St Jude's. It wasn't just that it was, by anyone's definition, a far better school that the one he had been in for so long (it was, however you chose to measure such things, better than most schools in the country), it was that he knew he must move on. How had it happened? What the hell had he been thinking of? And, most importantly of all, how had no-one found out about it? He couldn't imagine what it would be like if news got out. He knew that moving to St Jude's wouldn't make any of it go away – it would still be a disaster if his employer found out – but there was something about a fresh start in a new institution that made him think, misguidedly perhaps, it might reduce the risk of exposure.

He still couldn't believe he'd done it. It was the kind of thing that other teachers did, the kind of thing you read about and snorted at in disbelief. How could anyone be so stupid?

Now the stupid one was him. Any thoughts that he might be able to keep it quiet had disappeared completely as soon as he had seen the note.

It had been tucked into the inside pocket of his jacket and it was only at the end of the day when he hooked the jacket off his chair and reached for his Oyster Card, that he noticed it.

The cut-out letters of his name on the front of the envelope unnerved him. The message on the sheet of paper inside made him shake.

I know all about you and the pupil you slept with. If you don't want anyone else to know then do what I say. Instructions to follow.

(from *Schooled in Murder* by Ben Joseph)

15

Sasha Ambrose would usually spend the first weeks of the summer holiday, and if possible the entire summer holiday, having no contact at all with teachers from school. That was what holidays were for. Not that she didn't like her colleagues, or at least the few of them she regarded as her friends, but simply because she needed a break.

But this holiday had begun like no other, and when Ewan called her and asked her out for a drink she had been quick to say yes. She was so worried by what had happened that the chance to talk it over with someone who might know more seemed a good idea.

It was a warm sunny evening and they sat outside a Richmond riverside pub.

'I haven't been sleeping too well,' said Ewan. 'How about you?'

Sasha looked at the deputy head, neatly turned out in chinos and a slim-fitting shirt. If he hadn't been sleeping well he didn't look too bad on it.

'Not too well, no,' said Sasha. 'I can't stop thinking about poor Liam.'

Ewan nodded, took a sip of his lager and licked his lips. 'Spooky, isn't it, someone killing him like that?'

'Yeah, straight out of his bloody book.'

'Why would anyone . . . I mean who . . .?'

'Exactly. Who on earth would want to kill him and why the fuck would they do it like that?'

'And then the police asking questions. They made me feel like a suspect.'

'Me too.'

'I guess it's because we were with him the night before he was found. We may have been the last to see him.'

'But it's not just that, is it?'

Ewan gave another slow nod. 'Yeah. *Schooled in Murder.*'

Sasha had never had a proper discussion with Ewan about Liam's novel. They had engaged in gentle banter about how the fictional school was clearly recognisable as theirs and had light-heartedly dismissed the idea that Liam had based his characters on St Mark's teachers. The idea was ludicrous. None of the characters bore a physical similarity to any of the staff, and as for the secrets those characters were harbouring, it was impossible to think that any of their colleagues might be hiding the same things.

And yet Sasha couldn't describe how uncomfortable she had felt when she first read the novel. Was she the only one to have experienced the same unease? Was she the only one who regretted confiding so much in Liam Allerton, or were there others who had taken the long walk to his classroom at the end of the Maths department and who now wished they had kept things to themselves? Was she the only one to have worked out what Liam had done?

'It's like we're *guilty* or something,' said Sasha. 'Just because we were with him in the pub and his drink was spiked . . .'

'But why would any of us have done it?' said Ewan.

The silence that fell between them was unnerving. Sasha

looked at Ewan. He held her gaze and for a fleeting moment she wondered whether she should tell him.

'The police,' she said, resisting the urge. 'They made me feel very uneasy.'

'They had to talk to us. We knew him. We were in the pub with him.'

'Did they ask you about his book?'

Ewan laughed. 'They couldn't stop. '

'Weird, eh? What do you make of it?'

Ewan reached for his beer. 'I have no fucking idea. But I can tell you one thing for free. Whoever did it must have read it.'

'Unless it's a coinci—' Sasha didn't bother finishing the word. She knew how unlikely it was. 'Have the police seen Ruth and Armit?'

'Yeah. I spoke to Armit yesterday.'

'How was he?'

'Shaken up like the rest of us. Ruth the same. Didn't enjoy the police questioning. But the thing you've got to remember about the police, Sasha, is they're thick as shit. You could tell from the way they spoke to us—'

'That Garibaldi cop didn't seem thick at all. He freaked me out.'

She could still remember the way the inspector had looked at her, the impression he gave that he was thinking much more than he would let on, that behind those eyes was a load of judgement.

Yet again, she wondered whether she should tell Ewan the truth. Yet again, she resisted. The stakes were too high.

She thought of the times she had sat with Liam working away at the *Guardian* crossword and remembered how much he had liked playing. That's what he had been doing – playing with her, playing with them all.

She thought again of what she had said to him that night in the Sun after his talk, when she'd managed a quiet word with him on the way to the loos. She hadn't said much, just enough to let him know she'd cracked it, that she knew what he had done. She could still see his face – a mixture of guilt and pleasure, the look of a man who had done something he shouldn't but who was pleased someone else had recognised it.

Ewan carried on talking and Sasha nodded and smiled as if she were listening.

But her mind was elsewhere.

On Liam Allerton's face in the Sun Inn, and on the pages of *Schooled in Murder* .

Excessive alcohol and the prospect of the long summer holidays did strange things to you. It clouded the judgement.

That was the conclusion Armit Harwal reached when he had woken up the morning after the end-of-term party lying next to Ruth Price. At first he thought it might turn out to be nothing more than an ill-judged one-night stand but they had slept together several times since and he wasn't quite sure what he had got himself into. This wasn't what he had planned. In fact he had planned on quite the reverse, a carefree summer in which he could do whatever, and whoever, he liked. But, in the scale of things (and he always liked to take the balanced view) hooking up with Ruth Price was proving to be the least of his worries.

Compared to Liam Allerton's murder, it was nothing.

That bloody novel. Of course he'd laughed about it when news of it reached St Mark's. And of course he'd joined in the laughter whenever anyone had speculated in the staff room about any possible correspondence between Allerton's characters and St Mark's teachers. What else was he supposed to do? He remembered looking round and wondering whether he was the only one who felt so uneasy about it, whether he was the only one who regretted his intimate conversations with the Maths teacher.

And on top of that there had been the visit from the police. All those questions about the book, Liam's talk at the OSO and their trip to the Sun. He had never felt more guilty.

He looked at the woman opposite him as they ate breakfast in the kitchen of his Roehampton flat. In one sense they were in the same boat – both there on the night and both questioned by the police – but Ruth couldn't possibly be feeling the same as him.

He scrolled through his laptop and pointed at the screen.

'Everyone's talking about it,' he said.

Ruth peered over. 'What are they saying?'

'All kinds of things. They can't let go of the book thing. Speculation that Liam based it on real life.'

'And we know that's not the case, right?'

Armit tried to catch Ruth's eye, but she had turned away and picked up the newspaper. 'Of course it's not the case,' he said, 'which is why the police asking all those questions about the book is so fucking ridiculous.'

'But they have to, don't they? Barnes Pond. Rohypnol. And we were with him the night before.'

There was something about the way Ruth said this that made Armit uneasy, but he couldn't put his finger on it.

All he could think of was what he had felt when he first read *Schooled in Murder* – a sense of shock and a feeling of regret that he hadn't kept his mouth shut.

16

'So tell me what happened,' said Garibaldi, looking across the Caffè Nero table at his ex-wife.

He tried to limit his dealings with her to phone calls, but there were times when a face-to-face couldn't be avoided.

This was one of them.

'It was all very silly,' said Kay.

'Silly? From what Alfie said it sounded pretty serious.'

'He overreacted. That's all.'

'OK. And what, exactly, did he overreact to?'

'Do you know what? I can't even remember. I think we might have asked him about his plans or something.'

'His plans? I thought we agreed to lay off him.'

'That's easy enough for you to say. He's not living with you.'

'Well he is, actually. That's why we're here.'

Kay shook her head with a tut. 'You know what I mean.'

'So you asked him about his plans. Plans as in jobs and things like that.'

'Yes, we—'

'Look, Kay.' Garibaldi tried to control his rising anger. 'After all he's been through—' He sensed that Kay was about to interrupt and raised his hand to stop her. '—And now's not the time to talk about who's to blame. After all he's been through we need to be thankful he's where he is. He's got through university. He's graduated from Oxford with a good degree. Let's be grateful for that, shall we?'

'I am grateful for that. It's just that he seems a bit . . .' Kay waved her hand dismissively. 'No, forget it.'

'Go on, say it. A bit what?'

'He's drifting.'

'You mean he hasn't got a job.'

'Not just that, no.'

'He's not the only Oxford graduate who hasn't got a job.'

'Look, it's not just about jobs—'

'What is it about, then?'

Kay glanced round the café. 'OK,' she said, turning back to face him. 'What do you think of Alfie's girlfriend?'

So the row hadn't been about jobs at all.

'Alicia? She's great. Look, Kay, I think Alfie's happy, or at least I did until he turned up on my doorstep on Saturday night. And a lot of him being happy is down to Alicia.'

'I just think—'

'You just think, or Dom just thinks?'

'That's not fair.'

'History suggests otherwise.'

Garibaldi had turned up with the best intentions but here they were – in the middle of another Caffè Nero row. Maybe it was the place. Maybe it was something they put in their coffee.

'So what sparked it off?' said Garibaldi. 'You still haven't told me. And don't come out with that "I can't remember" crap.'

'OK. Alfie said something about not wanting any kind of job, wanting something meaningful and then Dom said—'

Garibaldi braced himself.

'Dom said something perfectly reasonable . . .'

'I find that unlikely.'

'Something perfectly reasonable about there coming a time when you need to put student idealism behind you and join the real world. And for some reason Alfie took exception.'

'I'm not surprised.'

'You mean you disagree?'

'Whether I agree or not, it wasn't very tactful, was it? Alfie obviously thought it was a reference to Alicia.'

'I have no idea what he thought—'

'Just because she's got ideals doesn't mean—'

'Anyway,' said Kay, cutting him off with a raised hand. 'That's when he exploded.'

'Exploded? What did he do?'

'Stood up and started shouting. At Dom. At me.'

'What about?'

'Everything. Right back to . . . everything.'

Everything. Garibaldi flinched. His depression, the discovery of Kay's infidelity, the split, the decision that Alfie should live with Kay and Dom. It may have been some years ago but the pain of it all was as raw as if it had been yesterday.

'Did Alfie mention Alicia in his . . . explosion?'

'He said they were happy together.'

'Of course he did. That's because they are.'

After Alfie's two previous girlfriends – the one from his private school sixth form, and the one he had met in his first year at Oxford who took him off to dinner parties when he should have been at QPR – Alicia was exactly what Alfie needed. When he'd started going out with Alicia at the beginning of his third year it had been cause for celebration.

120

But he knew Kay hadn't approved. She never said so explicitly but he could tell she was disappointed. Alicia wasn't the kind of person she had expected Alfie to hang out with, let alone go out with, at Oxford.

'I don't know what happened to him,' said Kay. 'He just laid into Dom. Came out with all this stuff about needing to respect differences, about not expecting everyone to conform to some idea of – do you know what? It was such undergraduate gibberish I can't even begin to repeat it. And he called Dom all kinds of names.'

'Like what?'

He shouldn't have asked but he was itching to know.

'The question is,' said Kay, 'what do we do?'

'He's more than welcome to stay with us .We've got room.'

'A bit small though, for the ... three of you.'

She said the last three words as if she'd just trodden in them.

'Do you want him back with you?'

'Of course. If he wants to come back.'

'And if he doesn't?'

'That's his choice. You say he can stay with you but I can't see that working long-term. I'm worried about him. He's losing his way.'

'His way or your way?'

'That's unfair. All I want is for him to be—'

'For him to be happy? Well I think he is, or at least I think he was until Dom slagged off his girlfriend.'

'He didn't slag her off. Alfie just flew off the handle. It was like it was all about something else, as if there was some other reason for the outburst.'

'So what do you want to do?'

'Can you talk to him?'

121

'Can I talk to him? You know what, I'd not thought of that.'

'You know what I mean.'

The unfortunate thing was that Garibaldi did. As with everything to do with Kay he knew only too well.

17

D CI Deighton looked at the notes spread on the table in front of her.

'And you found these in Allerton's house?'

Garibaldi kept his eyes on the cut-out letters. 'In a spare bedroom they called his study. Bundled up at the back of a drawer.'

'So hidden?'

'Not under lock and key but definitely out of sight. You'd have to look hard to find them.'

Deighton exhaled. 'So what do we make of them?'

Garibaldi stroked his chin, his eyes still scanning the notes on the table. 'First thing to say is the obvious. These are blackmail notes. Exactly the same as the blackmail notes in the novel delivered by Alex Ballantyne to the teachers at St Jude's.'

'I don't get it,' said Deighton. 'Why would Allerton have these hidden at the back of his drawer?'

'Exactly.'

'Could it be that ...' Deighton paused. 'No, that's ridiculous.'

'What are you thinking?'

'That he might have been actually—'

'That he might have been blackmailing his colleagues? I've thought the same myself, but I can't see it. Why would he do such a thing? What would be his motive? What—'

'Ballantyne's motive in the book was money.'

'Yeah,' said Garibaldi, 'together with a weird sense of power. There's no evidence that Allerton craved or needed either. And if he *was* actually blackmailing teachers at St Mark's then there'd be teachers at St Mark's with those secrets to hide. And there's no evidence of that.'

'No evidence yet, but that doesn't mean there isn't any. All we have is a load of teachers denying it.'

'One thing we do know,' said Garibaldi, pointing at the notes, 'is that he definitely didn't send these. They were in his drawer.'

'So we get back to the question – what were they doing there?'

'Maybe he was just playing around. He wanted to see what they'd look like so he made some mock-ups.'

Deighton stroked her chin, her eyes still fixed on the notes on the table. 'Or maybe he did these as practice. He could have made other versions and sent those. Or he could have made copies of them.'

'But there's no evidence that he was actually *doing* it, actually sending notes like these.'

'Still a bit weird, though, isn't it?' said Deighton. 'Especially when you consider where they were found.'

Garibaldi nodded. 'Exactly. Straight out of *Schooled in Murder*. DI Moriarty discovers Ballantyne is blackmailing when he finds notes in his drawer. It's the whole life and art thing again.'

Deighton raised her eyebrows.

'"Life imitates art far more than art imitates life".'

'Who said that? Larkin?'

'Oscar Wilde.'

'I'm not sure I understand it.'

'Nor am I. That's its beauty. And the thing about it is—'

'We need to brief the team,' said Deighton, cutting him off and walking back to her desk. 'And we need to keep this away from the media. God knows what they'd do with it. Where are we on everything else? Allerton's phone?'

'Nothing odd or unusual in what he kept on it or in his history. And the same's true of his messages and his call record.'

'What about calls on that Saturday night?'

'Right. Well the last call he made was on Saturday afternoon to his daughter. And the last call he received was on that Saturday night from his wife. Quite late. 11.00 pm. Given that Felicity Allerton left the Sun at 10.00pm she would have been at home by then. My guess is she was giving him a call to see whether he was on his way back.'

'OK,' said Deighton. 'We need to check that with her. Bank details?'

'Nothing suspicious, joint account with Mrs Allerton, who's still working as a freelance translator. Decent teachers' pension and the book's brought in a bit but not as much as you'd expect.'

'Anything more from the crime scene?'

'Yeah. Traces of fibre from Allerton's clothing on the gravel near the pond. Presumably Allerton was on the gravel when he was being strangled.'

'DNA? I'm assuming the body hadn't been in the water long enough for significant erosion.'

'None on the body. You'd expect some on the neck where he was strangled, so it looks like whoever did it wore gloves. Just like the book.'

'OK,' said Deighton. 'Anything else?'

'Digital forensics have come back on Allerton's computer

and the USBs and I'm a bit puzzled. I was curious to know whether Allerton had written, or started to write, anything else and I asked them to look out for it. They couldn't find anything, but what was really puzzling was that they couldn't even find any copies of *Schooled in Murder*, which I also asked them to look for. Nothing. It was in the emails he sent to his agent and in his correspondence with the publishers but there was nothing else. I expected there to be loads of drafts, loads of versions but no. Nothing. Almost as if he'd got rid of them . . .'

'Or hidden them somewhere else?'

'Like where? Another computer? There was nothing, and nothing backed up anywhere. Forensics said you'd usually expect back-ups somewhere. The cloud. A good place for that kind of thing apparently.'

'He was obviously pretty secretive about it. I mean, his wife had no idea he was doing it until he'd finished and showed it to her.'

'I just don't get it,' said Garibaldi.

'Right,' said Deighton. 'Along with everything else.'

She spoke with her eyes on the papers in front of her. Garibaldi couldn't judge the tone, but it felt like a criticism. He was tempted to point out that he wasn't the only one unable to come up with answers and that she seemed just as puzzled, if not more so, than him, but he managed to stop himself saying anything before he left the office.

Maybe a pastry from Gail's on his way to Felicity Allerton's might cheer him up.

'We'd like you to have a look at something.'

Gardner held her tablet towards Felicity Allerton and pressed the screen.

'We found them in your husband's room,' said Garibaldi.

Felicity peered at the screen as Gardner scrolled through photos of the blackmail notes.

'We've sent the originals to the lab,' said Garibaldi.

Felicity's eyes grew wider as she looked, her hand covering her mouth in shock.

'I don't believe it,' she said. 'These are the notes in—'

'Exactly,' said Garibaldi. 'The notes in Liam's novel.'

'But what—' Felicity lifted her eyes from the screen and looked at Garibaldi. 'Where did you say you found them?'

'In his room. At the back of his bottom drawer.'

'I don't understand it.'

'So you haven't seen them before?'

Felicity shook her head. 'Not at all. I mean, I never went in there. That room, it was very much Liam's place. As I said, I'd no idea he was even writing a novel until he showed it to me. I kept out. And I can't face going in there to sort out his things. I just can't face it.'

'We know this must come as a great shock to you,' said Gardner.

'What were they ... why ...? I don't understand.'

'We need to ask you some more questions about Liam's book,' said Garibaldi.

Felicity covered her face with her hands. 'That bloody book!'

Gardner leaned forward and spoke in a soft voice. 'We need to find out as much as we can, Felicity.'

'Of course you do! Of course you do. It's just ...'

'Let's start with the school in Liam's book,' said Garibaldi. 'It bears a close resemblance to St Mark's. Did Liam ever say anything to you about it?'

'He didn't need to. Its location, its physical description. Everything about it made it pretty obvious. I remember whenever he was asked he never said St Jude's was meant to be St Mark's but he never denied it either.'

'And,' said Garibaldi, 'what about the teachers at St Jude's and the teachers at St Mark's?'

Felicity's laugh sounded more like a whimper. 'You mean were the teachers in his novel versions of the teachers he worked with? He always denied it. And he always came out with the same line – he said everyone bases their invention to some extent on reality, on places and people they've known or observed. Where else were you supposed to get your ideas? Things can't come from nowhere. I can still hear him saying it. He said it that night when he was giving his talk. Someone asked the question at the end, I can't remember who.'

'He may have denied it in public,' said Gardner, 'but in private, when he was talking to you, did he ever say anything different?'

Felicity bowed her head and said nothing for a few moments.

'Are you OK?' said Gardner.

Felicity lifted her head. 'I'm fine. I'm just ... worried.'

'What are you worried about?' said Garibaldi.

'The way he was killed and now the notes ...'

'What are you saying?' asked Garibaldi.

'I don't know. I really don't know.'

'To get back to the teachers for a moment, Felicity,' said Gardner.

'Liam never said anything to me that was different from what he said to everyone else.'

'And did you believe him?' said Garibaldi.

'Did I believe him? Who was I to disagree? I didn't work up there. I didn't know these people. He never said anything to me about anyone having done those things. I mean, the whole idea's ridiculous. And yet—' Felicity shook her head as if ridding it of a ridiculous notion.

'And yet what, Felicity?' said Gardner.

'And yet those notes. What on Earth was he doing with them?'

'The thing about those notes,' said Garibaldi, 'is that they were in his drawer. He hadn't sent them.'

'But then why were they there in the first place?'

'Maybe he mocked some up to see what they'd look like. Maybe he was just playing around.'

'But then why hide them? And why stuff them away at the back of his bottom drawer? You don't think ... but no, that's ridiculous!'

'We're keeping an open mind, Felicity.'

'But that's crazy. He wouldn't ... no, that doesn't make any sense at all. But if what he wrote about was actually—'

'As I said, we have to explore all possibilities.'

'But how can any of it be true? Liam wouldn't ... he just wouldn't. And teachers can't have done those things. They just don't. Respectable, responsible people like that.'

'You'd be surprised,' said Garibaldi, getting up from his chair. 'They're often the worst. One last question before we go. Your husband's phone records show that the last call he received was on Saturday night at 11.00 pm. The call was from you.'

'It was, I remember.'

'What was that call about?'

'You may recall, Inspector, that I left the pub early and went home. I gave Liam a call to see what time he thought he might be back as I was thinking of turning in early. I wanted to know what time he'd be home because ...' Felicity's lip quivered. 'Because I wanted him to come

129

home . . .' She looked at Garibaldi, tears in her eyes. 'And I still do. I still want him to come home.'

She sat in the chair, hands clasped in her lap, looking up at Garibaldi and Gardner, her eyes wide with fear and incomprehension.

They all jumped at the sound of the doorbell. Felicity turned, looking through the open living room door into the hall, her face brightened by the absurd hope that her wish had been granted and her dead husband had just come back.

'Shall I——?' said Gardner, moving towards the door.

'No,' said Felicity, getting out of her chair. 'Let me. In case it's . . .'

Garibaldi and Gardner exchanged a glance, sensing what was going on in Felicity's mind.

Felicity left the living room, wiping her hands on her dress as if preparing herself for a royal handshake.

They heard her open the door.

'Oh. Hello.'

Garibaldi heard disappointment in her tone.

'Are you OK?' came a man's voice.

'Yes, I – I . . . The police are here.'

'The police? Shall I come back or——?'

'No, come in, please. I think they're nearly done.'

Felicity came back in followed by a man who raised his hand in greeting.

'I'm Ollie,' he said. 'I'm——'

'We've met,' said Garibaldi. 'You were with Felicity when we first came round.'

'Of course. Look, I'm quite happy to come back if I'm interrupting anything.'

'No, please,' said Garibaldi. 'Come in.'

Ollie pointed at an empty chair. 'Shall I . . .?'

Garibaldi nodded and Ollie sat down, looking at Garibaldi with raised eyebrows.

'Has something happened?' he said.

'They've found something ,' said Felicity. 'In Liam's study.'

'What have they found?'

'Tell me, Ollie,' said Garibaldi, 'did Liam talk to you about his book?'

'Talk about it? He never stopped. Not when he was writing the thing. I mean, I was as surprised as Felicity and Fran when he produced it. But when we knew about it and when he knew it was going to be published, yeah, he spoke about it a lot. Difficult to stop him.'

'When you read the book, Ollie, did you get the sense that Liam was basing it on anything?'

'Of course. I mean that school's obviously St Mark's, isn't it?'

'And the characters?'

'I know where you're going, but no, I can't believe he based them on teachers he worked with.'

'Why not?'

'It all seems a bit unlikely, doesn't it ? Difficult to believe.'

'So you don't think Liam's novel describes things that were actually going on?'

Ollie shook his head. 'No, I can't see it.' He paused. 'But it's strange that he should have been found in the pond like that, isn't it? I mean, that *is* straight out of his novel.'

'Can you think of anything else?'

Ollie looked thoughtful. 'Wait a minute, Didn't Felicity—' He turned to her. 'Didn't you just say they found something in Liam's study?' He turned back to Garibaldi. 'Isn't that what happens in his book? Don't they find something, cut up letters or notes or something? That's how they find out about the bloke who's been doing the blackmailing.'

'I think they do,' said Garibaldi, 'but—'

'So Liam . . . he's found on Barnes Pond like in the book and now you've found something in his study. They're not notes, are they?'

'We'd better be off, said Garibaldi, nodding to Gardner, 'but if anything occurs to you – either of you – please do get in touch.'

He took a card from his inside pocket and handed it to Ollie.

Ollie gave an extravagant shrug of his shoulders. 'I just don't get it,' he said. 'I don't get any of it. I'm confused.'

Garibaldi headed for the door, sensing that Ollie would be even more confused when Felicity told him what it was they had found in Liam's study.

18

'I told him to fuck off.'

So Alfie had beaten him to it – ever since he'd set eyes on his ex-wife's partner Garibaldi had wanted to do the same.

'OK.' Garibaldi tried hard to hide his approval. 'Was there anything that . . . I mean did Dom say something?'

'Yeah,' said Alfie, 'he said something all right. He was talking a load of shit about growing up, facing reality. And the next thing I know he's having a go at Alicia.'

'Alicia?'

'Yeah. He didn't name her specifically but it was pretty clear who he was talking about. All these young "woke" people. That's what he said. All these "snowflakes". They need to grow a pair. Grow a pair! He actually said it. And that's when I lost it. You know what? I can't go back there. Not now. Maybe never.'

'You're very welcome to stay here.'

'Thanks, but I can't really, can I?'

'Why not?'

'The three of us . . .'

'Look, I know the house in Putney's very big and this place . . . well this place isn't, but—'

'Dad, please, I'll be OK.'

'If you don't stay here where will you go?'

'I'll find something.'

'What? Rent somewhere? You'd be throwing your money away. Better off—'

'We – me and Alicia – might find somewhere together.'

That sounded more promising. Garibaldi felt himself relax.

'But it won't be for a while. Alicia's mum needs looking after so we'll have to sort that out first.'

Garibaldi thought of Alicia's mum in her Camden council flat and suddenly it wasn't Alfie on the sofa but someone else.

There she was in front of him, Irish eyes twinkling over her knitting as she half-watched the TV. He could even see the programme – *The Generation Game*. Where was his dad? At the pub probably, or maybe at the Catholic Guild where he hung out with other Italian immigrants. Where was his sister? At a party maybe, or a disco. That's what they called clubs back then. Discos.

The clack of knitting needles stopped and his mother's eyes turned from Bruce Forsyth.

'You can't go out, Giacomo.' Only his family called him Giacomo. To everyone else he was Jim. 'You can't go out. You're too young. But your time will come and it will come soon enough.'

How long was this before she died, before he lost them both? And how old was he? Fourteen perhaps, maybe fifteen, young enough to be at home with his mum on a Saturday night, aching to watch different programmes on the telly, or to slope into his room to read or listen to the radio until *Match of the Day*.

'Mum—'

134

'What did you say?'

She'd gone. He was looking at Alfie again on the sofa.

'Did you just call me Mum?'

Garibaldi blinked. 'What? Mum? No.'

'I swear you just called me Mum.'

Garibaldi laughed. Another of those moments. So many years ago and they still kept coming. He'd never told anyone. Kay. Rachel. His sister. No-one.

'Are you OK, Dad?'

'I'm fine, Alfie, fine. Just worried—'

'Don't worry about me. I'll be all right.'

'I know. I just—'

Alfie got up. 'OK. I'm going up to Alicia's. I'll be back later.'

When Alfie had left Garibaldi poured himself a whisky and put on some music. Bill Callahan. Richmond Fontaine. Lambchop. The Felice Brothers. And, given that Rachel had a parents' meeting, he turned the volume up high.

As he listened he couldn't stop thinking about Liam Allerton and the blackmail notes, but the more he thought the less things made sense. They were no closer to finding the killer and no closer to answering the central questions. Why had he been killed? And why had he been killed in a way that echoed the murder in his novel? Why did he have blackmail notes in his bottom drawer?

And why did everything come back to *Schooled in Murder*?

He reached for his copy and flicked through it. Had he missed something?

He was still reading when Rachel returned.

After her bath, an important part of her work-recovery routine, she joined him on the sofa, her hands clasped round a mug of hot chocolate.

'Bad meeting?' said Garibaldi, putting down his book.

Rachel picked up the remote and flicked on the TV. 'No worse than usual. 'She looked towards the spare bedroom. 'Where's Alfie?'

'He's gone to see Alicia.'

'OK. And any more on the row?'

'Seems it was pretty big. And it turns out it was more about Alicia than it was about jobs. Look—' Garibaldi turned to her. 'You're OK with . . .?'

'Please stop asking. I'm fine. In fact, I like having him here. I enjoy seeing you together.'

'So he's not in the way?'

Rachel eyes made a dramatic sweep of the room. 'Doesn't look like it, does it? And by the way, I've checked the Half Moon and I've got a couple of tickets for next week. I know you mighty be busy , but thought I'd do it anyway.'

'Who's on?'

'Margo Cilker.'

Garibaldi raises his eyebrows. The name was new to him.

'Check her out on Spotify. You'll like her.'

'I will.'

Garibaldi leaned towards Rachel and kissed her on the cheek, remembering the morning after their first night together when she had picked up his Townes Van Zandt CD and nodded her approval.

Sometimes he couldn't believe his luck.

19

Ruth was regretting her end-of-term hook-up. There was no future in it. Even if it lasted through the summer (and Armit had made ominous noises about a last-minute package deal to Crete) she couldn't see it surviving once they went back to school in September. Schools were difficult places to conduct a relationship.

Or maybe schools were just difficult places full stop.

Her teaching career so far had been marked by many difficult moments, but none had been as tricky as the publication of *Schooled in Murder*. As soon as she was told that Ben Joseph was, in fact, Liam Allerton she had, like most of the teaching staff and management, rushed to get hold of a copy.

And when she read it she yet again wished she hadn't told him so much.

This particular regret was dominating her thoughts as she walked from the Kingston bus stop back to her flat, and was still turning over in her mind as she picked the post up off the mat and greeted her cat Bunsen.

It was only when she had made a cup of tea and given Bunsen some food that she sat at the table and looked at the post. As usual, it was mostly junk and promotions, and she was about to chuck it all in the bin when she came to the bottom envelope.

Her heart fluttered when she saw the cut-out letters:

Ruth Price

She ripped open the envelope and took out a card.

I know you've been stealing funds from the school. If you don't want anyone to know do what I say. Instructions to follow.

She recognised it immediately. The same note as the one received by Prisha Bedi in Liam Allerton's novel.

Who had sent it? And why?

She picked up the envelope and looked for the postmark. There it was. SW13.

What was going on?

She peered closely at the letters cut out from newspapers and stuck down in ransom-note style. It must have taken ages.

And it wasn't true. Not a word of it.

She'd never stolen funds from the school. She'd never stolen anything. OK, the odd bit of stationery and photocopying paper, but who hadn't done that?

What should she do? Maybe if she said nothing no-one would ever find out. But then if someone *did* find out, and especially if the police found out, what would they make of her silence? They'd think she had something to hide – and that was the last thing she wanted.

But if she did contact the police protesting she was innocent (which she would do in the absolute conviction that she was), it would look as though she had nothing to hide at all.

There was only one thing for it.

Ruth took a breath and reached for her phone.

Ewan Thomas was reassured after his drink with Sasha that someone else had been as spooked by events as he had been and that he wasn't the only one to have been made to feel guilty by those detectives.

But the reassurance wasn't enough to make him feel less anxious. Things had been bad enough when Allerton's book had been published. He could still remember the ripples it had caused – the fevered speculation about whether Allerton, who had obviously modelled his fictional school on St Mark's, had also based his characters on any of the St Mark's teachers. Everyone agreed that if this is what he had done he had disguised it well. None of the teachers in his book shared the characteristics of any of the St Mark's staff he had worked with. There was no bald Geordie Geography teacher, no moustached member of the History department who walked with a limp, no PE teacher who had worked as a bodyguard for Madonna, no teacher of Politics who was also a stand-up comedian, no Physics teacher with bad body odour, no head of Maths who couldn't pronounce his 'R's.

The teachers in Allerton's novel shared none of the quirks, idiosyncrasies and easily identifiable features of the St Mark's staff.

But that didn't stop the speculation.

The head had been the worst. In his role as deputy, Ewan had witnessed in close up Harry Reed's hysterical reaction to Allerton's novel. Reed was convinced that he was the model for Rhodri Maine, the head of St Jude's in *Schooled in*

Murder, and whenever the book was discussed (which, when it came to his conversations with Ewan was very often), he made a point of insisting that he, unlike Rhodri Maine, was not sleeping with the wife of a member of staff. He insisted so much that Ewan began to doubt him, but he kept the suspicion to himself.

It had been a difficult time, but Reed and the school weathered the storm and *Schooled in Murder* soon became a thing of the past – if not forgotten, then at least no longer the subject of daily speculation. But with the discovery of Allerton's body in the reeds of Barnes Pond the storm had returned, more dangerous and threatening. The book was in the news again and St Mark's was in the glare of a media spotlight much harsher than the one that had shone on them before.

All of this had made for the worst beginning to a summer holiday that Ewan could remember. This had always been a time when he could get away – usually for a couple of weeks to somewhere sunny – and indulge himself with a freedom not possible during term time when, as deputy head at one of the country's leading public schools, he felt eyes were on his every move.

He had assumed that recent events would not necessitate a change of plans, but a voice in his head now kept warning him that such an assumption could be misguided. If things took a turn for the worse – and difficult though it was to imagine anything worse than Liam Allerton's murder, Ewan could see this happening – he might not get away this summer at all.

Struck by such a possibility, Ewan decided, as he munched on his muesli in the flat on Lonsdale Road he had lived in since moving to St Mark's, that he would go into town to cheer himself up. A bit of shopping, a drink with a friend in Soho, perhaps an art gallery in the afternoon – maybe that would take his mind off things.

Had he not paused to pick up the mail from the mat on his way out, the day he planned might have worked its magic. But once he had seen the lettering on the envelope and read the card it contained, he knew that he was not going anywhere today or that if he was, he was unlikely to be able to think about anything other than the card's message:

I know all about your coke habit. If you don't want anyone else to then do what I say. Instructions to follow.

He knew exactly why it was so familiar – he had seen this very message, reproduced in the same ransom-note style in the pages of *Schooled in Murder*.

Ewan took the note into the kitchen, put it on the table and sat down.

He picked up the envelope and looked for the post-mark. SW13.

Anyone could have sent it. The question was, why would they?

On one thing Ewan was absolutely clear. This accusation had no truth whatsoever. He may have taken some in his youth and he may have had acquaintances who still indulged, but he definitely didn't have a coke habit.

But that didn't mean he wasn't freaked out.

What should he do? Could he sit on it and say nothing?

If he kept quiet no-one might find out. But what if they did? What if the police got to know about it? How would that look?

He stared at the note in front of him, elbows on the table, his chin resting on his fists.

He had no choice.

Soho and the art gallery would have to wait.

Sasha Ambrose looked at the note she held in her hand and felt her world disintegrating.

> I know all about you and your sideline. If you don't want everyone to know about it do what I say. Instructions to follow.

As soon as she saw the cut-out letters on the envelope she knew what it contained, and when she looked at the card inside she knew immediately where she had seen it before.

Her hands were trembling and her mind was spinning. Who had sent it and why? And what the hell should she do?

It didn't matter that the allegation was untrue. What mattered was that the note was identical to that received by one of the characters in Liam Allerton's book. When everyone got to know about it, they would look even more closely at *Schooled in Murder* and that would do nothing to improve her state of mind.

She picked up the envelope and looked at the postmark. SW13.

Who the fuck had sent it and why?

First all the questions from the police about Liam. And now this.

What would they say when they found out? It could only mean more questions, more probing.

But what if the police didn't find out?

What if she kept this quiet? Or better still, what if she destroyed it? If she burned it now, who would ever be able to say that she received it? They need never know.

Was she thinking straight? She shook her head to try to clear it.

What could be the possible consequences if she burned the card and envelope?

On the other hand, what would happen if she told the police? After all, she knew the allegation was untrue and wouldn't her contacting the police show that she was innocent, that she had nothing to hide?

She couldn't decide, so, with her eyes still on the card she thought things through again.

Armit was still pinching himself after last night. How good had that been? He considered himself pretty experienced in sexual matters and he knew last night had been one of the best – and he sensed that Ruth felt the same about it too. Things were suddenly looking up. Maybe this thing with Ruth might not be a bad idea after all. Who knows, with seven weeks of holiday ahead (and with many repeats of last night in store), it might even help him forget about the whole Liam Allerton thing. The book. The murder. The questioning by the police. Everything had been shit, but maybe now he could put it behind him and enjoy himself.

His mind was so much on Ruth that he didn't at first notice anything unusual about the way his name and address had been put on the envelope. Given that most of the mail he was opening was junk he thought it was merely another desperate marketing gimmick.

But when he saw the card inside, Ruth was no longer in his thoughts.

I know all about you and the pupil you slept with. If you don't want anyone else to know then do what I say. Instructions to follow.

20

Whenever Garibaldi looked at DCI Deighton addressing the team or whenever he was sitting on the other side of her desk from her, as he was now, he couldn't stop thinking about the night she had opened up to him about her private life, when she told him about Abigail. He had thought that the revelation, and the realisation that they were both living with teachers, might mark the beginning of a more open relationship between them. Maybe they'd bond over gags about being in trouble with Miss, or being put in detention. Maybe they'd go out for another drink.

But the jokes hadn't materialised, nor had the drink. Despite that, things seemed to have loosened a little in their relationship. Whenever Deighton gave him her pastoral-care look and enquired after his well-being she did it in a different tone, almost with a wink, as if acknowledging what they had said to each other on their evening out. And when Garibaldi reciprocated he may have stopped short of asking after Abigail directly but his questions about his boss's well-being always had a knowing inflection.

The truth was that Deighton still remained a mystery. Not just her aloofness. It was something else, and Garibaldi often wondered whether it was simply that, at some level, he found her attractive.

'And Felicity Allerton had no idea about them?' said Deighton, her head bent over copies of the blackmail notes spread on her desk.

'None at all,' said Garibaldi. 'She says she kept out of his study.'

'What did she say when you showed them to her?'

'Couldn't understand it. Couldn't believe her husband had actually sent notes like that.'

'Do you think the same?'

'I think so. I can't imagine Allerton was actually doing what Alex Ballantyne does in his book and blackmailing his colleagues. On the other hand . . .'

'But if he was . . .'

Garibaldi left the 'were', unspoken, mouthing it internally.

'If he was,' continued Deighton, 'his colleagues would have those secrets and be prepared to pay to stop them being revealed.'

'How do we know they don't?'

'We don't for sure, but they all strongly deny it.'

'Exactly. All very Mandy Rice-Davies.'

Deighton looked at him over her reading glasses. 'Sorry?'

'Mandy Rice-Davies. You know, the Profumo scandal. When she was told that Lord Astor had denied sleeping with her that's what she said – "Well he would, wouldn't he?" She was only a teenager at the time . . .'

Deighton's nod suggested she didn't find this helpful. 'So my question is whether we've investigated St Mark's closely enough.'

'A bit of me wonders whether we might be investigating it too much,' said Garibaldi.

'What do you mean?'

'You said right at the beginning that we were detectives, not members of a book club, but that's how we've been behaving. We keep going back to the book as if that's how we're going to crack it.'

'Given how Allerton was killed, we have to assume a link with the book, don't we?' Deighton pointed at the notes. 'And now these . . .'

'Maybe we need to consider alternatives.'

'Such as?'

'I'm not sure. I just think we might need to get our heads out of his bloody book.'

Deighton laughed. 'And that from a man whose head's always in one.'

Garibaldi smiled. 'The problem is where to look. We already know Allerton was pretty good at keeping things to himself. I mean, neither his wife nor daughter knew he was writing a novel.'

'Has the daughter seen the notes?'

'She hasn't seen them but we spoke to her about them.'

'And what did she say?'

'Pretty much the same reaction as her mum.'

'OK,' said Deighton. 'I think you could be right. We're looking at the book because the murder directed us to it and these notes do the same, but we need to look elsewhere. We need to assume—'

'Assume nothing. Exactly.'

Deighton pointed at a pile of papers on one side of he desk. 'Have you seen this?'

She picked a paper off the top of the pile and passed it to Garibaldi.

147

COPY CAT KILLER?

The team investigating the murder of Liam Allerton are said to be investigating links between his death and the novel he wrote under the pseudonym Ben Joseph. In the novel, *Schooled in Murder*, a man's body is found in Barnes Pond. He has been strangled and drugged. It has now emerged that Liam Allerton may have been murdered in an identical manner.

This has led to increased interest in Allerton's book and to speculation that clues to the identity of his killer might be found within its pages.

Araminta Warburton of the Barnes Bookshop said demand for the book had rocketed since the discovery of Allerton's body. 'Liam's death is unbelievably sad and tragic. He was a well-known figure in the local community and his loss is distressing for all. The circumstances of his death have definitely led to an upsurge in demand for his book. We've had to reorder copies several times.'

His death has also turned attention towards St Mark's School, where Allerton taught for many years. The murder victim in *Schooled in Murder* blackmails fellow teachers at St Jude's School, an institution which bears close similarity to St Mark's. The question that is being asked is whether any of the fictional teachers are based on Allerton's former colleagues.

A spokesperson for St Mark's commented, 'We

are all greatly saddened by the death of Liam Allerton. He taught here for many years but we have no reason to believe that he based any of his novel on events or characters at the school.'

DCI Deighton, in charge of the investigation, said, 'We are well aware of *Schooled in Murder* and are including it in our enquiries. But it is only one element of a complex case and we would encourage everyone not to be too keen to see parallels.'

But despite the police warning, the gossip continues, particularly in Barnes. Araminta Warburton said, 'everyone who comes in to buy a copy talks about it.'

Garibaldi put the paper down. 'You said it would be difficult to keep a lid on it.'

'Who leaked it?' said Deighton.

Garibaldi shrugged. 'Could have been any of the teachers we interviewed.'

'Why would they do that?'

'I can't believe it's his family. Maybe it's—'

His phone rang. He looked at the screen. A number he didn't recognise.

'Go ahead,' said Deighton.

He took the call. 'DI Garibaldi.'

'It's Ruth Price here. I think there's something you need to know.'

'What's happened?'

'Something came through the post this morning.'

Garibaldi looked at Deighton as he listened to Ruth.

'OK,' he said, 'we're on our way round.'

He hung up. 'Guess what Ruth Price got through the

post this morning? A blackmail note. Exactly the same as one of the notes in the book.'

Deighton leaned back in her chair and sighed. 'So much for getting our heads out of it then.'

'Life and bloody art, eh?' said Garibaldi, as Gardner drove them down the A3 towards Kingston.

'Yeah,' said Gardner, 'all a bit difficult to believe, isn't it?'

'Like the rest of this bloody case.'

'Who the hell has sent Ruth Price a blackmail note?'

'Well, I know one person it can't be.'

'Who's that?'

'Liam Allerton.'

'So the idea that he'd actually been blackmailing teachers—'

'We can't rule it out. He could have been doing it and these could have been sent by someone else.'

'But who? Why?'

Garibaldi looked out of the side window as they passed Putney Vale Cemetery.

'We have no idea, do we? All that shit about finding out how the victim lived. We seem to have forgotten it. We need to look at Liam Allerton in the real world, not in the pages of his bloody book. I was telling Deighton only this morning that we should be looking somewhere else.'

'You were saying that this morning?'

'Yeah. Why?'

'That's weird.'

'What's weird about it?'

'Because that's exactly what I've been doing.'

'What do you mean?'

'I've been looking somewhere else. I was getting into

a complete tangle so I decided to go back to basics. So I looked at Ben Joseph's talk, the one you were at. I went through the list of people who'd bought a ticket and had a closer look at them.'

'All of them? There were about a hundred there. And nothing happened at his talk. I was there, remember. If his drink was spiked it happened in the pub not at the OSO.'

'I was trying to see if there were others in the audience who knew him. We know about the teachers and we've been looking at them, but he'd lived in Barnes for years. Must have had friends who went along. But I didn't know who on that list of ticket-buyers was a friend so I ran it against people doing other things we know Allerton got up to. Tennis. Spanish. Choir.'

'Any luck?'

'As it happens, yes.'

'What have you got?'

'Three people who did those things with Liam Allerton. I'm following them up.'

'That's great work.'

Garibaldi looked at his sergeant. She was trying, and failing, to suppress a smug grin.

He felt like he'd just given her a gold star.

21

Helena Redwood liked tennis. She'd liked it ever since she was a child, when her parents introduced her to the pleasures of the game at their local club. She'd never been particularly good at it. Despite her parents' encouragement and investment she never made the progress either they or her coaches expected. She could hit the ball on both forehand and backhand (though topspin was beyond her), she could get a serve over the net and into the service box and she could hit the occasional winning volley. But she was never one of those slim, agile, athletic girls who made the game look easy, hitting powerfully and elegantly, even mastering the grunts that the professionals were so fond of.

She played at school in teams (always the Bs unless the As were short) and she played at university, but for her it was always a social thing rather than a serious athletic activity. When she started work she stopped playing completely. And when she married and had children, playing tennis became even less of a priority. It was only when the kids had grown up and left home, and when her husband decided their marriage was over and that it would be a good idea if he left home as well, that she started playing more frequently.

Playing tennis would not only give her something to

do, it would also help with her fitness and weight and be a way of meeting new people. Not that she didn't already have a large circle of friends. Far from it. She had got to know many people over the years they had lived in Barnes, but most of them knew her as one part of a couple, and she felt the need to branch out and be with people who knew nothing of her history. If she were honest, she saw taking up tennis again as part reinvention and part reconnection with something she associated largely with her pre-married (and therefore happier) days.

It worked out well. She avoided joining the Riverside or The Roehampton or Bank of England clubs (places which were too expensive and populated by people she would rather avoid, namely those who could both afford such places and might possibly know her) and went for a more relaxed and less expensive option. The informal gathering of 'senior' players at Barn Elms proved the perfect solution. When she turned up for the first session she found a group of players whose age range seemed to be fifty to seventy and whose ability range seemed to be from near-beginner to once-expert. It looked like just what she needed.

Doubles also suited her. She was past the years in which she could cover the court in a singles game. Playing with someone else was perfect. You served less, you got more chance to stand at the net and you had someone else to share the load (and to be on the receiving end of polite apologies). Over the months she got to know the group well, even meeting some of the women for coffee and arranging extra doubles sessions with those who were free at times other than Sunday mornings.

The tennis group was where Helena met Liam. At first they knew each other only as tennis players whose conversation was mainly limited to the weather and the game, but when he came along for coffee after a midweek session she found out more about him. And when she discovered that he had published a novel she was quick to get hold of a copy. She liked a good whodunnit and she enjoyed his.

Curiosity had brought Helena to Liam's talk at the Barnes Book Festival. He was a good speaker and he'd kept the crowd entertained. Of particular interest had been his answers to questions about whether he had based his book on real people and events – Helena had listened closely to Liam's responses, but despite his confident denial that his fiction was based on any kind of reality she had left the talk still slightly concerned that the woman at the tennis club in *Schooled in Murder*, the woman with the voracious sexual appetite who had given new meaning to the term mixed doubles, might possibly be based on her.

And now she would never get the chance to ask him.

Dead. And dead in such a strange way.

When the group had gathered at Barn Elms the Sunday following the discovery of his body, they marked Liam's absence with a minute's silence. They stood in a circle, heads bowed, rackets resting on the ground and thought of the departed player.

As they did, Helena sneaked a look at those in the circle, in particular the other three women, wondering whether when they had read Liam's book they had thought the same as her.

When Ariadne Fowler decided she wanted to learn a language in retirement she spent a good deal of time deciding which one it should be. French was a possibility, but she already had some of that from her schooldays (an average O-Level – and, yes, she was old enough to have done

O-Levels) but there was something in her that felt learning French, and being able to speak French (and affectedly peppering your English with French phrases), was nothing more than a status symbol, a sign of snobbery which said to the world you were well off, educated and spent much of your time holidaying in France or at your French second home. There was something about France and the French that simply put her off – and as soon as she imagined the type of people who might turn up to a local French evening class she decided it probably wasn't the language for her.

Then she thought of Italian. She had a Latin O-Level (a bit better than her French one) and she sensed that might make picking it up quite easy, but, although Italian might not have had the same social cachet as French, she also associated it with a kind of snobbery. Whenever she thought of the type of people who enthused about all things Italian – the food, the art, the culture – and the type of people who spent each summer in Tuscany she realised that those who wanted to learn Italian were likely to have the same smug knowingness as French enthusiasts.

She briefly considered the possibility of something not many people chose to learn – German, Portuguese, Arabic, Chinese or even something Scandinavian – but eventually opted, with some sense of inevitability, for Spanish. It was an obvious choice. There was something more democratic about it. Not only was it one of the most widely spoken languages in the world, it also, for her, had none of the associations of French or Italian. There may well have been as many Barnes residents spending time in Spain as there were in France or Italy but Ariadne somehow saw them as different and if there were many of them around she managed not to hear them quite so much. Maybe they were just a bit quieter.

That was why she enrolled for the weekly evening Spanish lessons for beginners at Rose House, the Grade II listed seventeenth-century house close to the Sun Inn.

She didn't regret it. The group was diverse (or as diverse as you were likely to get it in SW13) and the teacher was good, an elderly Spanish woman who had real passion for her country's culture. Ariadne enjoyed the regular weekly commitment, the idea of homework (it brought her back to her university days) and the chance to get to know the others in the group. Meeting new people hadn't been part of her motive for signing up – she was happily married with grown up children and a large circle of friends – but she grew increasingly fond of the other class members as the weeks progressed and as, in faltering, error-strewn, badly pronounced Spanish, they started to reveal things about themselves and their lives.

That's how she discovered that Liam was a writer. When, some time into the second year of their lessons, he had to give a presentation to the rest of the class on his interests and hobbies he had told them all about his book – *Educado en Asesinato* – his translation of *Schooled in Murder*.

The revelation that Liam had been writing under the pen-name Ben Joseph took her , and the rest of the class, by surprise. Liam didn't look like a writer (not that she knew what that look would be) but when he had told them it made sense. In all the lessons he showed a shrewd percep-tiveness, as if he were weighing everything up before saying what he thought. And often what he thought was expressed (in English that is – his Spanish was as faltering as everyone else's) clearly and cogently.

From the moment Liam made his revelation to the class Ariadne regarded him differently. She couldn't be precise about the difference but sensed that she started to find him in some strange way more attractive than he had been before. Maybe it was something about her and creative artists – anyone who managed to make things up from nothing, to conjure works from nowhere, held a strange fascination for someone who had spent her working life in accountancy.

And when she had read *Schooled in Murder* she was even more fascinated. Her reading had perhaps qualified her feeling that artists conjured their works from nowhere. The school in his book was clearly based on the one he had worked in – St Mark's, next to Hammersmith Bridge – and she would be surprised if some of the teachers in his fictional school hadn't provided the inspiration for his characters.

But it was his portrayal of Alex Ballantyne's Spanish class that had fascinated her most, in particular Alex Ballantyne's erotic fantasies about the retired accountant who was a fellow class mate. It wasn't a huge part of the book – it didn't amount to more than a paragraph from the early section when Ballantyne was still alive, but it had leaped out at her from the page and she had read it so often that she could even recite it, something she found herself doing to her surprise when she lay beside her husband unable to sleep.

That's why she had gone to his talk. Liam was a witty speaker and engaged the audience, answering questions with intelligence and charm. But when it came to the question about how much of the book was based on real people and places and things, Ariadne hadn't been at all convinced by his response. All that stuff about the creative process, about the reshaping and the refashioning of reality – it cut no ice with her. She had the strong sense that Liam had stitched up some of his ex-colleagues and she also had the strong sense that he had done the same to her. She had no doubt that she was the model for the object of

Alex Ballantyne's fantasies when his attention wandered in his Spanish class, but would now never have the chance to have it confirmed.

Liam was dead. Not just dead. Murdered. And not just murdered. Murdered like Alex Ballantyne.

Fred Tolley had always sung. Whenever the mood took him he would burst into song, much to the annoyance of his wife, Charlotte. The problem was Fred liked to sing at times and in places when Charlotte would much rather he didn't. In the bath or shower was OK, especially with the door shut and the radio on loud, but she was less tolerant on other occasions – at breakfast or dinner, for example, or when they were watching TV or, most annoyingly, when she was driving.

The choir was Charlotte's suggestion. If Fred had somewhere to go to sing it might mean that he would do less of it at home or that if he did still insist on singing in the house he might at least start to do it a bit more in tune. What's more, it would get him out of the house. The idea of a regular weekly commitment for her husband greatly appealed to Charlotte and Fred hadn't needed much persuading to pick up on her suggestion. The truth was he had always harboured the desire to sing with others. In his youth this ambition had taken the form of singing in a rock band, but the chance had never arisen. He now regarded himself as too old to be in a band, but he knew age was no barrier when it came to singing in a choir and he embraced the opportunity with enthusiasm.

He was nervous when he made his first appearance at the rehearsals but the director made him welcome and so did the other choir members. There were twenty in all, most of them women, and everyone seemed pleased at the addition of another male voice.

The good thing about the choir was that it genuinely catered for all abilities. Not everyone could sing well, but this seemed to pose no problem. It wasn't that sort of choir. It was about people singing together and enjoying it. It was about giving it a go and having fun. That's why they sang what they did. Yes, there were a few traditional songs, classic choral stuff, but the repertoire was broad, encompassing show tunes, pop songs and gospel.

Fred enjoyed it and didn't regret joining. It was good to do something for himself on one night each week and he sensed that Charlotte enjoyed it as well – every marriage needed space, even those that were going well.

He particularly enjoyed the trips to the pub after each rehearsal. That was when he got to know some of the other choir members and that was when he got to know Liam Allerton. They had joined at the same time and shared an uncertainty about their own vocal competence. It was inevitable that they would bond and that's what they did on their first trip to the pub. He liked Liam. He was an intelligent, entertaining conversationalist and they had hit it off immediately. Soon they were meeting up for drinks on other nights of the week, giving themselves the chance to talk at greater length and away from the other choir members.

Fred couldn't remember when it was that he opened up to Liam about the state of his marriage but he knew it wasn't until they had both been in the choir and drinking together for about six months. He remembered the night well. He had drunk more than usual and was feeling particularly vulnerable after a bad row with Charlotte. He couldn't remember what the row was about – they'd reached the stage where it hardly mattered. Slightly tipsy and feeling the need to unload, he had told Liam about his suspicions, his sense that Charlotte was being unfaithful to him, his belief that she had encouraged him to join the choir to give her a free evening on which she could entertain her lover.

Liam had listened in an understanding way, not passing judgement or recommending any course of action. He simply listened.

At the time Fred had no idea that Liam was a writer. It was only a year later that he revealed to the choir that he had written a novel under the pseudonym Ben Joseph, and that it was about to be published. His announcement was greeted enthusiastically by the choir who all rushed out to buy his book.

When they read it they may all have felt that the choir Alex Ballantyne sang in bore a strong resemblance to their own, but it could surely only have been Fred who saw a resemblance between the out-of-tune bass and himself – the out-of-tune bass who was convinced his wife was having an affair because of his own inability to satisfy her, and who was equally convinced she had encouraged him to join a choir to give her a regular weekly slot in which she could get from her lover what he was unable to provide.

He never had the nerve to challenge Liam about this, to ask whether he had based his fictional character on him. All he had said was how much he had enjoyed the book, asking him pointedly whether there had been any complaints from the school he had taught in before he retired.

And now he would never have the chance. Liam Allerton's singing days were over.

22

Garibaldi and Gardner stood beside Ruth Price looking at the card on the table.

'What do you make of it, Ruth?'

Ruth turned to Garibaldi, 'What do *I* make of it? I don't know. You're the detective. What do *you* make of it?'

'My first question is whether there's any truth in the accusation.'

Ruth threw back her head and laughed loudly. 'Of course I haven't been embezzling funds from the school!'

'And if you had, I daresay you wouldn't admit to it.'

'Don't you believe me?'

'If you haven't been embezzling school funds, can you think of any reason why you might have been sent this note?'

'I have no idea. And that's the question you should be asking – who the hell has sent this to me and why?'

Spiky. That's the word Garibaldi would use to describe her. Everything came at you with an edge.

'We've seen this note before, of course,' said Garibaldi.

'Of course we have. That bloody novel!'

'And can you remember who gets this note in that bloody novel?'

'Yes, I can. Prisha Bedi. And before you ask I do not think for one moment that Prisha Bedi is supposed to be me. For a start she's Indian. On top of that she teaches ... do I need to go on? Someone's murdered Liam and instead of finding out who killed him you're sitting around talking about his bloody book.'

'We'd be foolish if we didn't, don't you think, Ruth? Given the similarities—'

'Are you saying that whoever killed Liam sent me this note?'

'Not at all. We're simply exploring all possibilities.'

Ruth put her hands on her hips and huffed, a teacher displeased with her student's shoddy effort.

Garibaldi pointed at the note and envelope. 'We need to take these with us.' He nodded to Gardner who picked up the note and envelope in her gloved hand and put each into an evidence bag.

'Do let us know if you think of anything.'

'Like what?' said Ruth.

'Anything that could be relevant.'

'Such as?'

'I'll leave that to you,' said Garibaldi, heading for the door.

'Hard work, isn't she?' said Gardner as they drove back to Hammersmith.

'You're telling me,' said Garibaldi. 'And she puzzles me.'

'In what way?'

'She's like all teachers. Thinks she's clever.'

'*All* teachers? I see, so that includes Rachel, does it?'

'It's not a problem with Rachel because she *is* clever, but most teachers think they're cleverer than they are and Ruth's no exception.'

162

'We're looking at her bank accounts and financial trans-actions and we've asked the school's finance department to have a look, but there's no evidence yet.'

'There's something about her though, isn't there?' said Garibaldi.

'What do you mean?'

' She's too confident, too assertive. All of the teachers are like that. They're so used to being right about things, so used to having the answers, so used to being believed. But Ruth's worse than most. Ben Joseph nails it in his novel, gets it exactly right. The thing about *Schooled in Murder* . . .'

Garibaldi broke off and looked sideways at Gardner.

'You know what?' he said. 'No matter how hard we try or wherever we look we can't escape that book, can we? And what gets me is that it's at the heart of our investiga-tion and there's still only two of us who've read the bloody thing!'

'You're wrong there,' said Gardner with a smirk.

'You've read it?'

'Finished it last night.'

Garibaldi clapped his hands. 'So what did you make of it?'

'I enjoyed it. I mean the cop's completely unbelievable and as for the procedure . . . well, that's never realistic in these things, is it? If they made it realistic, if they actu-ally wrote it as it is, the whole thing would be so boring, wouldn't it?'

'But that's forgivable, right, in a novel?'

'I guess so. But anyway, I've read it.'

'And . . .?'

'And here's what I think. I was expecting more.'

'More what?'

'I don't know. There's a lot of school stuff, isn't there, and not much action.'

'What kind of action were you expecting?'

'I don't mean I wanted a serial killer on the loose in Barnes. I just thought there might be more, I don't know, threat or menace.'

'I don't think it's that kind of novel. It's more—'

Garibaldi's phone rang. He checked the screen. Deighton.

'Hi, boss.'

'Where are you?'

'We're on our way back.'

'Well get here quick. We've had three phone calls. Three more blackmail notes.'

'Who's got them?'

'Ewan Thomas. Sasha Ambrose. Armit Harwal.'

'The other three who were at his talk and with him in the Sun.'

'Exactly,' said Deighton.

23

Deighton stood at the front of the room beside a screen displaying photos of four blackmail notes.

'This morning four St Mark's teachers received these through the post. All posted in SW13. All in the same cut-up ransom note style. All worded in exactly the same way as the four blackmail notes in *Schooled in Murder*. First the murder of Liam Allerton. Then the discovery of notes in his drawer. Now those notes being received by four teachers. All, it seems, from the pages of Allerton's novel. What are we supposed to make of it all? Who's sent these notes? Are they connected to Allerton's murder? If so, how? And why have the notes been sent to the four teachers who were at the talk in the OSO and with Allerton in the pub afterwards? All four tell the same story. They – no surprises here – deny the things they are accused of – and they all say they've never received such notes before. If so, we have to ask why they're getting them now. We also, of course, have to ask who sent them.'

She looked round the room.

'Could it be the killer?' said Gardner.

'Why would the killer send blackmail notes?' said Deighton.

'Maybe he . . . or she . . .' Gardner shook her head as her sentence fizzled out. 'No, doesn't make sense, does it?'

'How about the notes found in Allerton's study?' asked Garibaldi. 'Anything back from the lab?'

'Allerton's fingerprints and DNA all over them. No-one else's.'

'So we still have to ask what he was doing with them,' said DC Hodson.

'Exactly,' said Garibaldi. 'One possibility is that he *was* blackmailing these people. But that assumes those people had those secrets to hide. It also assumes that Allerton had some motive for doing it. One thing we can be sure of and that's Allerton didn't send these notes. SW13 may be many people's idea of heaven, but I don't think Allerton's posted them from there.'

A few laughs.

'OK,' said Garibaldi, 'so if we assume that Allerton *wasn't* blackmailing his ex-colleagues, and if we assume that those four teachers are innocent of those accusations—'

'We assume nothing,' said Deighton.

'I know,' said Garibaldi, 'but what I'm saying is—'

What was he saying? He had no idea. Just like he had no idea about everything else in the case.

'The media love the story already,' said Deighton. 'God knows what they're going to do when they find out about these notes.' She paused and gave another look round the room. 'Any questions?'

Gardner put her hand up. 'When I read *Schooled in Murder*—' she broke off and gave a sideways glance at the team, as if trying to catch the eye of those who had yet to read it '—I obviously looked for the similarities we all know about, but I also found myself looking for other things, things that weren't there.'

'What do you mean?' said Deighton.

'Allerton's killer copied the way his character was murdered. As I read I kept looking for other things the killer might want to copy. Other murders, other big events. But there was nothing. Just the one murder.'

'There's the notes, though,' said Deighton, pointing at the screen. 'Someone copied that. Maybe not the killer, but someone.'

'Sure,' said Gardner, 'someone copied the way Ballantyne was murdered and now it seems that someone has copied the notes, but what I mean is there are no other violent events. One murder and that's it.'

'Maybe we should be grateful,' said Deighton.

Garibaldi looked at Gardner. He wasn't sure what point she was making, and she looked as if she wasn't too clear herself.

She seemed baffled, like everyone else in the room.

'What about the head's wife?' said DC Hodson. 'None of the teachers in the book *kill* Ballantyne, do they? It was the head's wife. Do we need to speak to her?'

'Yes,' said Deighton. 'I think we do. No stone unturned.'

'What about the Sun CCTV?' said Gardner.

'Nothing clear or obvious,' said DC Hodson. 'We know when Allerton left the pub and we know that he left alone. And the times those who were with him left roughly corresponds to the times they gave in their statements. No big discrepancies.'

'And do the cameras show the table Allerton was sitting at?' said Garibaldi.

'Yes, but not clearly enough or close enough to see whether anyone did something to his drink.'

'What about the other people in the group?' said Gardner. 'We know who the teachers are but there were three or four others who seemed to be close to them. We see Allerton talking to them. Do we know who they are?'

'Nothing yet,' said DC Hodson.

'OK,' said Garibaldi. 'And we still don't know why Allerton didn't go straight home, how he ended up in Barnes Pond.'

'One thing we haven't considered,' said Gardner, 'is whether whoever spiked the drink and whoever murdered him are the same person.'

The room turned to look at her. It was a good point.

'We've made that mistake before,' said Garibaldi, thinking of a previous case where a similar assumption had been made.

'Where are we on house to house?' asked DC McLean.

'We've done all the houses bordering the pond. And we've looked at footage from those with CCTV, but none show Allerton and, as expected, none of them reach the pond. And nothing's come from the appeal for dashcam footage.'

'We're not getting any closer, are we?' said Garibaldi.

'No,' said Deighton, 'and I keep thinking of that phrase "getting lost in a book". Yes, we need to look at it but we need to keep our heads up, keep looking at real life. Liam Allerton's murder is real. It happened. And we have a duty to him and to those he left behind to find out who did it.'

Garibaldi nodded again. The lack of progress worried him. However he looked at things, whatever angle he chose to take, whatever unusual path he tried to pursue, he ended up nowhere.

MURDER BY THE BOOK?

A bizarre twist in the Barnes Pond murder case was revealed yesterday. The body of Liam Allerton, a retired Maths teacher, was found in the reeds of Barnes Pond last Sunday in circumstances that bear remarkable similarity to the discovery of the murder victim in *Schooled in Murder*, the crime novel he wrote under the pseudonym Ben Joseph.

It has now emerged that four teachers at St Mark's School, the school at which Allerton taught for many years and said to be the model for St Jude's School in his novel, have received blackmail notes identical to those received by teachers in the novel.

In *Schooled in Murder* teachers at St Jude's are asked to pay money in return for silence about secrets which include drugs, sexual relations with students, embezzlement of school funds and working as a prostitute.

DCI Deighton, in charge of the case said, 'We are aware of Allerton's book and it continues to form part of our investigation.'

No-one was available from St Mark's for comment.

24

Garibaldi cycled down Shepherd's Bush Road to Hammersmith Broadway, cut down Queen Caroline Street beside the Apollo, joined the towpath and headed towards Fulham. As he passed the River Café he looked up at the Craven Cottage floodlights and wondered, not for the first time, how different things might have been if his dad had taken him here when he was a boy rather than to QPR. What if Fulham rather than QPR had been passed down from father to son? What would it have been like to stroll to games with Alfie along a picturesque stretch of the Thames rather than head up to the buzz and grime of Shepherd's Bush and White City?

Soon he was lost in a game of what-ifs, turning over all kinds of alternative lives that could have resulted from a different choice at a particular time. It was a game he played too often.

He locked his bike outside the Crabtree and walked into the garden where Ollie Masters sat at a table, reading a paper and sipping a coffee.

'Ollie?' said Garibaldi as he walked towards him.

Ollie looked up and put down his paper. 'Can I get you a drink?'

Garibaldi held up his hand. 'I'm fine.'

'We could have met at the Day Centre,' said Ollie, 'but I thought it might be easier here.'

'The Day Centre?' said Garibaldi, sitting down opposite him.

'I don't attend,' said Ollie with a laugh. 'I volunteer. Three days a week in Bishops Park.'

'I see,' said Garibaldi.

'I started a few years ago when I stopped work. I know it's a cliché, but I decided to give something back.'

Garibaldi nodded his approval.

'I'd just lost my wife and it was time to reassess a few things.'

'What was your work?'

'Marketing. H.J. Heinz. Tomato Ketchup. Baked Beans. Not exactly what I had in mind when I studied English at university but, hey, that's life. Never know where it's going to take you.' Ollie took a sip of coffee and picked up the paper. 'Before we start can I ask you about this?'

He turned the paper towards Garibaldi. It was the *Daily Mail*. 'Not my usual read, I hope you'll understand, but I saw someone reading this at the Centre so went and got a copy.' He pointed at the headline – *Murder by the Book*? 'Have you seen it?'

Garibaldi nodded. 'We're not sure how they got hold of it, but, yes, we've seen it.'

Ollie shook his head. 'It's incredible, isn't it? I mean what's going on?'

'We're pursuing every possible line of enquiry.'

'I'm sure you are, but – look, however I can help. This whole thing, it's so distressing.'

'Can I ask you a few questions about Liam?'

'Of course, please do.'

Garibaldi took out his notebook and pencil. 'How did you know him?'

'We met at university, or as it now seems to be known, uni. Never called it that when we were there. Anyway, that's where we met and it carried on from there. I got my job with Heinz, Liam went into teaching and we kept in touch. I met Marion, Liam met Felicity.'

'So you knew him well? '

'Couldn't have been much closer, I guess. But ...' Ollie gave a slow shake of his head. 'But something like this happens and you start to wonder. I mean, you can never know anyone completely, can you? They can always surprise you.'

'And was that the case with Liam?'

'Did Liam surprise me? Over the years I'm not sure he did. Not often. But then he wrote the book – and, yeah, that was definitely a surprise. Came out of nowhere.'

'He never mentioned anything about wanting to write?'

'Never. He never even hinted at it. And then a couple of years after he retires there it is – *Schooled in Murder*. Have you read it?'

'I have, yes.'

'What do you reckon? I've never been much of a fan of crime fiction myself.'

'It's not the type of novel that matters,' said Garibaldi. 'What matters is whether it's any good.'

Ollie nodded his agreement. 'Sure. But in the case of Liam's novel whether or not it's any good seems to have become very much a secondary issue. It's bizarre, isn't it? Not just the way he was killed, but those notes in the drawer. Felicity told me about them. And now–' he pointed at the *Daily Mail* – 'these notes to teachers. All straight out of the book. What do you make of it all?'

'We're exploring all possible avenues.'

172

'Yeah, but this book stuff, so many things ... you can't ignore it, can you?'

'We're not ignoring it at all. Far from it. In fact it's one of the reasons I want to talk to you.' Garibaldi opened his notebook. 'Tell me, Ollie, did Liam ever say anything to you that suggested he was worried about the book at all?'

'Worried in what way?'

'That it might have caused offence.'

'You mean that it might have put him in danger of some sort? Not directly, no. I mean, he never said "I think someone's going to murder me because of what I've written".'

'I wasn't imagining that he might have,' said Garibaldi with a smile.

'When we spoke at Felicity's the other day you said that you could see that Liam had based the school in his novel on St Mark's but not the teachers. Why are you so sure?'

Ollie hesitated, looking from side to side as if he were considering whether or not to reveal something.

'Look,' he said eventually, 'I said he wouldn't have based his characters on the teachers he worked with because I didn't want to think that what happened to him was a consequence of that. I said what I want to believe ...'

'What do you mean?'

'I want to believe that Liam would never have done what the victim in his novel does, blackmail those teachers, but ever since he died, ever since he was murdered in that way, and especially since I found out about those notes in his drawer, I've been thinking back over some of the things he said to me.'

'Things about the book?'

'Not specifically, but they could be things related to it. Look, when I read the book it was clear that Liam had put quite a bit of himself into Alex Ballantyne. I guess all

173

writers put themselves, or bits of themselves, into their characters. Ballantyne's a bit of a cynic, just like Liam was, and he has the same interests. But Ballantyne's also a huge gossip. That's how he finds out about the teachers' secrets, and I'm not saying Liam did exactly the same but there were many occasions when we went out for a drink and he'd tell me things that were going on at school, things he'd discovered. People told him things.'

Garibaldi flicked over a page in his notebook. 'Did he say anything specific about what he'd discovered?'

'You won't need your notebook,' said Ollie, pointing at it. 'He didn't say some of the teachers he worked with were drug addicts or escorts or embezzlers or whatever. It's just that he gave the impression that he knew things about his colleagues.'

'So you think,' said Garibaldi, 'that Liam found out about secrets and put them in his novel?'

'I'm not saying that. I can't believe for one moment that . . .'

'Do you think there's also a chance that Liam was himself doing what Alex Ballantyne does in his novel?'

'You mean blackmailing teachers? No . . . I mean those notes in his drawer, they don't prove anything, do they?'

'A bit strange, though, don't you think?'

Ollie laughed. 'Very strange. Like everything else. Nothing makes sense does it? And the more you think about it the less you feel certain about anything. I mean, maybe . . .' He trailed off, as if thinking better of what he was about to say.

'Maybe what?'

Ollie spread his arms wide. 'I don't know what to say. I can't believe he's gone. Poor Felicity. Poor Fran. They were so good to me, all of them.'

'In what way?'

'I lost my wife three years ago. Nothing like Liam. Nothing like the shock of a murder. It was expected, but even so . . . they looked after me. Now it's my turn, I guess. I need to look after them.'

'Liam and Felicity, what were they like as a couple?'

'They were great. Good fun. We spent a lot of time together, the four of us. We even went on holidays together in the early years, before they had kids.'

'They got on with each other OK?'

Ollie looked at Garibaldi through narrowed eyes. 'I'm not sure what you mean. Yes, they had the occasional row, but what couple doesn't?'

'When you say the occasional row, can you remember what any of them were about?'

Ollie laughed. 'Not really. They were typical . . . couple rows. Nothing serious.'

'According to the St Mark's head Liam could be difficult.'

'Difficult? Yeah, I imagine he could have been. He wasn't one for suffering fools. But, look, he wasn't like that with Felicity. As I said, they may have had rows but any that I saw were the usual stuff, the kind of rows I used to have with Marion the whole time.'

'You mean the kind of rows you were prepared to have in front of other people?'

Ollie looked taken aback. 'Well, I guess so. By definition, if they're the ones I saw then . . . I'm not sure what you're getting at here, Inspector.'

'Do you remember them ever having a row about the book?'

Ollie shook his head. 'All I can remember is Felicity being completely surprised when she found out he'd written it. Totally gobsmacked. And when she'd read it I remember her saying she was worried about the St Mark's thing.'

'The St Mark's thing? Was she any more specific?'

'She just said she hoped people didn't look too closely at it. I didn't think much of it at the time but, after all that's happened, I keep coming back to it.'

'Look too closely? What do you think she meant?'

'I don't know, but these recent events, the way they all point you to the book ...' Ollie shrugged his shoulders. 'I don't know. I really don't know.'

'But as far as you know, things were all OK between Liam and his wife?'

'Yeah. As far as I know.'

Something about the way he said it and the silence that followed made Garibaldi think he was holding something back.

'OK,' he said, shutting his notebook. 'Thanks for your time, Ollie. 'If you think of anything else ...'

'Of course.'

Garibaldi stood up and pointed to the *Daily Mail* on the table.

'And don't believe everything you read in there, will you?'

25

Garibaldi lay on the sofa listening to Nick Lowe with his eyes closed, his copy of *Schooled in Murder* lying on his chest.

He'd loved reading ever since he was a kid when his mother took him to Hammersmith Library every week. The habit had stayed with him – he popped into the local libraries in Castelnau and East Sheen whenever he could and carried a book with him wherever he went (the latest Anne Tyler currently nestled in his jacket pocket). He still felt grateful to the library and could recall every detail of those weekly trips – the smell of the pages, the gummed labels, the click of the librarian's rubber date stamp, the library cards, the wonders of the pre-digital age when public libraries were still places of reverential hush, no noisy kids and parents, not a playgroup or storytime in sight.

And he still felt grateful to his mother for setting him on the right track.

Reading lay at the heart of his job. Reports, documents, statements – they all needed careful scrutiny, but much of the reading he did was metaphorical. Faces, signs, situations, scenes, clues – these also had to be read but in a different, more subtle way.

In no case, though, had reading ever been as central as it was proving to be in the Liam Allerton investigation.

In no other case had a book mattered so much.

Garibaldi opened his eyes, picked up his copy of *Schooled in Murder* and flicked through it.

He had never doubted his own intelligence and he seldom felt completely stumped. Quite the reverse. He prided himself on his ability to see things from a different angle, to pursue possibilities and develop hypotheses others failed to, often doing it with a reference, sometimes a quotation, that he thought illuminated his ideas but that he knew irritated others.

Thinking outside the box is what he liked to call it.

Being a smart arse is what others liked to call it.

But now, lying on the sofa with the book in his hand, he didn't feel like much of a smart arse. He didn't need to think outside the box – he needed a new box entirely.

First the murder of Liam Allerton and now four blackmail notes received by St Mark's teachers. Who had done it and why?

He had no idea.

Maybe it was the strain of having Alfie in the flat, his worry about what having him there might do to his relationship with Rachel.

Or maybe it was too much country music and QPR's loss of form.

'Don't worry, Giacomo.'

Garibaldi recognised the voice immediately.

'It's important to read.'

The voice again.

Garibaldi lifted his head and there, in the corner of the room, was his mother, sitting in her chair, looking up at him over clacking knitting needles.

'Do you hear me?' she said.

Garibaldi's mouth fell open. 'I don't understand,' he said.

'What don't you understand? If it's a word, you look it up in a dictionary. That's how you learn.'

'It's not the words,' said Garibaldi. 'I understand the words. It's the way they fit together, the picture, the big picture. That's what I don't get.'

His mother laughed and turned her head to the TV in the corner. Bruce Forsyth had just said something funny.

'You need to be patient, Giacomo. It will come to you if you let it.'

'But what if everyone else gets it,' said Garibaldi, 'and I don't? What do I do then?'

His mother turned back to him and smiled. A gentle, reassuring smile.

'Don't you worry about other people, Giacomo. You just worry about yourself. Life can be difficult enough without creating more worries.'

'You don't understand,' said Garibaldi. 'You don't get it, Mum.'

He lifted himself up from his supine position, got off the sofa and walked towards her, but as he drew closer his mother faded, growing smaller and fainter.

Garibaldi reached out his arms. 'Mum? Mum. I—'

'Did you just say "mum"?'

'What? I—'

Garibaldi turned to see Rachel standing in the doorway.

'You just said "mum". Very loudly.'

'Did I? I—'

'Are you OK?'

'Fine. I'm fine.'

Rachel looked at him, unconvinced.

'I was just thinking aloud,' said Garibaldi. 'I often do it.'

179

He knew this wasn't true. He knew exactly what it was and he had lived with it for years without telling anyone.

Maybe now was the time.

Rachel raised her hand. 'I've had a shit day so I think I'll go straight in the bath, OK?'

Garibaldi said nothing. Experience had taught him that it was never wise to come between Rachel and her bath, so he gave a nod, went back to the sofa and picked up his copy of *Schooled in Murder*.

Something was unsettling him, something more than the conversation with his latest vision. An idea was nibbling at the edges of his mind, but it had yet to take a recognisable shape.

He flicked through the book, scanning the pages to remind himself of some details. Then he reached for a sheet of paper and a pen, and jotted down the names of the four St Mark's teachers who had received the blackmail notes:

Ewan Thomas
Sasha Ambrose
Ruth Price
Armit Harwal.

He looked at the list. All four had been at Liam Allerton's talk and with him afterwards in the Sun. All four could possibly have spiked his drink. All four had received blackmail notes identical to those received by characters in *Schooled in Murder*.

He flicked through the book to check he'd remembered correctly and then, beside the list of the St Mark's teachers, he scribbled down the names of the four St Jude's characters in Allerton's book who received notes.

Ashley MacDonald
Ted Fox
Harry Antrobus
Prisha Bedi.

Nick Lowe's voice filled the room as his eyes darted between the lists.

Did anything connect them, or was he looking for something that wasn't there?

His eyes carried on jumping from one set of names to the other.

Nothing.

He kept looking, unable to rid himself of the sense that he was missing something, and all he had to do was look harder.

He looked harder.

And then he saw it.

26

G aribaldi stood by a flip chart at the front of the incident room.

'As you know, Liam Allerton was murdered in a manner identical to the manner in which Alex Ballantyne, the character in his book, was also killed. As you also know, blackmail notes were discovered in Liam Allerton's drawer, just as they were in Alex Ballantyne's. And now four St Mark's teachers have received notes identical to those received by the characters in the book.'

He reached for his copy of *Schooled in Murder* and held it up. 'So many things come back to this book. And last night I read it again. What a swot, eh? Anyone would think I was doing an exam. Anyway, I noticed something I want to share with you.'

He turned to the flip chart and turned over the top page to reveal his best marker pen writing:

St Jude's	St Mark's	Blackmailed over
Ted Fox	Ewan Thomas	Drugs
Ashley MacDonald	Sasha Ambrose	Escort
Prisha Bedi	Ruth Price	Embezzlement
Harry Antrobus	Armit Harwal	Sex with student.

'OK. So the names on the left are the St Jude's teachers in Allerton's novel who are blackmailed by Alex Ballantyne. The names on the right are teachers at St Mark's who received blackmail notes identical to those received by the teachers in the book. You're familiar with them already because these are the four who went to Allerton's talk at the book festival and who went to the Sun Inn with him afterwards. On the right are the secrets those St Jude's characters on the left are blackmailed over, the secrets that are also on the blackmail notes received by those St Mark's teachers. All of them, understandably, deny any connection. They say nothing links them to those characters in the novel. But when I wrote down the lists of names last night I noticed something that does. Does anyone see it?'

Garibaldi looked at the team as they scrutinised the names. He was enjoying this more than he perhaps should, relishing their bafflement.

'Remember,' he said. 'Allerton was a Maths teacher. And he loved crosswords.'

'Is that supposed to help?' said Gardner.

'Look for a pattern.'

'What kind of pattern?' said Deighton.

'It's in the names.'

'Give us a clue,' said Gardner.

'What is this?' said Deighton, unable to hide her frustration. 'Some kind of quiz show?'

'OK,' said Garibaldi. 'Look at the first name on the left and then look at the whole name on the right.'

'Ted Fox and Ewan Thomas,' said DC Hodson. 'So Ted and Ewan Thomas.'

Garibaldi nodded his encouragement. 'Go on,' he said. 'Ashley MacDonald and Sasha Ambrose. So Ashley and Sasha Ambrose.'

'Prisha and Ruth Price,' said DC McLean, continuing. 'Harry and Armit Harwal.'

The room fell silent.

'Now look at the first two letters of that name on the left,' said Garibaldi.

More silence.

Then a shriek from Gardner. 'I've got it! I've got it!'

The room turned to her.

'What is it then?' said Garibaldi.

Gardner was bouncing up and down on her chair, unable to contain her excitement. 'Take the first two letters of the name on the left and reverse them and you've got the initials of the name on the right. So Ted is ET that's Ewan Thomas, Ashley is SA that's Sasha Ambrose, Prisha is RP that's—'

'Exactly!' said Garibaldi.

Garibaldi looked at Gardner. A beam had spread across her face and she kept sneaking smug sideways glances at her colleagues.

'This is all very well,' said Deighton. 'But I don't see where it gets us.'

'OK,' said Garibaldi. 'The first thing to say is this has to be deliberate. If it's not and if it's an accident ...'

'We can't rule it out,' said Deighton.

'No we can't, but the chances of the pattern coming up by accident in four pairs of names ...'

'It's a bit like the way Allerton was killed,' said DC McLean. 'That could be coincidence too, but it's pretty unlikely.'

'Exactly,' said Garibaldi. 'And remember Liam Allerton loved crosswords. Used to do the Guardian cryptic every day in the staff room. And what are crosswords? Smart-arse word games. And what's this?' He pointed at the flip chart. 'A smart-arse word game. But that's not all,' said Garibaldi.

He reached for the marker pen and added a name to the St Jude's list.

Rhodri Maine

Beside it, in the St Mark's list, he wrote:

Harry Reed

'He's done the same with the head. Rhodri Maine isn't blackmailed in *Schooled in Murder* but remember he's having an affair with the wife of another teacher and his wife's also having an affair.'

'Crikey,' said Deighton, 'did Allerton do the same trick with *all* of his characters?'

Garibaldi held up his hand. 'Just one more.'

He wrote another name at the bottom of the St Jude's list.

Alex Ballantyne

Beside it he wrote:

Liam Allerton

'So, yes, maybe there was quite a bit of Liam Allerton in that blackmailing teacher, the one who, like Liam, is found in Barnes Pond.'

'This is all very well,' said Deighton,' but there's still the question of where it gets us. First we're in a book club. Now we're doing crosswords and playing *Only Connect*! Where does this get us?'

Garibaldi nodded. The truth was he had no idea.

'OK,' he said in a tone that he hoped suggested he knew

exactly where his discovery got them. 'What we've got to remember is that those four teachers –' he pointed at the first four pairs of names '– are the ones who happened to be at Allerton's talk and with him in the pub. Is that a coincidence as well? And those four teachers have received notes identical to those received by those characters whose names are linked, by this smart-arse method, to their own. Surely, on this basis alone, we need to talk to all four again and to look even more closely at the possibility that they may have done those things and that they may have been blackmailed.'

'Are you saying one of those might be the murderer?' said Gardner.

'I'm not saying anything,' said Garibaldi. 'All I'm saying is we need to talk to them again.'

'Good work, everyone,' said Deighton with a nod at Garibaldi. 'That's a lot to take in. So let's think about it and then let's . . .'

'Let's get on it,' said Garibaldi, finishing the line under his breath.

27

Milly Gardner could tell that Garibaldi had been impressed by her initiative of running another check on those who'd bought tickets to Allerton's talk. And he'd also been impressed that she was the first to get the connection between the lists of names – not by herself, admittedly, but she'd definitely been the quickest to pick up on the hints he was throwing out.

The whole thing had been typical Garibaldi – all very clever, but it hadn't come from nowhere. She knew he would have worked hard on it and that's why she herself had made a point of doing her own homework. She'd gone back to *Schooled in Murder* and found the parts that described those with whom Alex Ballantyne played tennis, learned Spanish and sang. No-one could say she was unprepared – she'd even stuck Post-its on the relevant pages.

She held the book in her hands now, yellow and orange stickers sprouting from the top of its pages, as she spoke to Ariadne Fowler in the high-ceilinged, elegantly furnished living room of her Riverview Gardens mansion flat just south of Hammersmith Bridge.

'I really don't know why you want to speak to me,' said

Ariadne, 'I hardly knew Liam. We just happened to be in the same Spanish class.'

'But you went to hear his talk at the Book Festival.'

'I did. I knew he'd written a novel and I thought it would be interesting to hear him talk about it.'

'You've read *Schooled in Murder*?'

'I have, yes.'

'And are you aware of the circumstances of Liam's death?'

Ariadne shook her head. 'Yes. Quite unbelievable!'

'It's about the book that I'm here, Ariadne. There seem to be all kinds of parallels between Liam's novel and things that were going on in his life. And in the book Liam's character, Alex Ballantyne, is in a Spanish class.'

Ariadne held up her hands, as if seeing where Milly was heading and stopping her in her tracks.

'You think the woman in that class is based on me, don't you?'

Milly reached for her copy of the novel. 'I can read you the description if you like—'

'There's no need to do that. I can quote it to you myself. Let me see, how does it go? "The petite red-headed woman in her fifties whose casual dress of jeans, converse and leather jacket gave the impression that she would rather be seen as an ageing rock chick than a retired accountant living in a block of mansion flats close to Hammersmith Bridge." Have I got that right?'

Milly nodded.

'And here's the bit that got me,' said Ariadne. 'She may have not been the best student of Spanish but Alex was grateful for her presence. When his mind wandered off the topic in hand he indulged in pleasant erotic fantasies about her.'

'The book obviously made a big impression,' said Milly.

'You've remembered it word for word. Did you ever say anything to Liam about it?'

'Funnily enough, no.'

'And did it upset you, this representation?'

'I was amused more than annoyed, but—' She broke off, struck by a sudden thought. 'Hang on, you don't think I'm in any way . . . involved, do you?'

'I'm just trying to find out more about Liam and his book.'

'The very idea that I might . . .'

'I'm not accusing you of anything, Ariadne. I just want to find out more about what was going on in Liam's life. If you find out how the victim lived you'll often find out how he died.'

Milly winced at the cliché.

'I'm shocked,' said Ariadne. 'I'm sure everyone is. I can't imagine why anyone would want to kill him.'

'Did Liam say anything in the classes that you think might be relevant?'

'Relevant in what way?'

'Anything that, looking back on it and knowing what happened to him, strikes you as odd or strange.'

Ariadne paused, giving it some thought.

'You know, there is something now I come to think of it, something that struck me as strange even at the time, something Liam said. Not in Spanish – he wasn't actually very good. We were talking about our families and he told us his wife was a translator which, given that we were in a language class, everyone found pretty interesting. And then someone asked him what she translated and he turned to the teacher and said, "how do you say 'truth into lies'?" Everyone thought it was very funny. As I say, it may be absolutely nothing, and it may have just been Liam having a joke, but I've always remembered it. Truth into lies. I reminded him of it in the pub after his talk.'

'You went to the pub after the talk?'

'Yes, he asked me along. Said he was going to the Sun with some friends and did I want to come. My husband was away so I thought . . .'

Milly's mind was racing. So Ariadne Fowler was one of the group at the pub.

'Who else was there, Ariadne?'

'I didn't know all of them. Some were teachers from his old school. I spoke to a few of them.'

'What about?'

'Nothing special. Liam's talk mainly, and his book of course. I should imagine you're looking at those teachers pretty closely, aren't you? I mean, being seen as the subject of erotic fantasies I can just about cope with and I certainly don't regard it – and nor could you possibly regard it – as motive for murder. But that blackmail stuff . . .'

Ariadne raised her eyebrows and exhaled through pursed lips.

'What time did you leave the Sun?'

'I can't remember exactly, but I only had one drink.'

'And was Liam still there when you left?'

'Yes. I remember saying goodbye to him.'

Milly scribbled in her notebook, snapped it shut and got up to leave.

'Well if you do think of anything else, Ariadne, please do get in touch.'

Ariadne took the card Milly held out to her. 'I will.'

Fred Tolley sat at his kitchen table.

'Yes, I went to Liam's talk. I wanted to hear what he had to say.'

'I see,' said Milly, flicking through her notebook. 'And you knew Liam through the choir?'

'That's right. He joined about the same time as me.'

'How well did you know him?'

'Difficult to say. How well do you know anyone? We went out for a few drinks after choir practice.'

'Have you read Liam's novel?'

'*Schooled in Murder*. Yes. I enjoyed it. And I read in the news that he was murdered in the same way as the victim in his book. Extraordinary.'

'It is, yes.'

'And what do you lot make of it?'

Milly took a breath. 'We're pursuing several lines of enquiry,' she said, reaching for another cliché.

'But I guess you're looking pretty closely at that book of his, aren't you?'

'As I said, we're exploring several possibilities. And one of those is that Liam might have put people he knew into his novel.'

Fred laughed. 'Just like the t-shirt, eh?'

'Like what t-shirt?'

'I saw a t-shirt once in a book shop. Funny place for a t-shirt, you might think, but not this one. It said – "be careful or I'll put you in my next novel". A t-shirt for writers. Anyway, I can see where this one is leading to. And you might also understand why I'm glad my wife is out.'

Milly reached for her book and opened it at one of the Post-it-marked pages. 'The thing is, in *Schooled in Murder* there's a description of a man in the choir Alex Ballantyne sings in—'

Fred held up his hand to stop her. 'You don't need to read it to me. There's a man Alex sings with in the choir who's unable to satisfy his wife and who thinks his wife's having it

191

off with someone who can and is doing it every week when he's out at choir practice. And you want to know whether I think that bloke is supposed to be me.'

'Well, yes, I was going to ask you—'

'You don't think I'm a suspect, do you? That I'm so angry about it that I killed Liam Allerton?'

'No, I'm not saying that. I'm just—'

'Look. Do I think Liam was using me as his inspiration for that character? I can't say, but am I going to admit to being in the same situation as his character? Of course not. Did I murder Liam? Of course not. Why would I? To be perfectly honest, detective . . . er . . .'

'Detective Sergeant Gardner.'

'To be perfectly honest, I don't understand why you've come to speak to me at all.'

'OK, well, look, what would be really helpful would be anything you can remember about Liam, anything he said in the times you were with him, when you went out for a drink that, looking back on it, strikes you as odd or significant in any way.'

'So you're not accusing me of anything? I'm not a suspect?'

'Not at all. I just want to know what you made of him, what you make of what's happened. In particular, did he say or do anything to you that struck you as odd or interesting?'

Fred Tolley looked relieved, as if being told he wasn't a suspect had made everything easier. He clasped his hands in front of him and considered the question for a few moments.

'OK, well there is one thing Liam said that always struck me as strange. I have no idea whether or not it's relevant to what happened to him, but I'll share it with you.'

'Please do. What did he say?'

Fred paused. 'We were out for a drink one night after

rehearsal. We were talking about our wives and, again, may I stress that I did not confess to him about my wife seeing a lover every time I was at choir rehearsal – I have no idea where he got that from but it wasn't from me. Anyway, we were talking about our wives and, almost out of nowhere Liam leaned towards me over our pints and he said, 'Fred, you just wouldn't believe what my wife and I have got up to, the things we've done.' Well, I was shocked. I thought he was about to give details, you know, intimate details but no, that was it. That's all he said.'

'Did you ask him what he meant?'

'I waited for him to elaborate, but he didn't, so I thought it best to leave it.'

'Did you ever meet his wife?'

'Never. I saw her at the talk and he introduced me to her and she was with him briefly at the pub afterwards but again I didn't have the chance to talk. I did keep looking at her and wondering about those words – "the things we've done", "the things we've got up to". She didn't look the sort but you never can tell, can you?'

'What sort do you mean?'

'The sort that are into stuff. You know, strange stuff.'

'Did you say you saw her in the pub?'

'Yes. Liam asked me to go with his friends for a drink.'

Milly jotted down a note. 'I see. And when did you leave the pub?'

'Can't remember precisely, but about 10.30, I guess. Liam was still there with his friends, most of them teachers from St Mark's as I remember.'

'Did you notice anything strange about Liam's behaviour?'

'In the pub? No. Looked like he was enjoying it.'

'What about his friends?'

Fred shrugged. 'They were just having a drink and a chat.'

'We have reason to believe that Liam's drink might have been spiked while he was in the Sun. 'Did you—?'

'Did I see anyone spike his drink? Don't you think I would have got in touch?'

Milly looked at her notes. 'To get back to what Liam said about the things he got up to, do you think he was talking about something sexual between him and his wife?'

'That's what it sounded like. What else could it be? The things we've got up to.'

'And how do you think this might be relevant?'

'I have no idea. You're the detective, you tell me.'

Milly tried to think of a witty comeback but nothing came to her. She closed her notebook, gave Fred Tolley her card and said goodbye.

Maybe her next interview would go a little better.

'Did I join the tennis group after my husband walked out on me? Yes I did. Did I do it to meet lots of men and sleep with them? No.'

Milly's interview with Helena Redwood was going no better than the previous two. As soon as the possibility of a resemblance between Helena and a tennis-playing character in *Schooled in Murder* was raised, Helena had become as aggressively defensive as Ariadne Fowler and Fred Tolley – protesting her innocence with similar forcefulness, making Milly wonder, as she always did when faced with exaggerated confidence, whether all three might in fact have something to hide.

And like the other two, Helena gave Milly no chance to read from her Post-it marked pages.

'Tell me Helena, how well did you know Liam?'

'You mean did I know him well enough to let him satisfy my voracious sexual appetite like the woman his character played tennis with?'

'I'm not suggesting that—'

'You wouldn't be here if you weren't.'

'Helena, without assuming that I'm suggesting any parallels, how well *did* you know Liam?'

Helena sat back in her chair and looked through the window of her apartment. It may have had a great view of the Thames but that wasn't enough to convince Milly it was a good idea to live in Harrods Village, the gated modern complex beside the Thames, built on the site of the old Harrods Depository.

'The truth is,' said Helena, ' I probably know more about how Liam played tennis than about him as a person. Strong forehand, weak backhand, very soft second serve and couldn't volley his way out of a paper bag.'

Milly opened her notebook.

Helena laughed. 'I'm sure you don't need to write that down.'

'I'm not,' said Milly, unable to hide her irritation.

'OK,' said Helena, sighing in a way that suggested the whole process irritated her and she wanted it to end as soon as possible. 'How well did I know Liam Allerton? Well we didn't talk much at the weekend sessions. He came for a coffee afterwards but the group was quite large and we never had the chance for a proper conversation. But when he started to come along to the midweek sessions we did manage a couple of conversations.'

'What did you talk about?'

'Nothing significant. Nothing, I'm sure, that will give you a clue about who killed him. I mean, it's not as though he said "I'm in terrible trouble, Helena, I've put people in my book, given them terrible secrets and because of that they want to kill me—"'

'I didn't for one moment expect that he did,' said Milly, now in no doubt that Helena Redwood was proving to be the worst of the three.

'But we did have one conversation which I do remember. I'd found out he was a writer, we all had, and I'd read his book and I asked him about it. I remember I asked the thing everyone always asks writers – where did he get his ideas from? And, before you ask, I did *not* ask him whether the sex-starved tennis player in his book was based on me – even though I had a sense that it might have been. Not the physical description, you understand, but the circumstances – joining the group after her husband walked out on her, that kind of thing. I kept well away from that, though I did ask how it had gone down at his old school because, let's face it, that was the meat of the novel. The tennis stuff was only really a page or two—'

'What did he say when you asked about the school?'

'He just laughed and came out with all that guff about the creative act, how all ideas derive from some kind of reality, all fiction being based on people and places et cetera et cetera. Exactly the stuff he said at the talk.'

'Why did you go to his talk, Helena?'

'Why not? I knew him, I played tennis with him and I'd read the book. I was interested. Surely I don't have to justify going to Liam Allerton's talk?'

'Of course not, I'm only—'

'I'm right, I'm a suspect, aren't I?'

'I'm not saying that. We're—'

'Look, I went to the talk because I was interested and I'm glad I did. It was a good talk. Liam said some interesting

196

things. I wanted to follow them up with him in the pub afterwards but I didn't get the chance.'

'You went to the pub afterwards?'

'You make it sound like I wasn't allowed to.'

'No, I don't mean that. I—'

Milly jotted down a note. 'To get back to your conversation with Liam. You were saying . . .'

'I was saying I asked him about where he got his ideas from and then I asked him what it was like to write, how he did it, and I was struck by what he said. I can't believe this is in any way relevant to anything but I do remember it because it wasn't the answer I expected.'

'What did he say?'

'He said writers were con artists. That's the phrase he used – con artists. Writers were con artists and writing was a con trick.'

Milly jotted the phrases down in her notebook. 'What do you think he meant?'

'I have no idea.'

'Did you ask him?'

'I was about to but then someone came over and joined us and the chance had gone. As I say, I can't believe it's in any way significant but given what's happened to him . . . by the way, where *are* you in this investigation? For him to be killed like that. How do you explain it?'

'We're still pursuing several lines of enquiry,' said Milly, getting up to leave.

'But that book seems to be at the heart of it, doesn't it?'

'As I said, we're exploring many avenues.'

But as she spoke the words Milly knew how far from the truth they were. Everything still seemed to point in one direction only – *Schooled in Murder,* Liam Allerton's first, and last, foray into fiction.

197

When Milly was back in her car she looked over her notes. The interviews had, in her view, not gone well, but she knew she had something – the identity of three members of the group in the Sun Inn after Allerton's talk. It might not lead anywhere but even Garibaldi couldn't say it wasn't significant.

As for the other stuff – truth into lies, the stuff Liam got up to with his wife, writing as a con-trick – she didn't know what to make of it. The more she thought about it the less it seemed to make sense.

28

When Sasha Ambrose heard from the police that she was not the only one to have received a blackmail note she was shocked. When she discovered who the other three were the shock turned to something more complicated.

She wanted to know more. What had the other notes said? And what had the other three said to the police?

There was only one way to find out.

'It's Sasha,' she said to Ewan when he picked up the phone.

'Sasha. I was meaning to call—'

'I hear you got one as well.'

'A note? I did, yes.'

'You know who else got them?'

'Yeah, I do.'

'What the fuck is going on?'

'I don't know, Sasha, I really don't know.'

'Have you spoken to the others?'

'Not yet.'

'When are the police seeing you?'

'Later today. And you?'

'The same.'

Sasha took a breath. There was so much she wanted to say, so much she wanted to ask, but she sensed the caginess. It was like a game of poker.

'What I don't get,' she said after a short awkward silence, 'is that it's the four who were at his talk, the four who were in the pub with him afterwards. So does that—'

'Does that make us suspects? The police seem to think so.'

'But that's, that's ridiculous!'

As soon as Sasha said the word she realised how wrong it was. There was nothing ridiculous about it at all. Of course they were suspects. If the police thought they actually *had* been blackmailed, if they thought each of them actually *had* those things to hide, then each of them had a pretty good motive, and yet . . .

'Look,' said Ewan. 'This is a horrible question but I need to ask it and I think we all need to know. What did your note actually say?'

'It implied I worked as an escort. And yours?'

'Drug habit.'

'So we're the same as those characters in the book, then?'

'Look, Sasha, I'm assuming you don't need me to tell you this but I'm going to tell you anyway. I don't have a drug habit.'

'And I don't work as an escort. Never have.'

'Right,' said Ewan, 'at least that's cleared up then. I suppose the question now is whether there's anything we should do.'

Anything we should do? Sasha couldn't see many options.

'I mean, we need to talk to Ruth and Armit, obviously, but is there anything else we need to tell the police?'

'About what?'

'Anything. Liam. The book. The school.'

'I think all we can do, Ewan, is tell the truth. Don't you?'

Ewan was silent for a few seconds. Sasha got the sense that he was considering alternatives.

'Well, look,' he said. 'Let's keep in touch. I'll talk to the others and I guess you should speak to them too. And let me know how it goes with the police.'

'OK.' Sasha hung up, not knowing what to make of the call, but sensing from Ewan's manner that he wasn't telling her the whole truth. She was used to this in her professional dealings with him. As deputy head, Ewan was at the heart of senior management, so dealing in partial truths and political evasions had become part of his nature. But what they were dealing with now was a far cry from quibbles about the timetable, staffing levels or pupil behaviour. They were dealing with murder.

Liam Allerton. Why had she spent so much time with him? What was it about him that tempted her to open up, to share things that should remain unshared?

And that novel.

Why the hell had he written that fucking novel?

Ruth Price took it as a bad sign that she should be told about Armit's blackmail note by the police and not by Armit himself — that a couple who were sleeping together shouldn't share such information struck her as ridiculous. OK, so she had chosen not to tell Armit about her own note, and so could be regarded as equally culpable, but as far as Ruth was concerned that wasn't the point. The whole episode, their lack of communication over something of such importance, confirmed what her gut had been telling her — that this whole thing was a mistake and she should do her best to finish it as amicably, and as soon, as possible — and definitely before he booked up a holiday in Crete.

She had been stunned when the police told her who else had received notes. Four notes to the four teachers who had been with Liam the night before his body was found – no wonder they wanted to talk to them. She'd stated her innocence with confidence. No, she had never embezzled funds from the school. No, unlike any of the characters in Liam Allerton's novel, she had not been blackmailed. Yes, this was the first such note she had ever received, and no, she had no idea who might choose to send it to her.

But, as she had faced their questions, her own had been forming. What notes had the others received? What had they said to the police? Could any of them be guilty of the blackmailer's accusations?

And why hadn't Armit been in touch?

'Armit,' she said when she decided she could wait no longer and rang him. 'Why haven't you called?'

'I was waiting for you to call me.'

'Why?'

'I didn't know what to say.'

'That's not the point. The point is I'm completely terrified and I thought you might—'

'I'm sorry, Ruth, when the police told me you'd got a note as well I was all over the place so I—'

'Given our situation,' said Ruth, 'I'd have thought—'

'I'm sorry,' said Armit. 'I really am. But these notes . . . I mean what did yours say?'

'Embezzlement.'

'Embezzlement?'

'I need hardly add that it's absolutely untrue.'

'Of course it is. I never thought—'

And yours? What did yours say?'

'That I slept with a student. Ridiculous!'

'Of course. And both of them identical to the ones—'

'The ones in the novel. Exactly.'

'*Schooled in Fucking Murder*!'

'Have you spoken to the others yet?'

'Ewan and Sasha? No, not yet. I'm waiting for ...'

'Waiting for them to call?' laughed Ruth. 'Like you were with me?'

'I'm assuming the notes they got were the other two from the novel.'

'Why do you assume that?'

'That's the pattern, isn't it?'

'Remind me. What were the other notes?'

'You really can't remember?'

'I just—'

'Drugs and prostitution.'

Ruth sighed. 'This is absolutely ridiculous. Do you have any idea who could have sent them?'

'Maybe someone's done it as a joke.'

'Pretty sick joke.'

'Maybe someone's read the novel and thought—'

'And thought what?'

'I don't know. It doesn't make sense. You wouldn't think anyone would do something like this.'

'You wouldn't think anyone would murder Liam but they did.'

'Do you think it's the same person?'

'I'm not saying anything. It's just ... look I ...'

Ruth listened to the silence.

'There's something I ...'

Armit trailed off, and a long pause followed. Ruth sensed he was on the verge of revealing something.

'Look, Ruth, can I see you tonight?'

'Tonight? I thought we were leaving it for a couple of days.'

'I know, but—'

'I think I need some time alone, Armit, time to take it all in. Maybe when we've both seen the police, when we've heard from the others.'

'OK.'

She could hear the disappointment in his voice.

'But you're OK?' he added.

'About as OK as I could expect to be under the circumstances. And one thing I'm totally OK about is the fact that I have never embezzled.'

'Yeah, me too. I mean about the student. I've never slept with a student.'

Ruth hung up, looked at the phone in her hand and wondered whether she should bite the bullet and give Ewan and Sasha a call as well.

But something was stopping her. In her head she kept hearing what Armit had said about his blackmail note. Something about his words, something about the way he denied the accusation troubled her, and she knew exactly what it was.

Then she thought about Liam Allerton, lying in the reeds at the edge of Barnes Pond. Why had she ever said anything to him? Why had she opened her mouth to the school's biggest gossip?

And why had he written that fucking novel?

'Ruth, I was going to give you a call.'

Ewan's plan had been to ring Ruth and Armit before they called him, just to be upfront about it all and show that he had absolutely nothing to hide.

But Ruth had beaten him to it.

'I've already spoken to Sasha,' he said. 'And what can I say? We're gobsmacked. Totally.'

'Your notes,' said Ruth. 'What did they say?'

'They were straight out of the novel,' said Ewan. 'Mine was drugs and Sasha's was prostitution. I don't need to add that both are completely untrue. I mean I know mine isn't true, and as for Sasha—'

'They're obviously not true, but the question is why the fuck have we got them?'

'I have no idea,' he said. 'And the police don't seem to have much idea either. They're all over the place.'

'I didn't like their manner at all,' said Ruth. 'Very accusatory. And that was before the notes. God knows what they're going to be like now.'

'I really don't know what to say, Ruth.'

'First the murder. Now four notes to four teachers. Straight out of *Schooled in Murder.*'

'And the four teachers ,' said Ewan, 'are the ones who were with Liam in the pub after his talk.'

Ewan knew why he had gone to Liam's talk but he had never been sure why the other three had done the same. Out of interest? To support him? Plausible enough, given that they all knew Liam and might have counted themselves as friends, but he knew that in his case it was more than that that had brought him to the OSO that Saturday night. Now, in the wake of the notes, he wondered whether the same might be true of the others.

'That can't be coincidence,' said Ruth. 'It's as if someone's out to get us, to set us up.'

'But who would do that? Why?'

'I have no idea, Ewan, but I'm worried.'

'Well, look, we need to keep in touch. All of us. The important thing is we know those notes aren't true. None of them. So we've got nothing to worry about.'

But, as he said the words, he knew he didn't believe

them. He couldn't speak for the others but he himself had plenty to worry about.

'Does Harry know?' said Ruth. 'Have you spoken to him?'

'The police have told him,' said Ewan, 'but I haven't spoken to him, no.'

'As if we haven't had enough bad publicity already.'

'These things have a habit of riding themselves out,' said Ewan. 'It'll blow over.'

He knew it was wishful thinking. He would be delighted if things blew over but at the moment, thinking about what Liam Allerton seemed to have known, he could only see things blowing up.

29

'We need to talk about Alfie.'

The words felt strange. They were usually Kay's being delivered to Garibaldi. Now they were Garibaldi's being delivered to Rachel.

They had just finished watching *University Challenge* and *Richard Osman's House of Games* and were about to move on to *Only Connect*. It was the latest leg of their ongoing weekly quiz competition, one in which they watched recorded episodes of the programmes, sitting side by side on the sofa, shouting out the answers and keeping a careful tally. Garibaldi liked to think he was ahead, but Rachel's scorekeeping suggested otherwise, leading him both to doubt her accuracy and wonder whether she was sneaking in some advanced viewing. Garibaldi also liked to think he was getting better, particularly at *Only Connect,* which, having started as the quiz he found almost impossible, was now the one he preferred.

'OK,' said Rachel. 'Alfie. What do we need to talk about?'

'Look, when he said he'd like to stay I thought it would be for a night or two. It's now nearly a week. And I'll be honest with you. When he's here it's beginning to feel a bit cramped.'

'It's not a problem,' said Rachel. 'Really. And even if it were what could you do? You can't kick him out.'

'I know, but . . .'

'You always say you don't see enough of him.'

'I'm worried about him, Rachel.'

Rachel reached out and put her hand on his arm. 'You've been worried about him ever since I met you.'

'OK. I hated him living with Kay and Dom. It was like I'd lost him and if I'm honest part of me hoped he might do something like walk out. But now that he has—'

'You need to chill.'

'Chill?'

Rachel stroked his arm. 'Yeah. Relax a bit. You're very tense.'

Garibaldi turned and looked into her eyes. He put his hand on top of hers and smiled.

'Is it the case?' said Rachel.

'Maybe. I just can't work it out. Ever since we went to that bloody talk.'

'So I'm to blame, am I?'

'Of course not. It's just that straight after it Alfie turns up and the next morning Ben Joseph's body's floating in the pond and since then I haven't been able to get my head straight. Nothing makes sense.'

Rachel yawned and looked at her watch. 'You know what's a good thing when nothing makes sense?'

'Tell me.'

'An early night.'

'Really?'

'Yes, really. I'm turning in.' Rachel started to stroke his arm again. 'Why don't you turn in as well?'

Garibaldi looked at Rachel's hand on his arm. 'On a school night?'

Rachel's raised eyebrows suggested that such things were possible.

'You know what?' said Garibaldi. 'That's not a bad idea.'

Rachel got up from the sofa , reached for Garibaldi's hands, pulled him up and led him to the bedroom.

The sound of a key turning in the flat's front door stopped them in their tracks.

'Hi!'

Garibaldi turned. 'Alfie!'

Alfie threw himself onto the sofa with a sigh and reached for the remote. 'OK if I watch TV?'

'Of course it is,' said Garibaldi, edging away from the bedroom door. 'You don't have to ask.'

Garibaldi looked at Rachel and carried out a quick risk assessment. If Alfie was in the living room watching TV could he and Rachel make love in their bedroom? Would he feel comfortable about it? He knew the answer. Even if Alfie put the TV up to maximum volume, even if they put on loud music in the bedroom, even if he could be certain that nothing would be heard beyond the bedroom door, it wasn't something he could do.

For all Rachel's reassurances that Alfie's presence in the flat made no difference, here was evidence that it did.

Garibaldi went back into the bedroom and closed the door behind him.

'I'm so sorry,' he whispered to Rachel.

Rachel slipped out of her skirt, a gesture which, under the circumstances, Garibaldi found painfully arousing.

'No problem,' she said, taking off the rest of her clothes and leaping into bed.

'This is exactly what I mean about it being difficult.'

'Relax. We're not a pair of desperate teenagers are we?'

'No, but—'

Rachel switched on the bedside light and reached for her book.

'It's OK,' she said. 'It really is.'

Garibaldi went to the door. 'I'll be back in a couple of minutes.'

'No hurry,' said Rachel from behind her book.

He closed the bedroom door behind him and sat down next to Alfie, who was watching Netflix – a drama about a bunch of millennials having problems being millennials. Garibaldi couldn't stand it.

'How's it going?' said Garibaldi, his eyes on the screen.

'Which bit of "it" are you talking about?'

'Whatever.'

Garibaldi winced. Had he really said 'whatever'? It wasn't just his sex-life that Alfie's presence in the flat was affecting.

'Well, QPR's prospects for next season aren't looking too good.'

'Tell me something new,' said Garibaldi. 'What about Alicia?'

'Alicia? You mean woke Alicia, Alicia the snowflake?'

'Those aren't my words – you know that's not what I think.'

'She's OK.'

'Yeah? Up to anything interesting?'

'We're going to an exhibition tomorrow.'

'An exhibition?'

'Yeah. At the Barbican. Art in the Sixties.'

Garibaldi laughed. 'And to think that you used to hate art.'

'I've always liked art, Dad.'

'Really? Not when your mum dragged you round the Tate, talking to you loudly so that everyone could hear what a great mum she was . . .'

So much for his pledge to stop slagging off Kay in front of their son.

'Talking of your mum . . .'

'I spoke to her earlier.'

'And? '

'I don't think she's forgiven me. Dom definitely hasn't.'

Their eyes were on the TV. It made conversation easier, the same way that it did when they sat side by side at Loftus Road. The way that it did when Garibaldi sat in the passenger seat beside Gardner.

'So . . .' Garibaldi took a breath. 'So you won't be . . .'

'Moving back to Putney? No.'

'Look, Alfie. You're not a kid anymore and you don't have to put up with stuff like . . . well, with stuff like that. And you know what I think about Dom.'

As he said the words he wondered how true they were. He'd spoken with Alfie about all that had happened over the years – his illness, the marital breakdown, the separation, the divorce, the decision that Alfie should live with Kay – but he had never let Alfie know the extent of his feelings about Kay's new partner. He'd always assumed that Alfie, being intelligent and perceptive, had worked it out for himself.

'Dad,' said Alfie. 'I'm not going back to Putney. End of.'

End of. He'd been spending too much time with his mother.

'OK, but don't think your only option is to move out somewhere else. You're welcome here. More than welcome.'

'I know, but . . . it's not ideal, is it? So I'm working on it, I really am. I've got a mate who's got a room in his flat—'

'But what about the rent? There's plenty of room here.'

'Look, Dad, I know there are loads in the same boat, moving back in with their parents.'

'Boomerangs.'

'Exactly. I just feel ... I guess ...'

Alfie trailed off and said nothing for a few seconds, his eyes still fixed on the Netflix millennials.

'I don't want to be in the way, Dad. I really don't.' He tilted his head towards the bedroom. 'You and Rachel. You need your time. You need your space. For ... you know. For everything.'

Garibaldi turned to look at his son in no doubt that he knew exactly what he and Rachel were about to do when his return had interrupted them.

30

Hi Ruth,

I expect you're surprised to hear from me. It's been a
long time, and a lot's happened to me since we last saw
each other. I bet a lot's happened to you too – I hope it's
been good because, to be honest, what's happened to
me since I left school has been shit.

I decided to get in touch when I saw about the murder
of that man who used to teach at your school. The thing
is I've thought about you quite a bit over the years but
when I read about that man and the book he'd written
I started thinking about you even more. What we did.
What you did.

It said the book was set in a school a bit like the
one he'd taught in – St Mark's. When I saw the name I
remembered it was the school you went to when you
left Ellison. I remember things like that about you, little
details. And that was one that stuck. I was interested in
this book so I got hold of it and read it. I do quite a bit of
that now – read. Helps the nerves. Helps me settle. So
I read it. And I couldn't believe it. Teachers with secrets
being blackmailed. And there was our secret. Couldn't
believe it. One of the teachers had done what we did. It

all came back to me – what we did, what I felt and what it did to me when you ended it.

I just want you to know that I still think of you. It may not have mattered to you but it really mattered to me.

Ruth stared at the screen. Why had she opened her emails?

She couldn't avoid it once exam results were out and the beginning of the new year loomed, but in the early weeks of the holidays she liked to give herself a break.

So why had she done it?

Nerves. That was the only explanation. She was nervous about everything. The murder. The note. That must be why she'd done it.

And when she opened the email there it was – exactly what she feared, come back to haunt her. No, more than haunt her. Terrify her.

What did it mean? And where would it lead?

At least she hadn't seen it before the police came to interview her. There's no way she would have coped with this running through her head. She may have said exactly the same thing, given exactly the same answers, but she'd have been more conscious that she wasn't being entirely straight.

Especially after the one called Garibaldi had shown her that thing with the names. Prisha Bedi. RP. Ruth Price. She hadn't needed to do any acting when that particular bomb had been dropped.

No, she had said. She couldn't possibly be the model for Prisha Bedi. And, no, she had never embezzled school funds.

Sasha wished whoever it was would stop getting in touch. Calls, texts, WhatsApps – they were pretty persistent and every time she received one she was tempted.

214

It was difficult. She'd been trying hard ever since she read the book, ever since there was the initial fuss that Liam might have been writing about St Mark's and some of its teachers. She'd managed to stop then, but when the storm died down and people stopped talking about it, when no one seemed to be looking for any parallels between Liam's story and any kind of reality, she'd started again.

It was all too easy – that was the nature of the beast. You thought you could control it, but you didn't need to be a genius to work out that it was the other way round and that it had you absolutely in its grip.

Liam's murder had changed everything. The book, the school, the teachers – they were all back in the spotlight and under even closer scrutiny. And then there was the note. She knew it wasn't true, but that didn't mean she wasn't shit scared.

She'd tried to answer the detectives as truthfully as she could, but when it had come to that thing with the names she had to pretend. Ashley MacDonald. SA. Sasha Ambrose. When she'd first read *Schooled in Murder* it hadn't taken her long to see what game Liam was playing. She hadn't done the *Guardian* crossword with him so often in the St Mark's staffroom without getting some sense of the way his mind worked. So when the detective had triumphantly revealed his code-cracking she had pretended that it all came as a complete surprise. Had she seen this for herself? No. She was amazed. How clever of you to have spotted it, Inspector.

She had said nothing about what else she had discovered in the novel – that Liam's game was a little more complex than they thought.

But she had answered other questions with absolute truthfulness, especially the one about the note. Had she worked as an escort? No. Absolutely not. Never.

The police may not have noticed anything but she couldn't be absolutely sure. She knew she had to tread carefully, especially when it came to the short one with the Italian name.

She was still very much in danger.

As Ewan Thomas sat on the bus on his way to the Bridge, the pub at the top of Castelnau on the south side of Hammersmith Bridge where he had arranged to meet Harry Reed, he went over recent events, trying to work out the likely direction of his conversation with the head and how he should answer his questions.

Under normal circumstances Harry would leave him alone at the beginning of the summer holidays. But these circumstances were far from normal. Liam Allerton's murder had been bad enough but those blackmail notes had once again thrown St Mark's into the spotlight. Each of the recipients had now been interviewed by the police and, from what he had been told, each of them had come out with the only possible line – no, of course they hadn't done the things the notes accused them of and yes, they realised that the notes were identical to those received by characters in *Schooled in Murder*.

But did the other three feel as worried as he did? Ewan knew he didn't have a drug habit – of that he was absolutely certain. And he knew that he had protested his innocence to the detectives with complete conviction. Neither of them could have been in any doubt that he was telling the truth.

As he had been speaking, though, as he had been answering their questions, his mind was thinking of other questions they could ask him, and one in particular that he would struggle to answer so easily. And he was so preoccupied with those thoughts that when the cops had sprung the name thing on him he had been completely poleaxed. Ted Fox. ET. Ewan Thomas. He hadn't seen it at all and couldn't believe for one moment that it was significant, but when they went on to reveal the same pattern in the names of the other blackmail note recipients he had to recognise the possibility that it was.

As the bus pulled up opposite the Bridge, Ewan wondered whether he should share the police's name theory with his head but decided, on balance, that it might be better not to.

Armit reckoned the interview with the police had gone well. Or at least it hadn't gone as badly as it could have. He'd been able to answer their questions with confidence. No he'd never slept with a student – he'd never do anything like that. And, no, he had no idea why anyone would send him, or the three other teachers, notes like that. He was, of course, well aware of the fact that the notes were identical to the notes received by characters in Liam's novel but he had no idea what to make of it – in the same way that he had no idea why Liam's murderer should choose to kill him in that particular way.

It had been more difficult when the detectives had asked why the four of them who had gone to Liam's talk at the book festival were the four to have received the notes. Wasn't this odd? Armit had given the only answer he could – that he had absolutely no idea – but they wouldn't let it go, especially the man. He kept coming back to the fact that the four people who had received those notes had been amongst the last to see him alive. Armit could see what they were implying. They were all suspects.

All through the interview he hoped they couldn't see

how uneasy he felt. The man called Garibaldi had some-times looked at him in a way that suggested he sensed Armit was holding something back – not lying as such, but not delivering the whole truth.

And when he saw Armit's response to the pattern of names and initials he looked at him even more strangely. The revelation came as a total shock. Harry Antrobus. AH Armit Harwal. No, he'd never seen that – either in his own name or the names of the three colleagues who had received the notes.

But Inspector Garibaldi had looked at him in a way that suggested he didn't think Armit had told the truth.

Or maybe that was just his paranoia.

31

Rosanna Reed seemed a far cry from Garibaldi's image of a headmaster's wife and an unlikely partner for Harry Reed. Whereas the St Mark's head had a pomposity bordering on the absurd, his wife had a down-to-earth informality. Garibaldi couldn't imagine the two of them together.

'It might seem strange that we want to talk to you,' said Garibaldi, 'but I hope you understand.'

'I quite understand,' said Rosanna, 'and it doesn't seem strange at all. You're here to ask about the murder of poor Liam and how it's connected to his novel.'

'That's exactly why we're here,' said Garibaldi.

'And, given that in his novel the murderer was the headmaster's wife you want to question me and find out whether I did it.'

'Well, I wouldn't put it quite so bluntly, but—'

'Maybe I should start by saying that on the night of Liam's murder – Saturday wasn't it?'

'Some time between late on Saturday night and early Sunday morning,' said Gardner.

'Right, well that whole weekend I was away. Staying with an old schoolfriend in Gloucestershire. So I have an alibi. You can check it out.'

'I wasn't going to ask where you were,' said Garibaldi.

'Well, there you go, you've got it for free. What else do you need to know?'

'You're absolutely right,' said Garibaldi, 'to say we're exploring connections between Liam Allerton's murder and his novel.'

'And that,' said Rosanna, ' is because of how he was killed and where he was found.'

'That's one of the connections, yes.'

'You mean there are more?'

Garibaldi nodded.

'Harry hasn't mentioned any more. I told him to keep me updated . . .'

Rosanna huffed with impatience as if she were talking about a naughty child.

'I should imagine your husband found things difficult when *Schooled in Murder* was published,' said Garibaldi.

'He did. There was a bit of media interest. Nothing like the interest there is now, of course.'

'What did your husband say about the book when he read it?'

'Haven't you asked him?'

'I'm asking you.'

Rosanna gave another huff. 'OK, so he said that Allerton had clearly modelled his fictional school – what was it called, St John's?'

'St Jude's,' said Gardner.

'He said that he'd clearly modelled it on St Mark's but he couldn't believe for one moment that he'd modelled his teacher characters on any of his staff. And as for the black-mail thing. Completely ridiculous.'

'And do you agree?' said Garibaldi.

'Of course I agree. Look, to be honest, much to Harry's

irritation I try not to get involved in the school. I'm not that kind of headmaster's wife. In fact, it's remarkable that Harry has done as well as he has with a wife like me. All I can say is that I am definitely not the model for the head's wife. I have never had an affair. And I can't believe that Harry is the model for the St Jude's head. He hasn't had an affair either.'

Rosanna leaned back in her chair. Garibaldi glanced round the living room of the Lonsdale Road house that came with her husband's job, trying to think of more questions.

He raised his eyes to Gardner who shook her head.

'Thank you for your time, Rosanna,' he said, getting to his feet and gesturing for Gardner to do the same.

'It's a strange one, isn't it?' said Rosanna as she showed them to the door.

'It is,' said Garibaldi, 'but we're making good progress.'

'I hope you had your fingers crossed,' said Gardner as they crunched across the gravel drive to their car.

'What do you mean?'

'Making good progress.'

'My fingers are always crossed,' said Garibaldi, climbing into the passenger seat. 'It's their default position.'

Ben Joseph kept haunting Araminta Warburton. Images of the dead writer came to her all the time. She might be in the Barnes Bookshop, serving a customer, or walking along the High Street, or sitting at home watching TV when a vivid picture of him talking at the OSO would flash across her mind, followed by thoughts of what he might have looked like floating at the edge of Barnes Pond. It was at its worst at night, when, as she lay in bed reading, she found herself

221

unable to concentrate on the words on the page. Usually she would read for half an hour before gently dozing off with the bedside light still on and the book fallen onto her chest – the perfect booklover's way of falling asleep. But since the murder, sleep had not come so easily and she often found herself tossing restlessly, turning over in her head thoughts about who might have killed him and why.

People still talked about it in the shop, probing her with questions, as if because he had spoken at the festival and she had introduced him she was privy to knowledge unavailable to the public. *Schooled in Murder* was still selling and was still on display in the window. She had thought of putting a simple memorial message beside it, but had decided against it. Given the press coverage and the level of local interest, all those looking in would know all about what had happened to the author.

Today as she parked her car and went to open the shop she was feeling out of sorts. The adrenaline thrill of running the BookFest had gone. In its place had come a sense of sadness and regret and she couldn't work out what was causing it. Part of her was still a little irritated that Liam Allerton's murder had taken attention away from the festival's success, but there had been enough favourable comment from those who had attended events, and from those who had spoken at them, to reassure her that everyone was appreciative of what had, by anyone's definition, been a successful event. The sadness was to do with more than that, and she kept coming back to the conclusion that it was all to do with what had happened to Liam.

Like the whole community, Araminta was traumatised by the brutality, the unexpectedness and, yes, the mystery of it all. She had experienced many bereavements, many of them of people much closer to her than Ben Joseph aka Liam

Allerton, but his had struck her in a way that others had not, and at times she wondered whether it was because, in selling *Schooled in Murder* from her shop, she had in some way been responsible for what happened to its author. She knew this was absurd but she also knew that whoever had killed him had clearly read the book – not necessarily bought from her shop, of course – and she couldn't help but feel there was a high likelihood that Liam Allerton's murderer was a local.

Her mind was so full of these thoughts as she turned the keys in both locks that at first she didn't see it.

It was only when she went into the shop, bent over to pick up some junk mail from the floor and turned to the right that she saw what was on the window.

It was sprayed on the front, so she had to read backwards, but Araminta had no difficulty making out the words:

THE IRONIC DEATH OF BEN JOSEPH

They were in bright-red paint, spread across the whole of the front window above the display of *Schooled in Murder*.

Araminta dropped the mail she had just picked up, put her hands to her mouth and gave a little whimper. Not even in her worst nightmares had she imagined she would ever see graffiti on the window of her bookshop.

She stood there transfixed, unable to take her eyes off the bright-red letters.

Who had done this and why?

She tried to think logically. It must have happened some time between closing yesterday at six and now, 9.30 am the following day. And someone, surely, must have seen it. You couldn't paint a shop window without being noticed, not in an area like this – a busy street with shops on either side.

Someone must have seen it happening. Someone walking

past. Someone driving past. Unless, of course, it happened in the middle of the night – at three or four in the morning.

But what about CCTV?

The camera inside the shop was turned off when it was closed and they didn't have an external one. But surely there were cameras in some of the surrounding shops?

Araminta opened the door and walked onto the pavement. She stood, hands on hips, looking at the window.

'Blimey!'

She turned to the voice. It was Justin from the charity shop next door.

'That's a bit much, isn't it?' he said.

'I don't believe it,' said Araminta. 'I'm speechless.'

'What's it mean?' said Justin.

'Ben Joseph's the writer who was murdered and ... do you know what? At the moment I'm more concerned with how to get it off than working out what it means.'

'You'll need something powerful,' said Justin. 'Like an industrial cleaner.'

'I'll kill whoever did this,' said Araminta.

'I wouldn't do that. We've had enough murders round here already.'

Araminta turned and saw that a small group had gathered on the pavement on the other side of the road, looking across at the window.

It was all too much. She needed help. Giselle, her assistant, was on the way in but she knew there was little she could do. She needed a whisky perhaps. Or a tranquiliser.

Or maybe a detective.

She went back into the shop and found the card.

32

Garibaldi looked closely at Fran Allerton's features. He could see her mother in the eyes and her father in the lower part of her face, particularly in the mouth, which turned down slightly at the edges as if it were permanently passing some kind of critical judgement.

'What was my father like?' said Fran. 'Where do I start? Everything about him was, I don't know, normal. Not without his faults, but then who isn't? And he had a habit of speaking his mind, yes, but not to the extent that anyone would want to kill him . . .'

Fran Allerton's high-ceilinged and elegantly decorated flat was on the fifth floor of a Victorian mansion block on the north side of Hammersmith Bridge. With large windows looking down on the bridge it would be the perfect place for a Boat Race party and Garibaldi could imagine Fran and her partner (whose job in banking had presumably provided the money for this prime riverside property) throwing one each year. He could also imagine the kind of people who would be there – the friends of a banker and a woman who worked at the V&A. The thought of it, together with thoughts of the Boat Race itself, made him shudder.

'Did your dad enjoy his job at St Mark's?' said Garibaldi.

'He did,' said Fran, 'but he was glad to retire. He said the time was right – he wanted to go while he was still enjoying it and was still able to deliver in the classroom. I remember him saying there's nothing worse than an old teacher who loses it in his final years. He didn't want to do that. I know he was worried about whether they'd have enough money but, being a Maths teacher, I'm sure he'd done his sums.'

'When you say money worries . . .'

'Nothing serious,' said Fran. 'You'd have thought a nice house in Barnes, dad teaching at St Mark's, mum working as a translator would mean we were pretty well off but it's not what it seems. The house is Mum's family home. She inherited it when her parents died. We were OK, but Mum always made the point about Dad being so much poorer than the kids he taught. It was a running joke with them. They were always – I don't know what the right word for it is – academic ,maybe, but that makes it sound as though they worked in universities. Cerebral, maybe that's it. They valued a life of the mind. They brought me up believing that money wasn't important, that it didn't matter as much as other things. And I'm glad they did, but now, looking back on it, I wonder whether money might always have been more of a worry than they liked to let on.'

'Do you have any evidence of money troubles?'

'No, and if you asked Mum about it now she'd deny it. I guess she'll get his pension . . .' Fran looked up at the ceiling, her eyes welling. 'I'll have to check. I'll have to make sure Mum understands. He was always the one who sorted out things, the finances, the bills. There's just so much to do. Thank God for Ollie.'

'Your dad was close to Ollie?'

Fran nodded. 'Yeah. They were at uni together, or as they always liked to say, college. And when Marion was alive they did a lot as a foursome. You know, holidays together, that kind of thing. Ollie was heartbroken, completely devastated when Marion died. To be honest I don't think he's recovered at all. But, yeah, he's been great at sorting things out. So much to do, isn't there? I came across a term for it the other day. Sadmin. That's exactly what it is – admin that's sad.' Fran reached for a tissue. 'It's just so sad. So fucking sad.'

Garibaldi gave her time to gather herself, then said, 'Was your mum worried about your dad retiring?'

'I think she was a bit concerned that he might not have enough to do and they'd get under each other's feet. I mean, mum's a freelance and works from home and they were used to him being around in his long holidays, but that was different to him being around all the time.'

'And how did it work out?' said Garibaldi.

'Dad spent a lot of time in his room,' said Fran, 'but that was nothing new. It was his man cave. He'd always been in there, listening to music, reading, working. Turns out he still was working but Mum had no idea – and nor did I – that what he was working on was a novel.'

'When I last spoke to you Fran, I remember you saying that your Dad could be difficult and you were about to say more when your mother came in. Do you remember that?'

Fran nodded.

'What were you about to say?'

Fran turned away and looked towards the window. 'Look, it's nothing important. I can't believe it's in any way relevant, it's just that – it seems ridiculous even to say this and it's almost like a betrayal – but all I'm saying is that Dad was no angel. I mean no-one is, are they, but he had his faults like the rest of us and I'd be lying if I said there weren't . . . tensions between him and Mum.'

'When you say tensions . . .?'

'There were times when . . . I don't know . . . look, every marriage, every relationship has tensions.'

'Were there rows?'

'There were some, yeah.'

'What were they about?'

'Nothing specific. I mean there probably were the usual ones about unloading the dishwasher and putting out the recycling but I can remember times . . .' Fran paused, as if reluctant to say any more. 'Look I loved Dad, don't get me wrong. I loved him to bits. But he could be difficult, and there were times when Mum seemed sort of doing what he wanted. Sometimes I looked at them and thought, she's doing that to please him and I never thought it was happening the other way round, that he was doing things to please her. And now he's gone I worry about her, of course I do. He was such a strong character . . . and Mum . . . she's . . . I worry about her.'

Fran paused and blew her nose.

'Did he have a temper?' said Garibaldi.

'No, it wasn't like that. Dad was always very controlled. There was nothing . . . explosive. Look, I'm not sure why I'm telling you all this. Dad's gone and I can't see how any of this is going to help. It's not going to bring him back, is it? And it's not going to help you find his killer.'

'We just need to know what was going on in his life.'

'What was going on in his life, or at least his life since he retired, was his book. First of all he wrote it without any of us knowing. Then he submitted it. And as soon as he knew it was going to be published it dominated everything. Then, when it came out earlier this year he started doing lots of book stuff. Suddenly he was very much the centre of attention and there was all this speculation about whether it was based on St Mark's.'

'What did your mum make of it all?'

'I think she found it difficult. She's never been one for putting herself in the limelight – not like Dad – and I'm not sure she was entirely comfortable. Don't get me wrong, she was supportive, she's always been supportive, but I don't think it's what she ever imagined might happen when Dad retired.'

'I see,' said Garibaldi, looking out at the Thames through the high windows. 'But your Dad enjoyed it all?'

Fran paused for a few seconds. 'Most of the time he was really positive and upbeat. Pleased to have done it and pleased to have got it published. There was just one moment . . . and it's stayed with me because I thought it was odd. I can't remember the exact words but he said something like if he knew it was going to cause that much fuss he would have thought twice about it.'

'Did he explain?'

'That's all he said.'

Garibaldi paused and consulted his notebook. He looked up. 'What do you make of the way your father was killed?'

'I find it completely baffling.'

'And you are aware that when we searched your father's study we found blackmail notes?'

'Yes, Mum told me, but that doesn't prove anything, does it? It doesn't mean he was sending them.'

'No, but it's odd, don't you think, especially as they were hidden away at the back of his bottom drawer.'

'Yes, but—'

'Your dad obviously put a lot of himself into Alex Ballantyne, didn't he? Tennis. Choir. Spanish. He gave him exactly the same hobbies. Strange isn't it? And, like Alex Ballantyne, the police found blackmail notes in his room.'

'But it's ridiculous to suggest that he might have been—'

'In addition to all that, four St Mark's teachers have received blackmail notes identical to those received by characters in the novel.'

'That's incredible. I mean, what the fuck's going on?'

Garibaldi leaned forward. 'Tell me, Fran, did your dad ever tell your mum or you whether he definitely *had* based those characters on his ex-colleagues?'

Fran shook her head, 'No.'

'When I was at your father's talk he was asked a question about how much of the novel was based on real life and I was surprised by the very polished way your dad answered it. He seemed very prepared, very confident.'

Fran nodded her agreement. 'Funny you should say that. Just after it came out I went to see them and Mum and Dad were going through how to answer questions he might be asked. It was almost like she was coaching him through the answers. I remember all this stuff about the creative act, about ideas having to come from somewhere.'

'Well, look Fran, thanks for your time and thanks for being so candid about things. If there's anything—'

'There is one thing,' said Fran. 'It's just come back to me. There's one other thing he said.' She bit her lip and turned away, looking out of the high windows. She turned back. 'No, it's probably nothing.'

Garibaldi fixed his eyes on her. Fran shifted in her chair. Garibaldi held her gaze and waited.

Fran cleared her throat. 'He said he wished he'd played by the book. That was the phrase, "played by the book". I had no idea what he was talking about or what he meant and I remember being puzzled at the time. I'd forgotten about it, but it's just come back to me. He wished he'd played by the book.'

'What do you think he meant?' said Gardner.

'At first I thought he was talking about his teaching career. From what I could make out he had a habit of speaking his mind and not following the usual lines. A kind of maverick. But maybe he meant something else.'

'The phrase "playing by the book",' said Garibaldi, 'usually means doing things according to the rules, doing things properly. Do you think your father could have meant anything other than that?'

'Like what?'

Garibaldi shrugged. He had no idea what else he might have meant but he was intrigued by the fact that Liam Allerton had said it.

Playing by the book.

He kept thinking of the words.

And then, as he looked out of the mansion flat's high windows, instead of words came thoughts of Larkin's poem of the same name.

He looked out into the deep blue air, thinking of nothing, nowhere and endlessness, seeing again the body of Liam Allerton in the reeds of Barnes Pond.

He was brought out of his reverie by the ringing of his phone.

He didn't recognise the number.

'DI Garibaldi.'

'Hello, Inspector, it's Araminta Warburton here from the Barnes Bookshop. Something's happened.'

'What is it?' said Garibaldi, getting up from his chair and motioning for Gardner to do the same.

'I think you'd better come and look.'

Garibaldi and Gardner walked across Hammersmith Bridge to where Gardner had parked the car and drove down Castelnau, taking a right into Church Road and pulling up opposite the Barnes Bookshop.

As soon as they climbed out they saw it, scrawled in bright-red paint across the front window:

THE IRONIC DEATH OF BEN JOSEPH

'What's Barnes coming to?' said Gardner. 'A body in the pond and now graffiti on local shop windows.'

'It's graffito,' said Garibaldi.

'No, it's graffiti.' Gardner pointed across the road. 'Look. There in the window. Graffiti.'

'Graffiti's plural,' said Garibaldi.

He couldn't resist. Why learn Italian if you couldn't show off your knowledge?

'Really?' said Gardner. 'I never knew that.'

'There you go. You'll end today wiser than you began it.'

'Who said that?'

'I did,' said Garibaldi, crossing the road and waving to Araminta Warburton who had seen their car draw up and had come out to meet them. 'Still, at least it's all spelled correctly. And where else but Barnes would you find the word "ironic" in graffiti?'

33

Garibaldi held his phone out in front of Deighton.

'And when did this appear?' she said, peering at the screen.

'Some time between shutting the shop yesterday at 6.00 and opening it this morning at 9.30.'

'CCTV?'

'None in the shop and we're checking out the neighbouring ones. We're also looking at CCTV all along the High Street and near the Red Lion junction. So far no signs of anyone walking along holding a can of spray paint. My hunch is it would have happened in the middle of the night.'

Deighton took the phone from Garibaldi and played her fingers on the screen to enlarge the picture.

'I don't get it,' said Deighton. 'What's the point?'

'Exactly. Why would anyone spray that on the bookshop window?'

'And why . . .?' Deighton screwed up her face. 'Why is Ben Joseph's death ironic?'

'Remember the opening of *Schooled in Murder* ?'

'Remind me.'

Garibaldi reached into his jacket pocket and pulled out

his copy of the novel. 'Always carry it with me now. It's become a kind of bible.'

He turned to the first page and read. 'During his long teaching career Alex Ballantyne liked to point out to his pupils that "ironic" was one of the most misused words in the English Language.'

'So someone doesn't want anyone to forget about the book,' said Deighton.

'Exactly. That opening page is all about irony. Shows how it's a tricky word, often misused. And what that graf-fito . . .' Garibaldi paused to see if his boss had registered his use of the Italian singular. 'What that's doing is reminding us of it. Liam Allerton aka Ben Joseph's death is ironic because—'

'Because he died in exactly the same way as the victim in his book,' cut in Deighton. 'Yes, I get that.'

'I'm not sure, strictly speaking, whether his death *is* ironic, but most people reading the window are going to know what it's getting at which is, as you say, the similarity between his murder and the murder in his book.'

'So it's, what, a reminder?'

'Looks like it.'

'But it feels like something else as well.'

'What's that?'

'A taunt. It's like someone out there's taunting us.'

'About what?'

'About our progress. Reminding us that we haven't found his killer.' Deighton peered more closely at the screen. 'Is it too much to hope no-one's got a photo of this?'

'No chance. There was a crowd on the pavement by the time we left. All waving their phones about.'

Deighton sighed. 'The media will love it. Another thread in their narrative.'

Narrative. Never had one of Deighton's favourite words been more appropriate to a case.

'The question is,' said Garibaldi, 'whether this connects to everything else. The murder. The notes. There's no evidence that the person who murdered Allerton sent those notes and there's no evidence that whoever did this is the same as either of them.'

'Tell me,' said Deighton. 'Those four teachers who got the notes. What do they have to say?'

'They all deny the accusations. So no surprises there. Ewan Thomas doesn't do drugs, Sasha Ambrose isn't an escort, Ruth Price hasn't nicked school funds and Armit Harwal hasn't slept with a student. And none of them had received notes like that before.'

'What did they say when you presented them with your code-cracking, the names and initials?'

'None of them had seen it, or at least that's what they claimed. And they all said they were nothing like those characters. Different physically. Taught different subjects. A couple suggested the pattern was just a fluke, mere coincidence.'

'But you still think it was deliberate?'

'I'm no statistician, but the odds on that being a fluke would be pretty long. I think Allerton was definitely up to something. The problem is I don't know what it was.'

'Anything back from the lab?' said Deighton.

'On the notes? Nothing. No fingerprints. No DNA. There's stuff from the recipients, but nothing else. Whoever did it used gloves.'

'And what about the notes we found in Allerton's drawer?'

'Allerton's prints and DNA but no-one else's.'

'How about Allerton's night at the OSO and in the Sun?'

'Nothing more from CCTV in the pub. From what we can make out the statements from those who were with him are confirmed by the footage. Times of departure and movement.'

Deighton reached for the copy of *Schooled in Murder* at the edge of her desk. 'Correct me if I'm wrong, but it doesn't happen in this does it? Graffiti on a bookshop window.'

'Nothing like it.'

'So unlike the murder and the notes this incident isn't lifted from here?'

Garibaldi nodded. They looked at each other and said nothing. It may only have been a few seconds but Garibaldi found the silence embarrassing, as if neither of them knew what to do or say next. He was usually never short of ideas, often left-field ones that might move investigations in completely different directions, but at the moment they seemed to have deserted him.

Maybe it was the strain of his domestic threesome.

'We do have a couple of other things,' said Garibaldi, trying to sound positive. 'Milly's discovered the identity of three of the people in the Liam Allerton group at the Sun Inn. They were all at the talk and Liam invited them to the pub.'

'Who are they?'

'People he knew from his various activities. Milly interviewed them all and reckons Liam put a little portrait of each of them in his novel. Not entirely flattering portraits.'

'Is there anything he *didn't* put in his bloody novel? It's driving me mad!'

'Yeah, me too. '

'So that's three possible suspects to add to the ones we already have. Rohypnol takes about thirty minutes, sometimes less, to work so the chances are someone spiked his

236

drink at the pub not long before he left and somehow got him to Barnes Pond before it took full effect.'

'Perfectly possible,' said Garibaldi, 'given how close the Pond is to the pub.'

'And there's nothing on the pub CCTV that shows Allerton leaving with anyone else?'

'The camera on the front of the pub shows him leaving at 11.05 pm, and he's by himself. No-one with him. Which, of course, raises another possibility.'

'What's that?'

'His drink might not have been spiked at the pub at all. Someone might have met him after he left the pub and done it then.'

'So Allerton left the pub carrying a drink?'

'Doesn't look like it on the CCTV.'

'Maybe someone met him on his way home and some-how got him to take a spiked drink.'

Deighton hooked the glasses off her nose.

'And the other thing,' said Garibaldi, 'is we spoke to Rosanna Reed, the headmaster's wife. If you remember in *Schooled in Murder*—'

'Yes, yes,' said Deighton. 'In the book it's the head's wife who's the killer. I'm assuming she didn't own up to it?'

'You assume right. She was as baffled by everything as . . .'

'As we are?'

'As everyone is.'

'So . . .' Deighton put her glasses back on and looked at the papers on her desk.

A knock on the door made them both turn.

Gardner stood in the doorway. 'We've just had a call,' she said, 'and it could be important.'

Deighton beckoned her in. 'What is it?'

'It's from a bloke who says he's been following the case

237

and has something we might like to know. No name yet – looks like it could be from a burner. He says there's a teacher at St Mark's who has definitely done what one of the teachers in the book is accused of.'

Gardner paused and looked at Deighton and Garibaldi, holding the silence as if she were enjoying the momentary power.

'He said there's a teacher at St Mark's who slept with a pupil at a previous school.'

'Who's the teacher?' said Garibaldi.

'Well, in the book, if you remember, it's Harry Antrobus, which according to your code makes it Armit Harwal—'

'So Armit slept with a student then?' said Deighton.

'No. The thing is it's not Armit at all.'

'Who is it then?'

'It's Ruth. Ruth Price.'

The three looked at each other, unsure what to say. Garibaldi's mind was spinning with possibilities.

'Hang on,' he said. 'So you're saying that Ruth hasn't nicked school funds but, if this call is to be believed, she *has* slept with a student. So when she says she hasn't done the thing her blackmail note accuses her of she's absolutely right, but the truth could be she's done one of the other things they're accused of.'

'Do we know this caller's telling the truth?' said Deighton. 'We've no idea who he is. It could be another . . . another I don't know what to call it. It could be like the notes, the graffiti.'

'But this is different,' says Garibaldi. 'This moves us on, this gives us a direction. It's as if . . .'

'This is going to sound crazy,' said Gardner, 'but I was thinking maybe Allerton . . .'

She trailed off, as if losing confidence in her theory.

'Maybe,' said Garibaldi, 'it's Allerton playing games again. He played around with their names and initials, maybe he's also playing around with what they've done. Maybe he's playing around with their secrets. Maybe he's—'

'Maybe he's swapped them,' said Gardner.

'Exactly!' said Garibaldi.

'Let's get this straight.' said Deighton. 'So you're suggesting they're all hiding something they could be blackmailed over, he points us in their direction by connecting characters to them through their names but then he gives them different secrets. Crikey, it's a bit complicated, isn't it?'

'The act of a crossword fan,' said Garibaldi. 'And a Maths teacher. It's all about patterns.'

'So if Ruth Price actually did sleep with a student, what did the others do?' said Deighton.

'Are you saying that one of those teachers killed him?' said Gardner.

Deighton shook her head. 'We can't assume, but on the other hand—'

'Maybe,' said Gardner, 'Liam Allerton actually *was* blackmailing those teachers over their secrets. That might explain the notes in his drawer. Then he goes further and puts it in his book, thinly disguising names, swapping around their secrets. And one of the teachers flips and kills him.'

'But why would they do that?' said Deighton. 'What do they gain?'

'Silence,' said Garibaldi. 'Dead men don't talk. Allerton could say no more about their crimes. The book would be there but the book gives them the wrong crimes, so they could quite rightly protest their innocence of what they're accused of.'

'But why kill him like that?' said Deighton. 'It turns everyone's attention back to the book.'

'There's one thing we're forgetting,' said Garibaldi. 'The notes those teachers received. They're the same as the ones in the book, and if this theory is right, if Ruth Price didn't embezzle but did sleep with a pupil, then those notes aren't based on the truth, they're based on the novel.'

'I don't know where this is leading,' said Deighton. 'I really don't.'

'I think it's leading to another chat to those teachers,' said Garibaldi, 'and another visit to Felicity Allerton.'

34

When Ruth Price opened the door she was surprised to find one of the detectives, the short one called Garibaldi, standing on the doorstep, cycling helmet under his arm.

Why did he want to see her again? She'd told them everything she could about Liam and about his book (or at least gave an answer to every question they'd asked) and they couldn't possibly think that Prisha Bedi, despite her name possibly being connected to Ruth's own through some code, was based on her. For a start Prisha was Indian and nothing like Ruth in appearance and she also taught a different subject. Most importantly, Ruth, unlike the fictional Prisha, had never embezzled funds from the school. None of this, though, stopped Ruth from feeling guilty. Every time the book was mentioned, every time anyone pointed out the similarity between Liam Allerton's fictional school of St Jude's and the real school of St Mark's she felt sick to the stomach.

She felt a similar sickness now, as she showed the detective into the living room, offered him a chair and sat down opposite.

'I have a few more questions for you, Ruth,' said the

detective, 'in relation to our investigation into the murder of Liam Allerton.'

'Are you any closer to finding his killer?' said Ruth, hoping she didn't look as nervous as she felt.

'We're getting close, very close. We—'

'And the notes,' said Ruth 'Who sent them?'

'Again, we're getting close. There's—'

'I hear there was some graffiti—'

'Graffito, yes.' The detective looked irritated. 'We're well aware of all these things, but I'd like to ask you a bit more about the note you received. You say—'

'Have you found fingerprints on it? DNA?'

'We know what we're doing, Ruth.'

'I'm sure you do. I'm worried, that's all.'

'The note you received threatened to reveal the fact that you've been embezzling funds from the school, didn't it?'

Ruth nodded. 'And as you know I—'

'And the wording of this note was exactly the same as the wording of the note received by Prisha Bedi in Allerton's book.'

'We've been through all this, Inspector, and as I've told you it's not true.'

The detective gave a tight-lipped smile and nodded in agreement. 'You're right. It's not true, is it? And shall I tell you why?'

'It's not true because I didn't do it, I've never done anything like that.'

'But that doesn't mean that you haven't done something you'd rather no-one knew about, does it?'

Ruth's body tightened. Her mouth dried.

'What would you say, Ruth, if I suggested that the note you got was untrue but that had you received someone else's note that might not be the case?'

'What are you saying? I don't—'

'I think someone else got the note that applies to you, Ruth.'

'I don't know what you're talking about.'

'Don't you? We've had a call, Ruth, from someone who has read Liam's book, someone who knows you – or maybe that should be *knew* you. And I mean "knew you" in every sense of the word. A young man, though he was no more than a boy when you knew him.'

'I don't understand.'

'Don't you? Well, Ruth, why don't you listen to what he had to say in his phone call to us. As I say, he saw the news about Liam Allerton's murder, he knew he taught at St Mark's where you teach. He got hold of the book and when he read it he couldn't believe what one of the teachers was blackmailed about. It wasn't a woman, it was a man, but it reminded him of what had happened. Does this ring a bell, Ruth?'

Ruth wrung her hands. 'No, no it doesn't. I still don't know what you're talking about.'

'Before you taught at St Mark's you taught at Ellison School, is that right?'

'Yes, that's right.'

'Do you a remember a Matthew Rose?'

'I taught so many students. I can't . . .'

'He remembers you, Ruth. He remembers you very well indeed. And that's because he had a relationship with you, a sexual relationship.'

'That's simply not true,' said Ruth. 'I have never had a sexual relationship with a student. I never would. So whoever this . . . this Matthew is, he's wrong.'

'Why would he tell us it's true, then?'

'I have no idea. It's like all these things with accusations.'

His word against mine. Does he have . . . proof of this? He, whoever he is, could simply be making this up.'

'And why would he do that?'

'I have no idea.' Ruth's body had started to shake. She clasped her hands to try to stop it.

'This is a terrible accusation, Inspector. All I can say is that this boy, whoever he is, is wrong. It sounds like he's messing you about. He may have been taught by me, I can't remember. I've taught so many. Do you have any idea of how many pupils I've had?'

'When you say had . . .'

'Taught.'

'He's the only one to call us so far.'

'I mean—'

'I needed to ask, Ruth, and you need to know. We can't let this go uninvestigated. We will have to ask questions.'

'Yes, yes I understand.'

When the detective had left Ruth closed the front door and fell back against it, gasping for breath.

This was a nightmare.

Armit was pleased Ruth called him when she was upset. Not pleased because she was upset but because she chose to call him. It showed they were close.

At first she couldn't say anything. She was struggling for breath so much that no words would come. Whenever she tried to speak all that came out was a strange, troubled wail. Armit's initial attempts to soothe her met with no success but he carried on telling her to relax and take her time.

'The police,' said Ruth eventually. 'They've been again, and . . .'

More sobs.

'And what, Ruth?'

'I need to tell someone. I need to tell you.'

'Take your time. I'm here for you.'

'There's been an accusation,' said Ruth, 'from a boy at a previous school.'

'What kind of accusation?'

'That I slept with him.'

'You slept with him? But that's—'

'It's not true,' said Ruth 'not a word of it. I've never . . . but he called the police and now they're looking at all those notes again.'

'Why? What do they—'

'They think Allerton knew about the secrets and swapped them round.'

Armit's heart skipped a beat. His chest tightened.

'It's ridiculous,' said Ruth. 'I didn't do that, I swear, but this phone call – it's got them looking at everything again. It's too much, it's all too much. Can I . . . can I come round? I need to be with someone.'

'Of course you can.'

Armit's stomach was still tight. He could feel the flutters, feel the rush.

Right crime. Wrong person.

This was bad news.

Sasha Ambrose ended the call, sat down in her chair and looked at the phone she held in her hand, as if she couldn't believe the words that had just come through it. The news of a police investigation into an allegation against Ruth from a former pupil had thrown everything into a terrifying new perspective, confirming what she had feared ever since she first read *Schooled in Murder*.

She hadn't spent so many hours in the staffroom doing the *Guardian* crossword with Liam without getting some sense of how his mind worked, and she had been onto that name and letter code thing well before the detective. But she'd also been onto another trick that Liam had played in the pages of his novel – something far more sophisticated and far more revealing.

She'd kept quiet about it, though. Nothing would have been gained by alerting others to her discovery. Quite the reverse – it would have made things even more dangerous.

Maybe she should have said something to Liam earlier, let him know that she had worked out the game he had played. It might not have changed anything, but it could have made her feel better about things. Still, at least she managed to let him know before he died. It may only have been hours before he was murdered but she was glad she had done it. She hadn't made a big thing out of it, just a snatched conversation in the Sun Inn when they crossed paths on their way to and from the loos and were away from the main group. A quick word, Liam. That's what she said as she had bent her head towards him and whispered in his ear. I know what you did. The code. I got it.

It was like telling him she'd got the answer to fifteen across.

Liam hadn't said anything. Just smiled and nodded, and made his way back to the table.

But now Ruth had been accused of sleeping with a pupil and Sasha saw the pattern unfolding.

What should she do?

There was only one option. Sit tight and ride it out. No-one yet had any evidence and the last thing she should do was confess.

Sit tight and wait. That's what she'd do.

*

Ewan could tell from Armit's hello that something was wrong.

'What's happened?' he asked.

'Where are you?'

'I'm walking into town.'

'Can you talk?'

Ewan looked around. He saw a side alley and headed towards it. 'Go ahead.'

'The police are investigating an allegation against Ruth.'

'What is it?'

'A boy from a previous school has contacted them to say that Ruth had a sexual relationship with him when she taught him.'

'And is this true?'

'Ruth says not, but—'

'But you don't believe her?'

'I'm not saying that, no, but if it's not true, who's made the accusation and why? And if it *is* true . . .'

'Hang on, so that character in the book, that note . . .'

'Exactly.'

'So first we're all connected by the names and letters and now you're saying one of us has committed someone else's—'

'Sounds crazy, doesn't it?'

'But does that mean . . .?'

Ewan stopped himself just in time. He didn't want to give anything away.

'I thought you should know,' said Armit.

'Yeah, well thanks for telling me.'

'I don't think there's anything we need to do, anything we should do.'

'No, of course, but . . . this allegation could be untrue. Someone who's read the book, seen the news and decided to have some fun. Like whoever sent us those fucking notes.'

247

'Yeah, could be,' said Armit.

Ewan could tell from his tone that he didn't really believe it. 'Does the head know?'

'I have no idea.'

'An actual allegation against a current member of staff. Surely the police have told him?'

'No harm in checking.'

'OK,' said Ewan.

He hung up and carried on walking into town.

Was it possible? Did each of them have a secret to hide? And in the unlikely case that they did, could one of them be Liam Allerton's murderer?

35

Garibaldi lay on the sofa listening to Laura Cantrell with the volume up high and singing along. This was something he hardly ever did, but it was now so unusual to be in the flat on his own he reckoned he might as well make the most of it.

Ever since the night of Ben Joseph's talk his life had become more crowded. Alfie and Rachel. Rachel and Alfie. He was concerned about both, but his priorities kept shifting. One moment he'd be more concerned about Alfie's well-being than he was about his relationship with Rachel. At another he'd do anything, even ask Alfie to leave, to preserve what he had come to regard as the most valuable thing in his life.

He felt his phone vibrate in his pocket. He took it out and looked at the screen. Gardner.

'Milly,' he said, turning down the volume with the remote. 'What's up?'

'Time for a quick word?'

'Sure.'

'You know the three people I interviewed who came to Allerton's talk and went to the Sun with him afterwards. I've gone back to the CCTV and can see all three of them there in that group. It's Allerton and his wife, the four teachers from St Mark's, and these three.'

'Anything interesting?'

'Not really. They're not there for long and they leave pretty much when they said they did. They talk to Liam a bit and have a word with each other and some of the teachers.'

'So you don't think any of them killed him?'

'No. But some of the things they said have made me think.'

Garibaldi resisted the urge to make a joke.

'I didn't think much of it at the time, but I keep coming back to them and I want to run them past you.'

'Go ahead.'

'The thing is each of them mentioned things about Allerton and his wife. Taken by themselves they probably don't amount to much, but taken together ... I just don't know. So in his Spanish class apparently he said his family wasn't what it seemed and he also made this joke about his wife being a translator.'

'A joke about being a translator? What was it?'

'He said she translated truth into lies.'

'That's a joke, is it? Doesn't sound very funny to me.'

'OK, but a strange thing to say, right?'

'Did he explain?'

'No. I think it was a corny wife joke. My wife lies, that kind of thing.'

'Why did he say that?'

'The woman, Ariadne, didn't know but she thought it was odd. And the more you think about it the more it is. And then Fred Tolley, the bloke he sang with in the choir, said that Allerton had said to him over a pint that he wouldn't believe what he and his wife got up to.'

'What was that about? Sex?'

'It sounded like it. This bloke didn't comment, all he said was that he found it strange. And then a woman in the tennis group spoke to Liam about his writing and he said it was all a con-trick, that writers are con artists.'

'He could be right there.'

'But don't you think it's an odd thing to say?'

'I'm not sure what point you're making, Milly.'

'That's it. Nor am I, but taken together these comments, they've ... I don't know. Something about them keeps nagging at me. They all make me think that things weren't as they seemed with Liam Allerton.'

'Well, they weren't, were they? No-one knew he was writing a novel for a start.'

'Yeah, but I mean between the two of them, Liam and his wife. Does this make sense?'

It made perfect sense. Truth into lies. Con trick. Things not what they seemed. The things they got up to. He recalled what Allerton had told his daughter about not playing by the book.

'You're right, Milly. Let's talk tomorrow.'

Garibaldi reached for his coat and headed out, trying to focus on the night ahead but unable to stop speculating about the enigma that was Liam Allerton and what might have been going on between him and his wife.

Felicity Allerton sat in the living room watching TV. Every now and then she glanced at the chair next to her and each time she did she saw him again, his critical gaze fixed on whatever they were watching as he voiced his disapproval. He had always talked at the TV, saying what he thought to news presenters, interviewers and, most entertainingly of all, to characters in dramas. 'You fucking idiot!' That's what he'd shout to someone on the screen he thought had said or done something stupid. 'What the fuck are you doing?' His voice was loud and aggressive and whenever he shouted Felicity worried that the neighbours would hear it and think Liam was hurling the abuse at her.

Fran had just left and Felicity felt again the sense of emptiness, her mind full of the thoughts and fears that were always there but that she managed to suppress in company when she did her best to put on a brave face. How had things come to this? And when did it all start to go wrong? In one sense things had been wrong for a very long time but there was no doubt they had deteriorated dramatically when Liam had retired. She may have been used to him being around during the day in the holidays (the long summer holiday in particular) but there was something different about knowing it was no longer a temporary thing and that he was never going back to work.

Having him around so much had brought its difficulties. Tennis, Spanish and the choir may have got Liam out of the house on a regular basis, but he still spent a lot of time at home, most of it in the room he had always liked to call his study. When he had been teaching, Felicity had always assumed most of what he had got up to in there was to do with his work – marking, preparing, report-writing. She would hear his music and give little thought to what he was actually doing. But once he'd stopped work she was more curious about what was keeping him occupied behind that closed door. Whenever she asked he simply said he was reading, listening to music or brushing up on his Spanish, and it had never occurred to her that it might be anything else.

His room remained largely untouched. The detectives

had been in there – that's where they had found those notes – but she still felt unable to begin the task of going through her dead husband's things. Many times she had gone upstairs, stood outside the door and tried to summon the courage to turn the handle, and many times she had failed.

Tonight, though, she left the living room and climbed the stairs thinking she felt brave enough to go in.

She opened the door and for a moment thought he was there. Liam at his desk, music on, sitting in front of his computer. It was so real, so vivid that for a moment she couldn't breathe. She closed her eyes and opened them again to find him gone.

Felicity went to the desk, sat down and gave a deep sigh.

It felt odd, as if sitting in his chair had moved her closer to her dead husband, as if, bizarrely, she had almost become him.

She closed her eyes, trying to imagine nothing had happened, that everything was as it had been before.

It all seemed so strange, so wrong.

This was not how it was meant to be.

She was so wrapped up in her thoughts that she didn't hear the sound of the letter box flap.

It was only when she left Liam's room and went downstairs that she realised something had been delivered.

Alfie and Alicia were in love. Garibaldi could tell. There was something about the way they were with each other, and, more tellingly, the way Alfie seemed exactly the same in her presence as he was when she wasn't there. A far cry from how he was with his previous girlfriends, one at school and one at Oxford, who had both changed Alfie so much that sometimes Garibaldi had hardly recognised him. It still pained him to remember the phase when Alfie had stopped coming to QPR in favour of high-class social events.

The meal out had been Garibaldi's idea. No agenda. No discussion of Alfie's future, just a chance to get together out of the flat and to get to know Alicia better. It had seemed a good idea when he first suggested it, but now the evening had arrived he wasn't quite so sure.

'Cheers!'

Garibaldi lifted his glass and the four of them clinked together.

'Cheers!' said Alfie. 'And while we're all here I've got some news.'

Garibaldi held his breath. The conversation so far had been easy, punctuated by a lot of laughter and avoiding all the serious stuff like Alfie's row with Dom and how long Alfie was likely to stay in the flat.

Was that about to change?

'Yeah,' said Alfie. 'There's something I – something we – want to say.'

Garibaldi shuddered. They were engaged. They were going to get married. Alicia was pregnant.

Alfie turned to Alicia with a smile. 'We're moving in together.'

Garibaldi exchanged a surprised look with Rachel. 'But what – how – what's happened?'

'It's a complete fluke, but someone Alicia works with is going abroad for six months and they want someone to move in to their flat while they're away. The rent's reasonable and we have to look after their cat, but—'

'You don't have to move out,' said Garibaldi. 'You can stay for as long as you like.'

'What? Both of us? And anyway, Dad, let's face it ...'

Alfie turned to Rachel and gave her a knowing grin. 'Its been a bit tricky, hasn't it?'

'Nonsense,' said Rachel. 'It's been great having you.'

'But what about your mum,' said Garibaldi, turning to Alicia. 'Is she OK about it?'

'That's the thing,' said Alicia. 'The flat's in Camden. In fact it's pretty much round the corner from where we are so I can keep a close eye on her, go round every day in fact.'

'But the rent,' said Garibaldi. 'Can you afford it?'

'It'll be OK,' said Alicia.

She smiled at him – a friendly smile, a warm smile, one that suddenly seemed very familiar.

'It'll be all right, Giacomo. Don't you worry. Everything will be OK.'

The voice was his mother's. There she was, smiling at him across the table.

'But—'

'No buts, Giacomo, you work hard, you do your best and everything will be OK. Trust God. He has a plan.'

'I'm not sure I bel—'

'You mustn't worry, Giacomo. You worry too much—'

'But Mum—'

'Sorry?'

'Mum. I—'

'Did you just call her Mum?'

Garibaldi turned to the voice. It was Alfie's.

He looked across the table at his mother. It was Alicia.

'Did I what?'

'You just called Alicia Mum.' Alfie turned to Rachel. 'Didn't he?'

Rachel looked at him. 'I'm pretty sure you did.'

'It sounded a bit like Mum,' said Alicia, 'but it could have been "um", I guess.'

'You OK, Dad?'

What should he say? Would he ever have the nerve to tell them? Would he ever tell anyone?

'I'm fine,' he said. 'Absolutely fine. I don't think I said that, did I?'

He looked round the table trying to give a reassuring look. 'What were we talking about? The flat! Moving in. What's happening?'

'You really sure you're OK?' said Alfie. 'I really did hear you say Mum.'

'Please, don't worry about it.'

Garibaldi looked at Rachel. This was the second time she had witnessed it – maybe that's why she looked more concerned than Alfie.

'Tell me about the flat.'

'OK, but there's something else,' said Alfie.

Something else? Alicia *was* pregnant? They *were* getting married? He'd had another, bigger row with Dom?

'The thing is,' said Alfie. 'I've got a job.'

A job? Had he heard correctly?

'Yeah. It's up near Alicia.'

Garibaldi raised his eyebrows, waiting for more.

'Not a big career thing or anything but we'll see how it goes.'

'Are you going to tell us or do we have to guess?'

'It's in a bookshop.'

'A bookshop?'

'Yeah. An independent bookshop in Camden. There was an ad in the window asking for an assistant and, yeah, I applied and I got it. The money's terrible but it's, you know, steady and the owner says there may be . . . opportunities.'

'This is fantastic,' said Garibaldi. 'Have you told your mum?'

He tried to imagine how Kay would take it. Then, to cheer himself up even more, he tried to imagine how Dom would take it.

As he did, his phone rang. A number he didn't recognise.

'DI Garibaldi.'

'It's Felicity Allerton, Inspector. Something's happened.'

'What is it? Are you OK?'

'I'm fine. Just a bit shocked. I've just received something and I think you ought to see it.'

Garibaldi looked at his watch. At least the meal was pretty much over.

And at least it had ended well.

36

Garibaldi stood beside the screen at the front of the incident room.

He pointed at the picture of a note –

I know what your husband did – that's why I killed him.

'As you can see it's exactly the same ransom note lettering as the other notes – the ones in *Schooled in Murder* and the ones received by the four St Mark's teachers. And, of course, the ones we found in the drawer in Liam Allerton's room.'

He pointed at the photo of the envelope. On it was written 'Felicity Allerton'.

'You'll already have noticed one significant difference between the notes those four received and this one. No postmark. The others were posted in SW13. This one, it seems, was pushed through Felicity Allerton's letterbox. What does this mean? Delivered by a local? Maybe but not necessarily. Sent by someone other than whoever sent the blackmail notes? Again, maybe, but we can't be sure. The note and envelope are at the lab, and we've taken Felicity Allerton's prints and DNA to eliminate her from anything we might find, but I'm not holding out much hope. We don't know the exact time this note was delivered. Felicity reckons some time between 7.30 and 8.00. She called me at 8.30.'

'Any CCTV in Cambridge Road?' said Deighton.

'No,' said Garibaldi, 'an outside chance some of the houses might have doorbell cams, especially the ones that have been recently done up by the kind of people who do that sort of thing. And we're doing house-to-house down there to see if we can get anything.'

'So do we assume that this note is from whoever killed Allerton?' said Gardner.

'We assume nothing,' said Deighton, 'but if it is then we have to ask ourselves why it's been delivered.'

'Most notes like that,' said Garibaldi, 'make a threat. If it's blackmail then they demand money. Or if it's something else, they say what it is – or if they don't they suggest it. This one doesn't. But that doesn't mean that Felicity Allerton, understandably, isn't scared shitless.'

'Again,' said Deighton,' the question is why has it been sent. What does it mean?'

'I know what your husband did,' said DC McLean, 'that could mean several things. It could mean I know he wrote that novel. Or, to get back to those notes we found, it could mean I know he blackmailed those teachers.'

'Yeah,' said DC Hodson, as ever spurred into speech by her fellow DC's contribution. 'Which brings us back to those four teachers up at St Mark's.'

'But why would any of them send it?' said Gardner. 'Why declare themselves like that?'

'Exactly,' said Garibaldi. 'It's a calling card. Literally and metaphorically.'

'And if it's Allerton's killer,' said Deighton, 'the same

question applies. Why do that? It's difficult to see any motive apart from wanting to frighten Felicity, but again, why? Why would anyone want to frighten her?'

'It draws attention,' said Garibaldi. 'And where does it draw attention? *Schooled in Murder*. Everything in this case brings us back to that book. The way Allerton was killed. The notes to those teachers. The graffito on the bookshop window. And now this.'

Deighton got up from her chair and stood by the board.

Garibaldi thought of sitting down but stayed where he was, the two of them flanking the screen.

'OK,' said Deighton, 'so we assume nothing. But if this note is from someone who isn't the killer, what are we supposed to make of it?'

'Could be a nutter,' said Gardner. 'A freak. I know it's a cop-out but someone could just be pissing us about. Could be anyone who's read that book. Everything that's happened since Allerton's murder could easily have been carried out by someone other than the murderer. We all know it happens. And it might not even be the same person—'

'That's a lot of nutters,' said DC Hodson.

'I can't believe that anyone who thinks they were implicated in that book did any of this,' said Gardner. 'At every turn we're being directed to the book, so why would anyone of them choose to do it? It doesn't make sense.'

Garibaldi listened as the discussion continued. They were getting no closer to knowing who had sent the note shown on the screen and why. If anything, the more they discussed it the further away they drifted from plausible explanation and from answers to all the other questions the case had thrown up.

Gardner was right. It didn't make sense. None of it did.

'If it's a veiled threat to Felicity Allerton,' said Deighton, 'what's the threat? That whoever it is will kill her? We can't rule it out. Killers aren't always rational and, yes, they are often nutters. Could it all be a series of taunts? Think of the graffiti. Call me paranoid, but it felt like a taunt, like someone was reminding us of what we're failing to do ...'

'It's like someone's playing games,' said Gardner.

Playing. The words of Fran Allerton came back to Garibaldi. Playing by the book – the thing Liam wished he'd done. But in a sense that's exactly what he had done. The names and the initials. What was it if not an elaborate game? And if Ruth Price was guilty of sleeping with a student and not of embezzlement, was he playing games there as well, swapping the crimes around?

'Ruth Price,' he said. 'Where are we on this allegation from a former student?'

'As expected, the call came from a burner,' said Gardner.

'The Ellison School head's aware of the allegation,' said DC McLean. 'But they claim never to have had a Matthew Rose there.'

'So anyone could have made that call,' said Garibaldi.

'But why would they if it isn't true?' said Gardner.

Garibaldi nodded. 'Exactly. We can't assume it *is* true, but on the other hand we can't ignore it.'

'And the head of this school?' said Deighton. 'Did he say whether any allegations had been made about Ruth Price in her time there?'

'Nothing on their records,' said DC Mclean.

'We'll only know for sure,' said Garibaldi, 'if this boy, probably now a young man, gets in touch again. There's no guarantee he will.'

'OK,' said Deighton, ' and what about the other teachers? Any evidence that they might be guilty of the other three things – drugs, prostitution, embezzlement?'

261

'We're still working on it, ' said DC Hodson. 'Looking at what we can in relation to all three. Bank details and the St Mark's accounts and finance departments for embezzlement. Usual contacts for drugs. And trawling escort firms. Nothing so far.'

'Look,' said Garibaldi. ' I think we're in danger of missing the obvious.'

The room turned to him.

'Books are a load of crap.'

He let the silence develop, enjoying the moment.

'It's just come to me. A line from Larkin. There's this poem called "A Study of Reading Habits" and that's the last line. "Books are a load of crap".'

Garibaldi looked at Deighton. She was giving him her stop-being-a-smart-arse-and-get-on-with-it look.

'Not sure Larkin really means it,' said Garibaldi. 'Irony and all that, but the line just came to me because I think Milly's right.' He looked sideways at Gardner who seemed surprised. 'Someone's playing games. Liam Allerton may have been playing games in his book, but if the things that have happened since he died are also games we know one thing for sure – Liam's not the one playing them. He didn't send those notes. He didn't graffiti the bookshop. He didn't send this note to Felicity. It's someone else and whoever it is keeps sending us back to *Schooled in Murder*. The boss is right. She said at the beginning of this case we're not in a bloody book club and she's right. Our noses have been stuck in its pages and we need to get them out. We've said it before but it needs to be said again. We need to lift our eyes.'

'And how do we do that?' said Deighton.

'Allerton said some odd things about his relationship with his wife. Truth and lies. The things they got up to.

Families not being what they seemed. Writing being a con-trick. And playing by the book. Look at Milly's interview notes – it's all there.'

'That's all very well,' said Deighton, 'but what does it mean? Where does it take us?'

'It takes us to Felicity Allerton.'

'So let's get on it,' said Deighton. 'Talk to her. See if you get any further. In the meantime our friends continue to have a field day.'

Deighton picked a newspaper off a table and held it up. Above a picture of the graffitied window of the Barnes Bookshop clearly showing the red letters 'The Ironic Death of Ben Joseph' was the headline.

Deighton read it out: '"Murder by the Book. Police still baffled by writer's murder"'.

She put the paper down and looked round the room.

'Police still baffled by writer's murder,' she repeated. 'Had they been here today to hear our discussion, they would, of course, be thinking otherwise.'

37

Garibaldi came out of Gail's carrying coffee and pastries and put them down on the table.

He pointed at the plate. 'Cinnamon bun and pain au raisin. Want to share?'

Gardner nodded and Garibaldi took a knife and cut each pastry in two.

'Always nice to have an excuse for a break,' said Garibaldi, taking a bite of the bun. 'We could even have a stroll by the pond afterwards and feed the ducks. What it is to live in a village!'

Gardner took a bite of the pain au raisin, sipped her coffee and licked her lips.

'What's put you in such a good mood?' she said.

'Alfie's moving in with his girlfriend.'

'The girlfriend you like, yeah?'

'The first one I've ever liked. And that's not all – he's got a job.'

'Never rains, eh?'

'Sorry?'

'Not just one bit of good news, but two. Like London buses. One doesn't come for ages and then ... So where's this job?'

'In a bookshop.'

'A bookshop, eh?'

'Yeah. I don't think his mum's very impressed, not to mention Dom, but I am. I'm all in favour of bookshops.'

'I'd run a mile if you offered me a job in a bookshop at the moment,' said Gardner. 'This case, it's put me right off books. Did that bloke really write that thing about books being a load of crap?'

'He did.'

'I can see his point.'

'Really? You couldn't get enough of them not long ago. You were worried you weren't reading enough.'

'Well, that was a mistake, wasn't it?'

'You're well off out of it,' said Garibaldi, remembering Gardner's attempts to impress her lawyer boyfriend. 'He wasn't good enough for you.' He took a bite of his bun. 'Anyone ... around?'

It came out clumsily, but he felt he had a duty to ask. Ever since he'd decided nothing would or should happen between him and his sergeant he had found it much easier to talk to her about these things and he liked to show her he cared. They had lived through each other's crises, exchanging front-seat confidences as Gardner drove them round. He knew all about her love life, from the end of her relationship with Kevin who she discovered had been cheating to her feelings of intellectual inadequacy with Smartypants Tim, and he had listened sympathetically to all she had said about her quest for The One.

In the same way she had listened to his own troubles, especially when he'd returned to work after his illness.

'Anyone around?' said Gardner. 'Not really. I mean ... no-one special.'

'No-one special?' Garibaldi had no idea what this meant. He waited for more but nothing came.

'Sometimes I envy you and Deighton. Both in steady relationships.'

'Nothing's what it seems, Milly. Nothing ever is. You know that's true with me and, as for Deighton, well, she's a woman of great mystery – there's still the sense we don't know the half of what's going on in her life.'

'That's the thing, isn't it?' said Gardner. 'You never know what lies beneath, do you? Like those swans on the pond. You look at them gliding along but you don't see their legs working away below the surface.'

Garibaldi smiled, trying to give Gardner the impression that her insight was both profound and original.

Half an hour later they were standing on the Cambridge Road pavement outside Felicity Allerton's house.

Garibaldi was on his phone.

'Is that Fran?'

'Speaking.'

'DI Garibaldi here. We need to speak to your mum again and we're at her house. We've rung the bell several times and she doesn't seem to be in. She's not picking up our calls either. Do you know where she is?'

'No idea. Maybe she's just at the shops. Or with a friend. She could be with Ollie? Strange she's not picking up, though.'

'Has she told you about the note ?'

'Yes, she has – and it's horrible. Hang on, you don't think . . .?'

'We don't think anything at the moment, Fran. All I'm saying is that we need to speak to your mother and we can't contact her.'

'But does that mean—?'

'You said she could be with Ollie.'

'She could be, yes. I mean Ollie mostly comes round to her, but she does sometimes ...'

'Do you have his number?'

'Sure. Hang on.'

Garibaldi gestured for Gardner to take out her notebook.

'Here it is,' said Fran.

Garibaldi repeated the number aloud and Gardner scribbled it down.

'If you speak to her before we do, Fran, could you let us know where she is and tell her we'd like to see her?'

'Sure.'

Garibaldi hung up and dialled Ollie's number. There was no answer so he left a message on voicemail and walked back to the car with Gardner.

Back at the station Garibaldi sat at his desk, going through the case notes, trying to do what he had urged the team to do – look beyond the book. It was difficult. Wherever he took his thinking, however lateral he tried to be, he found himself irresistibly pulled back to *Schooled in Murder*.

He reached for his copy on the corner of his desk, picked it up and looked at the cover. A pool of blood beside a pond at the bottom and a school's entrance at the top, both clearly intended to represent Barnes Pond and the fictitious St Jude's. Garibaldi opened the book and looked at the front pages. He checked the publication date – the book had come out earlier in the year – and chuckled as he read the usual disclaimer – 'This book is a work of fiction and, except in the case of historical fact, any resemblance to actual persons, living or dead, is purely coincidental.' He looked at the dedication, 'To Felicity and Fran, without whom none of this would have been possible' and flicked to the back of the book and read the Acknowledgements. They were short – mainly a list of names – none of the sentimental gush you so often saw in these things.

He scanned the names. None of them meant anything to him.

'Milly!' he called, looking over his computer screen.

Gardner looked up over hers.

Garibaldi held the book aloft, open at the Acknowledgements page.

'Did you read this?'

Gardner came over to his desk and peered at the page Garibaldi was holding towards her. 'Can't say I did. What about it?'

'It's the Acknowledgements. A list of people Allerton thanked. I don't recognise any of them but it might be good to find out who they are.'

Gardner looked at the page and, realising why Garibaldi was still holding the book out to her, nodded and took it.

Half an hour later she came back. 'Haven't got them all yet, but thought you might want to see these.'

Gardner handed Garibaldi a sheet of paper and pointed at two highlighted names. 'Frank Willock's his agent and Naomi Marsh is his editor. Do you want me to call them?'

Garibaldi shook his head. 'No, leave it to me.'

As Gardner walked away from his desk, his mind was already busy, trying to work out the questions he needed to ask. He jotted a few notes on his pad of paper and picked up the phone.

'Is that Frank Willock?'

'Speaking.'

'It's Detective Inspector Garibaldi here.'

'Is this about poor Liam?'

'It is. I was wondering if you could maybe answer a few questions?'

'By all means. I'm working from home today, but—'

'On the phone will be fine for the moment.'

'OK. How can I help? I can't tell you how distressing this has been.'

'I'm sure it has.'

'Everything about it. It's bad enough that he's died, but it's absolutely appalling that he's been murdered. And to be killed like that, straight out of his book. Not to mention all the other things that have happened since. I've spent my working life in books, but I've come across nothing like this. Nothing.'

Garibaldi looked at the questions he'd jotted down.

'As you say, Frank, the murder seems to be straight out of the book and ever since it happened a lot of people have been looking for more parallels. Did Liam ever say anything to you about where he got his characters and ideas from?'

'He never mentioned it. And, to be honest, I never thought to ask. Every writer draws on their own experience, we all know that.'

'But you knew he had taught at St Mark's?'

'Oh, yes, I knew that.'

'And you could tell that the school in his book bore many similarities.'

'Yes, but I didn't think . . .'

'What was Liam like as a client?'

'No problem. No problem at all. I know it was a risk taking him on, given his age and given what he was writing. It' s a very crowded market, crime fiction, and it's difficult to stand out.'

'Still I'm sure sales have boomed since his unfortunate demise.'

'I'm afraid I can't see it on those terms, Inspector. Any happiness at how well the book might be doing is more than offset by sadness about what happened to poor Liam.'

'Of course.' Garibaldi cleared his throat. 'I wasn't for one moment suggesting—'

'But, yes, he was very easy to work with. I took him on, suggested a few revisions and he took them on board. Came back with something much stronger.'

'Can you remember what changes you suggested?'

'Not offhand, no. I'd have to look at my notes, but from what I can recall they weren't major changes. Just tweaks.'

'Tell me Frank, what kind of deal did you get for Liam?'

'It was for two books.'

'I see. And the second book?'

'I hadn't seen anything, but Liam said he'd started and was well into it.'

'Well into it? That's interesting. Did it have a title?'

'Not yet, but just before he was murdered Liam said he'd be sending me a draft to look at in a couple of weeks.'

'And his publishers. Were they—?'

'Lotus Press. They loved it. Thought Liam might be the next Camilleri. You know, a late starter but prolific. Typical publisher hype of course. There'll never be another Camilleri, but they thought *Schooled in Murder* could be the beginning of a long series. Naomi's shattered by it all. Completely in pieces. Have you spoken to her?'

'I'm about to, Frank. Before I go, though, was there anything at all in your dealings with Liam Allerton that, knowing now what happened to him, strikes you as odd or interesting?'

'I've thought about this myself,' said Frank, 'but I can't think of anything. It all seemed pretty straightforward, nothing about Liam and nothing about the book that made me

270

think this is how it would all turn out. Liam just seemed . . . he just seemed so pleased about it. Maybe it was because it all came to him so late, maybe he never expected it to happen.'

'Did you know that his wife and daughter had no idea he was writing a novel until he'd finished it and showed it to them?'

'Is that right? No, he never mentioned that at all. Pretty strange thing to do, but on the other hand it's understandable and maybe quite wise. If you tell people you're writing a novel they expect to see in in Waterstones next week. And if you tell them and it doesn't appear in Waterstones at all then you have to face the consequences – embarrassment, humiliation, that kind of thing. So, yes, maybe it's a good idea to keep quiet about it. Or better still, given some of the stuff that lands on my desk, maybe it's sometimes better not to do it at all. Though that wasn't the case at all with Liam. Poor Liam. I still can't believe it.'

'One more thing, Frank. Ben Joseph was Liam's pen-name. Whose idea was that?'

'It was Liam's. He said he'd rather publish under a pseudonym.'

'Did he say why?'

'He just said he'd like a bit of distance between himself and the book.'

'Did you agree?'

'I didn't have a strong opinion. As it happened everyone seemed to know pretty quickly that Ben Joseph was Liam so I don't know what kind of distance it got him.'

'I see. Well, thanks for your time, Frank. Do get back to me if you think of anything else.'

'Of course.'

Garibaldi hung up and looked at the questions in front of him.

Something didn't add up, but he couldn't put his finger on it. He searched for the digital forensics report on Liam Allerton's computer and read through it. All as he remembered. No trace of another book. No drafts. Nothing. And yet he had told his agent he was about to deliver a draft of his second novel. If that was the case, then where was it? Maybe he'd given it an unlikely name or if Liam was so secretive maybe he'd put it somewhere you wouldn't look for it. He'd ask forensics to have another look.

He picked up his phone and dialled.

'Lotus Books.'

'Could I speak to Naomi Marsh?'

'I'll put you through.'

Naomi Marsh's voice was husky and grew even huskier the more she expressed her sadness and shock at Liam Allerton's fate. Garibaldi listened patiently as she went through her relationship with the writer from their first meeting to the moment when she heard he had been murdered.

'Tell me, Naomi,' said Garibaldi when he sensed she had finished, 'had you heard anything about his second novel?'

'We knew it was on the way. Frank said he was hoping to get it to us within the next couple of months.'

'And you were hoping for a series?'

'We were. And we were confident Liam could do it. There was something about his writing. Polished. Assured.'

'He came to it very late of course.'

'He did, but, you know, he was like so many talented people. A bit of a polymath. Taught Maths all his life then turned to novel writing. You never can tell with people, can you? But, yes, Liam showed that it's never too late. When we had our first meeting we had this lovely discussion about writers who started late. Penelope Fitzgerald famously didn't publish her first novel until she was sixty, then went on to win the Booker. Then there was Mary Wesley. And of course Camilleri.'

'And how was Liam to work with?'

'Fine. No problem. I must admit in that first meeting there were times when I wondered whether we'd taken too much of a gamble but it turned out fine. He was professional throughout. No problem at all. And when the book came out it was well received.'

'And after recent events,' said Garibaldi, 'it's probably sold a few as well.'

'That's hardly important under the circumstances.'

'Of course. So there was nothing about dealing with Liam and his book that made you think—'

'That made me think he'd be murdered like one of his characters?'

'Anything at all that, looking back on it, you find unusual.'

'It was all pretty straightforward. We had some editorial suggestions and the redrafts were absolutely fine. No problems with the copy edit. Then . . .'

Naomi fell silent for a few seconds.

'Then what?' said Garibaldi.

'It's probably nothing,' said Naomi, 'but now I think about it there was something a bit odd when it came to the proofs. Liam wanted to make some changes. Nothing unusual about that, it happens all the time. But now I come to think about it there was something a bit strange about his changes.'

'What was strange about them?'

'What was strange was that I really couldn't understand why he wanted to make them. There weren't many but I remember being puzzled. You can usually see straight away why a writer wants a change or the writer will explain it to you, but I distinctly remember being baffled by the ones he asked for. So I asked him about them and whether they were necessary and he insisted. He put his foot down. It's only just come back to me. You deal with so many of these things that details like that get lost, but, yes, I thought it a bit odd at the time.'

'Can you remember what the changes were?'

'Not off the top of my head, no, but I can dig them out for you.'

'That would be great.'

'Shall I email them?'

'Please do.'

Garibaldi gave Naomi his address.

'Thank you, Naomi,' he said when he had finished, 'that's been very helpful.'

But when he had hung up he folded his arms, leaned back in his chair and wondered how helpful it had actually been.

He felt no clearer about anything.

38

Garibaldi was surprised when Fran opened the door.
'Is your mother in?'

'No, she's not.' Fran Allerton looked distressed. Her voice was shaky. 'Wherever she is, she hasn't come back. I was worried that she might have . . . that something might have happened to her here in the house so I came over. But she's not here. I was about to ring you. I don't know what to do.'

'Still not picking up her calls?' said Garibaldi, standing with Gardner on the doorstep.

Fran shook her head.

'Has she done this kind of thing before?'

'No. Never. It's totally out of character.' Fran stepped back and held the door wider. 'Do you want to come in?'

Garibaldi turned to Gardner and nodded.

Fran closed the door and led them into the kitchen.

'Something's happened to her, I know it. I should have stayed. I know I should. But she said she'd be fine. I've called everyone I can think of. I've even gone through her address book.' Fran pointed at the book on the table.

'I wouldn't alarm yourself,' said Garibaldi. 'About three quarters of people reported missing turn up within twenty-four hours.'

'And how many turn up who've received a note threatening to kill them?'

'It didn't threaten her directly.'

'As good as, don't you think?'

'I understand your distress,' said Garibaldi.

'Do you? First Dad and now . . .'

'When did you last see her?' said Gardner.

'Yesterday morning. She said she was fine and I should go in to work. So she could have gone – or something could have happened – right after I left.'

'Can we look round the house?' said Garibaldi.

'There's no note. I've looked.'

'She definitely has her phone with her?' said Garibaldi.

'I don't know. But I've rung it from here and I haven't heard it ringing somewhere in the house. Could be on silent, I suppose.'

'How about computers?' said Garibaldi.

'Her laptop's here.'

'Could we have a look?'

'Sure.' Fran led them into the living room and pointed at the laptop on the table.

Garibaldi looked at it and then glanced at Gardner. When it came to the march of technology, he stood very much at the rear and he always deferred to his sergeant in these matters.

Gardner took her cue, sat down at the table and started tapping away with speed and confidence.

'Sometimes search history can give a clue,' she said. 'Train times. Maps. Places. Could have looked it all up on her phone of course but worth a try.'

Garibaldi and Fran hovered behind Gardner as she carried on tapping. 'Nothing obvious,' she said. 'Not that I can see. But I'll keep on looking.'

Garibaldi walked round the living room, taking in the books on the shelves, the newspapers piled in the corner and what he took to be Felicity Allerton's work on a desk by the window.

'Is your mother still working?' he asked Fran.

'Yes, still translating. More important now than ever, I guess. Something to keep her busy.'

Garibaldi walked into the hall and went upstairs. The door to Liam Allerton's study was closed. He pushed it open and found the room unchanged from when he last saw it. Closing the door behind him he crossed the landing and went into the bedroom. He stood in the middle of the room and looked at the double bed, struck by the sadness that, after so many years sleeping beside her husband, Felicity Allerton was now sleeping in it alone. Larkin came to him again – 'Talking in Bed' and the line about lying in bed going back so far. That's what Felicity had done with Liam, what he himself had done with Kay, what he was now doing with Rachel. He thought of the last line – the difficulty of finding words true or kind or, as Larkin puts it, typically avoiding anything too optimistic, words not untrue and not unkind.

He walked to the bedside table and picked up the notepad. He peered at the top sheet but couldn't decipher the scrawls. Putting it down, he went to the wardrobe and opened it. Liam's clothes were still there, occupying one side of the rail. Two suitcases sat at the bottom, still bearing the tags from the last holiday the couple had taken together.

He closed the wardrobe and walked back to the bed, looking down on it, wondering how well the two who had lain here knew each other, how every marital bed encouraged illusions of complete togetherness.

The bed was unmade, the duvet crumpled in a pile.

Garibaldi sat down on the side that must have been Liam's and looked at where he had slept. He thought of Felicity. What must it be like to have that new space beside you, to reach out in the night for someone no longer there?

When he went back downstairs Gardner was still on the laptop.

'Any luck?' said Garibaldi.

With a final flourish of keyboard tapping Gardner got up from her chair. 'Doesn't look like it,' she said. She turned to Fran and pointed at the laptop. 'We'll need to take this. Digital forensics might find something.'

'So what happens now?' said Fran.

'Let us know immediately if she turns up,' said Garibaldi. 'In the meantime we'll start looking into it.'

'Looking into it? You mean you'll start a search?'

'We'll put things in motion. Do the usual checks.'

'You think something's happened?'

'Too early to tell, Fran.'

'But what if—? I mean, that note. She gets a note threatening to kill her and then she disappears. Doesn't that make this high priority? First Dad, and now . . .'

'It is high priority,' said Garibaldi, 'and we'll do everything we can to find her.'

'Is that supposed to reassure me? You're not getting very far in finding Dad's killer, are you?'

'I know it must be difficult for you, Fran, but—'

Fran held up her hand in apology. 'I know. I'm sorry. I—'

'I understand your frustration,' said Garibaldi, heading for the front door, 'and your concern. And I want you to know that at the moment our priority is your mother's safety.'

Fran bowed her head. 'Of course. I'm sorry.' She reached for the door handle. 'Thanks,' she muttered as she pulled the door open.

Garibaldi and Gardner said goodbye. As they turned to walk away they saw a man hurrying towards them.

'Ollie!' said Fran, rushing out from the house to greet him.

Ollie gave her a hug and, looking at Garibaldi and Gardner over her shoulder, said, 'Any news?'

'Not yet,' said Garibaldi.

'Are you on your way?' asked Ollie.

'We were going, yes.'

'Could I have a quick word?'

'Of course.'

Ollie looked over his shoulder, as if someone might be listening. 'Maybe inside?'

They all stepped inside the house and Fran closed the door behind them.

'Shall we go and sit down?' she said.

Ollie turned to Garibaldi. 'I don't want to keep you.'

'No problem,' said Garibaldi, following Fran into the living room and taking a seat.

Ollie looked from one to the other. 'So no news of Felicity at all?'

'It's early days,' said Garibaldi. 'I was telling Fran that most missing people turn up very soon and there's usually an explanation.'

'Felicity is not most missing people. She's the widow of a murder victim who's received a threatening note,' said Ollie. 'She was absolutely terrified by that note and I'm really worried something's happened to her.'

'You think someone might have killed her?'

'I'm not saying that, I'm – I'm just really worried, that's all. That note came from Liam's killer.'

'We don't know that,' said Garibaldi. 'It's an assumption.'

'"I know what your husband did – that's why I killed

him". Seems pretty clear to me. Have you found anything on it? Fingerprints? DNA?'

'It's at the lab but we're not holding out much hope. The other notes showed nothing.'

'So you think those other notes were sent by the same person?'

'We don't know for sure.'

'I don't get it. Liam's murder. The notes. Everything's tied up with his book!'

'We're exploring all possibilities.'

Ollie looked incredulous. 'What other possibilities can there be? "I know what your husband did – that's why I killed him". What did Liam do that could possibly get him killed? Anyone who knew him would know that he wasn't that kind of guy. The only thing he did of any significance was write that bloody book and that's what got him killed. And now I'm worried that Felicity . . .' He shot an anxious look at Fran. 'How can we find her?'

'When you spoke to her,' said Garibaldi, 'did she say anything that made you think she might—'

'Might what?' cut in Ollie. 'Disappear? Do something stupid? No, nothing. All I heard was a frightened woman, a woman who had just lost her husband in the most disturbing way imaginable and who now thought she herself was in danger. I would have come round straight away but I knew Fran was here so . . . but I should have come round this morning, shouldn't I? The thing is I didn't think she needed twenty-four-hour protection or anything. Looking back on it, that's exactly what she *did* need and I have to say . . .' His look of disapproval moved between Garibaldi and Gardner. 'I have to say I think the police should have acted more responsibly on this. A woman in Felicity's position getting a note like that. Shouldn't she have had more support, more advice?'

'She said Fran was staying with her and that she would be OK,' said Gardner. 'There's a Family Liaison Officer and she had a number to call if she was worried about anything.'

'And look where that's got us,' said Ollie. 'She's disappeared. And if that note was from Liam's killer ...' He trailed off and bowed his head. 'What a mess. What a bloody mess.'

'We'll do everything we can to find her,' said Garibaldi.

'I just hope we're not too late,' said Ollie, lifting his head and looking at Garibaldi with pleading eyes. 'And what have you done about all those teachers? They were with him the night before he died. They could easily have spiked his drink. And if they really thought Liam had stitched them up in his novel, they would have had a motive.'

'We're well aware of that, Ollie.'

'I mean, I'm not trying to do your job for you or anything, but—'

'What puzzles us about that,' said Garibaldi, 'is the way he was killed. If it were one of those teachers why would they choose to kill him like that? And if the killer is behind the notes, why would they send them? If, as you're suggesting, it's because they're guilty of things they might be blackmailed over, why draw attention to the very thing they want kept quiet?'

'I have no idea,' said Ollie. 'Sometimes people aren't as clever as you expect them to be, especially when they're under pressure.'

'And do you think,' said Garibaldi, 'that the killer graffitied the Barnes Bookshop just to remind everyone of what they'd done – killed the writer of *Schooled in Murder* ? It doesn't quite add up, does it?'

'I don't know,' said Ollie, 'I'm just worried, very worried.'

'Of course you are,' said Garibaldi. 'That's understandable.'

Garibaldi got up from his chair. 'You have my number, Ollie. Give me a call any time.'

'If you find out anything—'

'We'll let you know.'

'He's in a bit of a state, isn't he?' said Gardner as they got into the car.

'Yeah,' said Garibaldi strapping on his belt. 'And he seems pretty clear where we should be looking. He's probably right. It's all very well saying lift our eyes from the book, we're not in a book club, books are a load of crap, we need to explore all possible lines of enquiry et cetera, but what other lines are there apart from the novel? It links everything. Those people in the pub that night with Liam. Why were they there? Because of the novel. That's why they went to the talk and that's why they went to the Sun afterwards. And it's those people who had the best chance to spike his drink.'

'So they have to be our main suspects.'

'But they all claim to have left the pub before him,' said Garibaldi, 'and CCTV bears that out. They could have waited for him, I guess. They could have waited by the pond.'

'They'd have to have been quick about it if they spiked his drink in the pub.'

'But the thing is we have no evidence that the drink *was* spiked in the pub.'

'So maybe they met him afterwards and did it then.'

'That's assuming they had a drink with them and that they got Liam to drink it. Did any of them leave the pub with a drink in their hand?'

Gardner started the engine. 'No. I'd have noticed.'

'If they had a drink with them they'd have hidden it.'

'Where could they have hidden it? It's summer. They didn't have coats or jackets.'

'You don't need a big drink, do you? A miniature would do it, or any small bottle. Something that would fit in a bag or a pocket.'

Gardner drove off, turning into Cleveland Road, then taking a left onto Station Road.

Garibaldi glanced towards Barnes Pond on his right and sighed. The tent had gone and the swans and the ducks slid gracefully over the water as they had always done. The place had returned to its former calm. Nothing about it suggested that this had recently been the scene of a murder.

And nothing in Garibaldi's head suggested they were any closer to finding the culprit.

39

Deighton looked at Garibaldi over the top of her reading glasses. 'Is Felicity Allerton still missing?'

'Still not answering her calls,' said Garibaldi from the seat on the other side of her desk, 'and her daughter's got no idea where she might be. She's tried everyone she can think of.'

'Where was her phone last used?'

'Close to her home the day she went missing. It's not a long time for a missing person but given the note she received the night before . . .'

'What do you think's happened to her?'

Garibaldi shrugged. 'At best she might have gone somewhere to lay low.'

'But why the phone silence? Why not tell anyone? You'd have thought she'd tell her daughter, wouldn't you?'

'Yeah. I agree – it's strange.'

'There's only one murder in Allerton's book, isn't there?'

'Just the one.'

'So . . .'

Deighton looked thoughtful, as if she were struggling with her own logic.

'We've moved beyond the book, haven't we? This note. The graffiti on the shop window.'

'Graffito.'

'Sorry?'

'Graffito. It's Italian and graffiti's the plural. One piece of writing is graffito.'

Deighton looked as if Garibaldi had just told her the earth was flat.

'I never knew that,' she said.

'Nor did I till I started learning Italian.'

It was the second time he had made the point. Had his grammar pedantry spread to other languages?

'You're right,' he said, 'we seem to have moved beyond the book, but "*The Ironic Death of Ben Joseph*" sprayed on a bookshop window and a note to Felicity Allerton saying "I know what your husband did – that's why I killed him". They may not be *from* the book. They're not like Allerton's murder, or the notes in his drawer or the ones sent to the teachers, but they both bring us *back* to it. Where was the graffito?' He paused, giving the 'o' some air. 'On a bookshop window, above the *Schooled in Murder* display. And what does it say? It reminds us of the ironic similarity between Allerton's murder and the murder of Alex Ballantyne. And that note – "I know what your husband did". We don't know for sure what it's referring to but there's one thing we know her husband did that might have got some people's backs up, and that's write the novel. So, yeah, we might seem to have moved beyond the book in terms of copycat stuff, but we haven't quite escaped it, have we? The book's still there, hovering over everything.'

Deighton tapped her fingers on the desk and screwed up her eyes as she looked out of the window.

She turned back to Garibaldi. 'Where are we on those teachers?'

'No more on, or from, the boy who accused Ruth Price.'

'What about the other three? Embezzlement. Prostitution. Drugs.'

Garibaldi scratched his head. 'We're looking at all of them in relation to all of the allegations. We don't know for sure, but if we're right in thinking Allerton swapped them around . . .'

'Anything come up?'

'Not yet.'

'OK, so getting back to Felicity Allerton's note, could it be that whoever killed Allerton did it to silence him and is making the same threat to his wife?'

'It doesn't make that threat, does it?'

'It's implied, though.'

'You're assuming that Felicity knows what her husband knew?'

'I'm assuming nothing, but—'

'But what might Felicity know that she needs to keep quiet about? It can't be the teachers' secrets. They're already out there in the book.'

'But *are* they out there in the book?' said Deighton. 'It's all so . . . so *tenuous*. There seems to be a coded link between the characters and four teachers, all of whom have received notes identical to those received by their counterparts in the novel. And it seems that if they're guilty of those things, they've been swapped around. Ruth Price didn't embezzle but she may have slept with a student. That's the only one we're anywhere near confirming, and that's not very near at all. As for the others, nothing. And these are the four teachers who went to Allerton's talk and were with him in the pub afterwards. We just keep going round and round. Nothing sticks.'

'Whoever sent that note,' said Garibaldi, 'must have known that Felicity Allerton would show it to us. So why would they do that?'

Deighton stroked her chin. 'It's almost a taunt, isn't it? Like that graffiti ... o. It's like someone's ... playing us.'

Playing. That word again.

'Boss?'

Garibaldi and Deighton turned to see Gardner standing in the doorway waving a file.

'We've got the digital forensics report on Felicity's laptop,' said Gardner.

Deighton waved her in. 'Anything interesting?'

'Well, yes.' Gardner sat at the desk and opened the file. 'There's something a bit odd. When they recovered what had been recently deleted they found a folder called "Stuff". And in this folder are a lot of files with the title *Schooled in Murder*.'

'What are they?' said Garibaldi.

'They're copies of the novel. They don't look like the printed book, they're typed.'

'The manuscript, then.'

'I haven't gone through them closely, but they looked to me like different versions of it. They're numbered.'

'How many are there?'

'Fifteen.'

Deighton leaned forward, resting her elbows on the desk. 'So what were they doing on Felicity Allerton's computer? No copies on Liam's computer and fifteen copies on Felicity's. What was going on?'

'Maybe he sent it to her,' said Garibaldi. 'Maybe she proofread it for him or edited it for him. I mean, she's a translator after all, isn't she?'

'But why would he not keep his own copies?' asked Gardner.

'Exactly,' said Deighton. 'Did forensics find any deleted copies on Liam's laptop?'

'No,' said Gardner. 'And we found that pretty odd.'

'So the question is,' said Garibaldi, 'why did Felicity have those copies of the novel and why did she delete them?'

'Do we know when she deleted them?' said Deighton.

Gardner consulted her notes. 'Looks like she did it the day before she disappeared.'

'So maybe . . .'

Garibaldi trailed off, remembering what Allerton had said when he'd been asked in his Spanish class what his wife translated.

Truth into lies.

The words danced round Garibaldi's head. Truth and lies. It was what he dealt with in every case. The search for the truth. The attempt to sift what was real from what was fabricated.

Other words rushed back to Garibaldi. Con-trick. Playing by the book. The things they got up to. Things not being what they seemed. Fran's mum and the limelight.

'We need to find Felicity Allerton,' said Garibaldi.

An idea was forming in his mind, but he wasn't yet ready to share it.

40

Whenever Garibaldi wanted to call Kay at work he went to the station car park, a place where he could raise his voice without being overheard.

'Have you called up to gloat?'

'Why would I gloat?'

'Because you've always resented him being with us. Ever since he stormed out and came to yours, you've had this feeling of . . . I don't know, some kind of victory.'

'You're talking bollocks, Kay. All I'm interested in is Alfie being OK and this news about him moving in with Alicia is fantastic.'

Kay fell silent.

'You don't think so, do you?' said Garibaldi. 'You don't like Alicia because you don't think she's good enough. You think, or rather Dom thinks, she's too woke, a snowflake.'

'That's not true.'

'Of course it's true. You preferred it when Alfie was arsing around with all those Oxford snobs. As soon as he meets someone more . . .'

'More what?'

'Closer to his background.'

'You mean closer to your background. Lives in a council flat so must be OK.'

'Don't be absurd.'

'I'm not being absurd. Alfie has – had – the world at his feet. Good school. Oxford—'

'Ah, yes, the school you – or was it Dom, it was certainly Dom's money, wasn't it —the posh school you sent him to for the Sixth Form. What a great idea that was!'

'It got him into Oxford.'

'Exactly.'

Another silence.

'That's the problem with you, Jim. You're so bitter.'

'I'm not bitter at all. I'm perfectly happy. It's all worked out OK for me and at long last it's all working out for Alfie.'

'Working out?'

'Weren't you the one – or am I wrong again, maybe this was Dom as well – weren't you the one who said he needed to stand on his own two feet, that he needed to make his own way or some other on-your-bike bullshit? Well, that's what he's doing now. He's moving out and he's got a job.'

'He's working in a bookshop for fuck's sake!'

'What's wrong with that?'

'What kind of money is he going to make in a bookshop?'

'There are more important things than—'

'Please, Jim, no! You're a grown man. You're a fucking detective. Don't come out with all this ridiculous kids' stuff. You know as well as I do that Alfie needs a proper job.'

'He's got a proper job.'

'It's not a . . . career, is it?'

'What the f—'

'What are his prospects in a bookshop?'

'The world's changed, Kay. When did you last take a close look at it? Not a look through your rose-tinted,

Putney-mansion glasses but the world as it is. It's not as easy as it was. Everything's changed.'

They both fell silent. Not a truce – more of a pause for breath.

'I hope you make clear to Alfie,' said Garibaldi, 'and to Alicia, that he'll always be welcome. You're his mother—'

'You think I don't know that?'

'He needs to move out on good terms.'

Garibaldi believed none of what he was saying. He'd be happy if Alfie never set foot in Dom's house again and, despite his recognition of the indisputable biological connection, he often thought he'd be happy if Alfie's contact with his mother was minimal. Unreasonable perhaps, but it's what he felt.

'I'm behaving like a grown-up, Jim. I don't know about you. Of course he'll be welcome. As welcome here as he'll be welcome with you and . . .' The pause. Always the pause before her name, belittling it, drawing attention to it. 'You and Rachel.'

Why had he called her?

Why hadn't he waited until Alfie had moved out and was settled?

Why had he been so impulsive?

Maybe Kay was right. Maybe he'd wanted to gloat.

'Giacomo.'

Garibaldi started. Where had that voice come from?

'Giacomo!'

There it was again. The voice of his mother coming down the phone.

'Giacomo, you must remember. You have an Irish mother and an Italian father. You have a fuse and you need to be careful.'

'I am being careful.'

'What are you talking about?' said Kay.

'Giacomo. You need to watch your temper. Sometimes you need to be less impulsive, less rash. Take your time.'

'I am taking my time.'

'Taking your time about what?' said Kay.

'Mum—'

'Did you just call me Mum?'

Garibaldi shook his head to clear it.

'No. I . . . look, Kay, I've got to go. Alfie. I just want—'

'Just want the best for him? Sometimes I wonder.'

Kay hung up and Garibaldi walked back to the building looking at the phone, trying to work out where his mother's voice had come from.

The phone rang in his hand. Not Kay trying to get another final word in. Surely not.

He looked at the screen. No name. Just a number.

'DI Garibaldi.'

'Inspector Garibaldi. It's Felicity Allerton here.'

Garibaldi and Gardner followed Felicity into the living room and sat down opposite her.

'Does your daughter know you're back?' asked Garibaldi.

'I've called her.'

'And you've told her where you've been?'

'I have, yes.'

'Maybe you could tell us as well.'

'Of course.' Felicity cleared her throat. 'It all seems so silly now. I feel a bit embarrassed.'

'Nothing to be embarrassed about,' said Garibaldi. 'Just tell us what's happened.'

'That note frightened me. It terrified me. "I know what your husband did – that's why I killed him". The message

292

is pretty clear, isn't it? Whoever killed Liam wants to kill me as well.'

'The note doesn't threaten you directly, does it?' said Garibaldi. '"I know what your husband did – that's why I killed him." More of a statement than a threat.'

Felicity reached for a tissue and wiped her nose. She clasped the tissue tightly in her hands. 'How else am I supposed to read it? What would you think if you got a note like that?'

'I know it's difficult, Felicity, but—'

'Are we any closer to finding who did it?'

'The note?'

'The note. Everything.'

'We're getting close, yes.' Garibaldi did his best to sound confident.

'So tell me, Felicity, you were frightened and you went away. Where did you go?'

Felicity bowed her head. 'I needed to be alone. I needed to be safe.'

'Where did you go, Felicity?'

Felicity looked up. 'This is going to sound silly.'

'Try me.'

'Littlehampton.'

'Littlehampton?'

'It's on the coast near—'

'I know where it is, I'm just puzzled as to why.'

'We used to go there, the three of us, when Fran was little. We stayed in a lovely little guest house and that's where I went. I wanted to get out of London. To feel the sea air. To be somewhere safe – where whoever sent that note wouldn't know I was. And, who knows, to feed on some good memories, to remember better times.'

'So while we were searching for you, you were holed up in a guest house in Littlehampton?'

'Yes. Not all the time of course. I went for long walks during the day. East Beach. West Beach. I had lunch in the East Beach café, looking out at the sea. '

Felicity seemed in another world, oblivious to the fuss her disappearance had caused.

'Why didn't you answer anyone's calls?' said Garibaldi.

'I didn't want anyone to know where I was.'

'But surely your daughter – did you not think how worried she would be, especially after that note?'

'I had to do it.'

'Fran was worried sick. She was fearing the worst.'

Felicity looked down at the floor. 'I thought getting away like that would help but I don't know that it did. All I could think of was Liam and what happened to him. I kept turning everything over, looking for explanations, looking for answers . . .'

'And did you find any?'

'Liam's life was pretty uneventful, you know. He was a teacher. A good teacher but that's all he was. We lived an unspectacular life. He had his work and I had mine and we got on with things in our quiet, understated way. Until, that is, *Schooled in Murder*. Suddenly things were different. And as I walked by the sea that's what I kept coming back to. The book. Liam was killed because of that bloody book.'

'Are you saying that someone didn't like what he wrote so they killed him?'

'Maybe I am. Maybe that's exactly what I'm saying.'

Garibaldi glanced at his notebook. 'So, Felicity, you think Liam was killed by someone who thought he'd put them in his novel?'

'Don't you?'

'You think he based some of the characters in the book on real people?'

'I know Liam denied it, but then he would, wouldn't he? But the school fits so why not the teachers?'

'You think there are teachers at St Mark's with the same things to hide?'

'You've looked into them, I assume?'

'We have, yes.'

'But found nothing?'

'We're still investigating. Tell me, Felicity, those notes in Liam's drawer, do you think there's a possibility that Liam may have been doing what Alex Ballantyne does in his novel – blackmailing teachers at his school?'

'I don't believe so, no.'

'But you're not convinced?'

'I find it very unlikely.'

'So what were they doing in his drawer?

Felicity shrugged. 'I have no idea, but I can't believe he was actually doing it. If he was doing something like that he'd either destroy them or put them somewhere a bit more difficult to discover.'

'What would you say, Felicity, if I were to tell you we have reason to believe that at least one of those teachers' secrets in the novel may well be true of one of the St Mark's teachers?'

'Really? Which one?'

'I'm afraid I'm not at liberty to tell you that. It seems that Liam may have been playing games with teachers' names and also playing around with their alleged crimes. Linking St Mark's teachers to characters and then attributing to those characters someone else's secret.'

'You mean ... I don't get it. You mean that there are teachers at St Mark's who actually *have* done those things?'

'As I said, we're investigating.'

Felicity threw her hands in the air in frustration. 'I don't believe it. I don't believe any of it!'

'I have a few more questions, Felicity, if you don't mind. Liam said a few things that people found strange. I'm sure they were entirely innocent, but I wanted to check.' Garibaldi opened his notebook and leafed through it until he found the page. 'One thing he said was that no-one would believe the things the two of you got up to. What do you think he meant by that?'

'The things the two of us got up to? I have no idea. Who did he say this to?'

Garibaldi consulted his notebook. 'Someone he sang with in the choir. Fred Tolley.'

'Maybe he was joking. He liked to do that, Liam.'

Garibaldi flicked over a page of his notebook. 'There are a few other things your husband said, Felicity, that I'm curious about. Apparently he said, and I quote, that he wished he'd "played it by the book".'

'Who did he say this to?'

'Your daughter, Fran. Any idea what he might have meant?'

'"Played it by the book"? I can only imagine he was talking about his time at St Mark's. He had a habit of speaking out about things. I can still remember him coming home sometimes and saying, "I've done it again, shot my mouth off. Why don't I just keep quiet about what I think?". Maybe he was referring to that but, to be honest, I don't really know.'

Garibaldi consulted his notebook again.

'What else did he say?' said Felicity. 'Is that notebook full of things he said about our relationship?'

Garibaldi held up his hand. 'Just a few more. You work as a translator, Felicity. In his Spanish class someone asked him what you translated and he replied, "how do you say 'truth into lies'". What do you think he meant by that?'

Felicity gave a rueful smile. 'Typical Liam. It was one of his stock jokes. He loved coming out with the line.'

'So he didn't mean anything significant?'

'Just a joke, I'm afraid.'

'To get back to his writing, Felicity. He said to someone else that what he wrote was a con-trick, that writers were con-artists. Any comment on that?'

'Who did he say this to?'

'Someone in his tennis group.'

'I hate to put a dampener on all of your theories, Inspector, but I don't think that line was his. I think he read it somewhere. In fact, I can remember him running it past me, asking me what I thought about it. I can actually remember our discussion. Liam may have taught Maths but he was always interested in literary things. Maybe, looking back on it, I shouldn't have been so surprised that he wrote a novel. I think his writing ambitions may have been bubbling under for some time. He just kept quiet about them and then, bingo, eight months after retiring there it was, *Schooled in Murder.*'

Garibaldi looked at his notebook and snapped it shut.

'And on the subject of *Schooled in Murder,* can you explain why when we searched Liam's computer, we could find no trace of the novel? It was there in his email folders and there were different versions of it in the to and fros with his agent and editor but there wasn't a separate folder anywhere. That surprised me.'

'It's no surprise, Inspector. I kept on at him about backing things up. In the cloud or on a USB but he insisted on doing it his way by emailing the latest versions to himself and keeping them in an email folder. He said it was as good as any other way. I did keep reminding him but he insisted.'

'The funny thing is,' said Garibaldi, 'that although we

297

didn't find his novel anywhere outside his emails on *his* computer we found a lot of versions of it on yours.'

'Really? But I—'

'But you deleted them?'

Felicity's mouth dropped open. 'I—'

'It's difficult to get rid of these things, Felicity. You think they've gone, but they're still there and all it takes is someone who knows how to find them.'

'Look, I can explain.'

'Please do.'

'I was his back-up. Once I knew he'd written the damn thing and when I knew it was going to be published I told him to send his revisions to me if he wasn't going to back them up himself. So that's why I had them on my laptop.'

'In a folder called "Stuff".'

'That's right.'

'That explains why they were there in the first place, but it doesn't explain why you deleted them.'

'OK,' said Felicity. 'Before I went away I couldn't stop thinking about that book. That bloody book! It had to be the reason poor Liam was killed and I couldn't bear to think of it. I didn't want to see it any more, didn't want to be reminded of it. So I took all the copies off the shelves, off the tables, even off his desk. I put every copy away, out of sight. I just didn't want to be reminded of it. And I also decided to remove everything to do with it from my laptop.'

'So it was, what, some attempt at a purge?'

'That's exactly what it was. I'm not sure it worked, in fact I know it hasn't, but that's why I did it.'

Garibaldi got up. 'Well, I'm glad you've been found, Felicity, and I'm sure your daughter will be very relieved to see you.'

Felicity got up from her chair. 'I feel a bit foolish, running off like that.'

'Please, don't worry.'

'Looking back on it, it was a stupid thing to do, but that note ... I just had to get away. From here. From everything. I didn't want to see anyone, I just needed to be by myself for a while. Does that sound silly?'

'It doesn't sound silly at all. I know exactly what you mean.'

Garibaldi walked to the door, wondering how overwhelmed you needed to be to think running away to Littlehampton might be the answer to anything.

41

Garibaldi leaned back, hands behind his head, and swivelled in his chair.

'Have you checked with the Littlehampton guest house?'

'Yeah,' said Gardner from the other side of his desk. 'All tallies with her account. Stayed two nights and checked out this morning.'

'Anything yet on those teachers?'

'No more on the Ruth Price sex thing. Nothing from Ellison School and nothing further from the pupil going by the name of Matthew Rose. So unless we get another call from him there's not much we can do, and there's still the chance it's someone making the whole thing up. And as for the other three, we're looking at each in relation to all the crimes but if any of them have been up to anything looks like they've kept it well hidden.'

'Possible, I suppose,' said Garibaldi. 'Millions manage to keep a drug habit hidden. Embezzlement I don't know about but it seems easy enough to shift money about and keep it out of sight. And as for escorts I can't believe for one moment that anyone would do that under their own name. They'd probably have some ludicrous alias. But I keep coming back to Felicity Allerton's laptop. All those copies of *Schooled in Murder* on hers and nothing on Liam's. And she deleted them. What do you make of it? Do you believe what she said about why she tried to get rid of them?'

'I'm not sure.'

'Nor am I. Something doesn't add up. I keep thinking about this book I read a couple of years ago. It was made into a film.'

'What was it?'

'It was called . . .' Garibaldi stopped himself. His idea was still forming and he wasn't ready to share it. 'You know what? I can't remember the title.'

'What was it about?'

Garibaldi gave a dismissive shrug, regretting raising it with Gardner. 'I can't remember the details,' he lied. 'I just keep thinking about it, I don't know why. All this talk about his book gets you thinking about loads of others.'

He picked up some papers from his desk. 'Where are we on the other three who were at the Sun?' he said, changing tack.

'Nothing. All squeaky clean. Like the teachers, they could have spiked his drink but there's no evidence from CCTV. Like the teachers, they could be said to have motives, though the way they're portrayed in the book is nowhere near as bad. Mostly references to sex, aren't they? A randy tennis player, a fantasy object in Spanish lessons and a bloke who can't satisfy his wife. I mean, they could be enough to provoke murder, but I don't really see it.'

'That's the thing about murder, Milly. Sometimes it's difficult to see what provokes it. And the danger is you can overcomplicate it . Most murders are driven by pretty basic desires. Money's one of them. Revenge is another. And so is sex. So when you say the way they're portrayed is nothing you can never be sure, can you?'

'All I'm saying is that if those teachers were up to any of those things they had more of a motive to silence Liam Allerton.'

'But what we keep coming back to is that if they wanted silence, if they wanted to turn attention *away* from their crimes, why kill him in a way that puts the whole thing right in the middle of a media spotlight?'

'Could be bluff. Could be them thinking they won't be a suspect for that very reason and doing it like that might give them some weird sense of satisfaction, of justice. I mean if you're prepared to kill someone like that, not in the heat of the moment but premeditated, you have to be pretty fucked up in the first place, don't you?'

Garibaldi stroked his chin. Gardner was talking sense.

'You know what?' he said. 'You're right.'

He got up and hooked his jacket off the back of the chair.

'Off somewhere?' said Gardner.

'Yeah. How about a lift?'

Felicity Allerton sat in her living room, hands clasped tensely in her lap, her eyes darting anxiously between Garibaldi and Gardner.

Garibaldi leaned forward in his chair, resting his elbows on his knees. 'Sorry to bother you again, Felicity, but I've been thinking about those copies of Liam's book on your computer.'

'I've explained that.'

'And I keep coming back to why you deleted them.'

'I've explained that as well.'

'I'm not sure I believe your explanations.'

'I don't understand.'

Garibaldi paused, sighed and sat back in his chair.

'There's something about your husband's book that's worried me all along and I'll tell you what it is. Neither you nor your daughter knew anything about Liam writing a novel until he told you he'd done it. I suppose that's just about plausible, though from what I've heard it does take a lot of time and effort to write a book, a lot of time sitting at a desk tapping away. Now it's possible that your husband spent a lot of time when he retired sitting in his study and you thought he was simply pursuing his interests – reading stuff about Chelsea, following the horses, brushing up on his Spanish, who knows what else he might have been into – but I find that very unlikely.'

'What are you saying?' said Felicity. 'I don't see—'

Garibaldi held up his hand to stop her. He glanced at Gardner who had turned to him and wore a look of surprise, as if she had no idea where he was heading.

'The other thing that puzzles me is the issue of Liam's next book. He told his agent and publisher it was well under way and that he'd be delivering a draft very soon but, strangely, there's no trace of a second book anywhere on his computer. Nothing at all. Zilch.'

'I can explain that,' said Felicity. 'He was stuck. He simply couldn't get going. Blocked – I think that's the word. He told me he had ideas, but just couldn't physically get started, and I—'

'There are other alarm bells, Felicity. Everyone at St Mark's was shocked and surprised when his book came out. Liam had never seemed that sort. Someone even said they had to send his reports back because they didn't make sense. Good at crosswords they said, but that didn't mean he could always string words together.'

'I don't know what you mean. School reports are hardly a way of judging whether or not a teacher can write.'

'I'd have thought they're a very good way.'

'Just because they were sent back, doesn't mean they're wrong. I think you should look at the teachers who sent them back. Maybe they're the ones with the problem.'

Garibaldi examined Felicity's face. Her confidence didn't fool him – he could tell from her eyes.

'All this stuff about you not knowing about Liam's book until he finished it, all this stuff about you proof-reading it when he was working on his edits after the book had been accepted – I don't believe it. Because I think you knew about this book a long time before that. Am I right?'

Felicity gave a thin-lipped smile and a slow shake of her head.

'The truth is there's a very good reason why everyone was surprised when Liam said he'd written a book. Everyone at school. Even his daughter. But not you. Because you always knew the truth, didn't you Felicity?'

Felicity continued to look straight at him.

'The truth is you wrote Liam's novel, didn't you? You wrote *Schooled in Murder*.'

Felicity's face lit up. '*I* wrote it? *Me*? Absolutely not! You couldn't be more wrong. That's ridiculous!'

'I didn't expect you to say anything else,' said Garibaldi.

'I say it because it's the truth! This is a difficult enough time for me. Everything I've gone through and now ... now this! What a ridiculous accusation!'

'Liam said some strange things,' continued Garibaldi. 'The things you two got up to. Wishing he'd played by the book. Writing being a con-trick. They all make sense now, don't they? The whole thing was a con-trick, wasn't it?'

'What can I say?' said Felicity. 'It's not true and even if it *were* true how could you possibly prove it?'

Garibaldi said nothing for a few moments, looking

closely at Felicity. She didn't turn away and her face still seemed confident, almost defiant. Too confident, perhaps. Behind the eyes, below the surface, Garibaldi could tell she was rattled.

'You and I know, Felicity, that the best way for this to be proved is for you to confess, to own up to it.'

'I can't do that.'

'Why not?'

'Because I didn't do it!'

'Well maybe I can let you think about it and then, when you're ready you can get in touch.'

Garibaldi got to his feet.

'Whenever you're ready, Felicity,' he said as he opened the front door.

42

'Why didn't you tell me you were going to do that?'
said Gardner as she drove towards Hammersmith
Bridge

'I wanted it to be a surprise.'

'It was that all right. When did you have that idea?'

'It came to me gradually. All those comments. So many
people saying things that pointed to their relationship, so
many things about the writing of the book that didn't make
sense. And then I remembered that book I read.'

'Oh, yeah, that book. What is it?'

'*The Wife*. Meg Wolitzer. A film with Glenn Close and
Jonathan Pryce. I don't suppose . . .'

'Never heard of it,' said Gardner. 'What's it about?'

'Pryce plays a Nobel Prize-winning novelist. Close is his
wife. And it turns out that she's the one who's been writing
his books all the time.'

'And you reckon the same thing's gone on with the
Allertons?'

'We're not talking Nobel Prize obviously, but Fran said
something about her parents' relationship that started me
thinking. She said Felicity sometimes did things not because
she wanted to but to please Liam.'

'What's unusual about that? Happens in every relation-ship, doesn't it? Every marriage.'

'The way she said it made it sound a bit more than that. She said that her father was very controlled. It was that word – controlled.'

'Controlled? What are you suggesting?' said Gardner. 'Some kind of coercive control?'

'It's a possibility, isn't it?'

'A possibility? Is that all? You were talking to Felicity as if you were absolutely convinced.'

Garibaldi smiled. 'It's sometimes the best way to play it. Gives you a more helpful response.'

'Hang on, so do you *really* believe it or are you just play-ing her?'

'I think there's a strong possibility. So many things don't add up. So many comments suggesting something going on between the two of them.'

'But I don't get it. Why would she write the book for him? Why couldn't he do it himself?'

'She's a translator, she works with words. He was a Maths teacher who worked with numbers. Maybe she was better at writing than him. And if she did things to please him, if she didn't like the limelight, if he had some kind of . . . control.'

'But how would she know about the school, the teachers?'

'Liam could have told her.'

'And that thing with the names, the code?'

'Again, Liam could have told her to do it.'

'But if there's any truth in those allegations about the teachers, how would she know about them?'

'Liam could have told her about them as well. She wrote it but Liam gave her the ideas, the info. And I'm sure he would have checked it over.'

'If Felicity wrote it,' said Gardner, 'how did Liam manage to talk about it at the book festival and answer questions?'

'Training,' said Garibaldi. 'They went through things together, I imagine, practising answers to obvious questions. Liam may have been a Maths teacher but he was a teacher and he knew how to address a group. And it's not as though we're talking about someone who was completely illiterate who didn't know the first thing about books. He was very confident when I saw him give his talk.'

'I just don't see it,' said Gardner, pulling up south of the bridge.

'I didn't see it myself at first,' said Garibaldi, as they got out of the car, 'but when the idea came to me it all fell into place. Funny things ideas, don't you find?'

He looked at his sergeant, unable to work out whether or not she did.

'So if your theory's right,' said Gardner, as they started to walk across the bridge, 'how does it help our investigation?'

What Westminster Bridge was to Wordsworth, Hammersmith Bridge was to Garibaldi. Crossing it gave him a view he would never tire of – long looping stretches of river on either side. To the right the Riverside Studios and the expensive apartments leading towards the River Café, Craven Cottage and Putney Bridge. To the left the riverside pubs – The Blue Anchor, The Rutland, the Old Ship – that lined the towpath on the way to Chiswick. Given his feelings about being north of the river he preferred the southbound view – the playing fields of St Mark's to his right, the Harrods Depository to his left – but walking across Hammersmith Bridge in either direction always made his heart flutter in a way that reminded him of the Romantic poet.

He felt the flutter now as he walked across with Gardner.

'How does it help?' he said, repeating his sergeant's question. 'It could lead us in all kind of directions.'

He said it with confidence, but as he looked up at the window of Fran Allerton's riverside flat and walked along the towpath with Gardner towards its entrance, he had no idea what those directions might be.

Fran Allerton sat on the edge of her chair underneath the high window looking out on the Thames. 'I'm relieved she's safe,' she said, 'but I have to say I'm also bloody angry. Why didn't she tell me?'

'I think she was in quite a state,' said Garibaldi.

'Even so. To go away like that without letting me know.'

'Did she give you any explanation?'

'The same as she told you. Needed to get away. Needed some space. It doesn't add up. I can understand that she might have been worried and frightened, but . . .' Fran paused, her eyes darting anxiously between Garibaldi and Gardner.

Garibaldi leaned forward. 'But what, Fran?'

'I wonder whether she's telling the truth.'

'About what?'

'About where she was.'

'Where might she have been if she wasn't in Littlehampton?'

'I don't know. Maybe whoever sent that note . . . it's ridiculous, isn't it? I keep wondering whether they might have . . .?'

'Might have taken her?' said Garibaldi.

'I just worry about that note.'

'No-one took her, Fran. We've checked with the guest-house in Littlehampton, the one you all used to go to when you were little and she was there. By herself.'

309

Fran looked down at the hands in her lap. 'Just shows how it's all got to me, doesn't it? I'm sorry.'

'No need to apologise.' Garibaldi sat back in his chair. He paused for a few seconds, looking up at the sun coming through the window. 'Could we get back to *Schooled in Murder* for a moment?'

Fran looked up. 'What about it?'

'Your mother said she was very surprised to find out your father had written a novel.'

'She was, yes. So was I.'

'She said she had no idea it was something your dad wanted to do. I'm going to suggest something to you, Fran, that you might find difficult to believe, but I'll get straight to the point. Has it ever occurred to you that your father might not have written the book at all?'

Fran's face froze. It was as if someone had pressed her pause button and turned down the colour.

'What do you mean?'

'Has it ever occurred to you that it wasn't your father, but your *mother* who wrote *Schooled in Murder*?'

Garibaldi waited as Fran struggled to process her thoughts.

'I don't understand. Whatever makes you think—'

'It's like this, Fran.'

Garibaldi kept his eyes on Fran as he explained his thinking: the deleted versions of *Schooled in Murder* on her mother's laptop; the absence of copies of *Schooled in Murder* on her father's laptop and no trace of his promised second novel; the general surprise that her father had written a novel at all; comments about the literacy of his school reports; the cryptic remarks he'd made to friends.

Fran gave a slow dismissive shake of her head. 'I don't see it. I don't see it at all. Why on Earth would she do it?'

'Your mother's a translator, works with words all the time.'

'That doesn't mean she'd be better at . . .' Fran trailed off, as if doubting what she was about to say.

'You said she did things to please your father.'

Fran laughed. 'I didn't mean things like . . . like this. I mean this is huge. If she'd written a novel, why wouldn't she say it was hers?'

'You also said she didn't like the limelight.'

'Why would they deceive everyone like that? No. I don't see it.'

'Stranger things have happened,' said Garibaldi, thinking briefly of telling Fran about the Meg Wolitzer novel, but deciding against it.

'Have you asked my mother about this?'

Garibaldi nodded. 'She denied it.'

'That's probably because she didn't do it.'

'When you next speak to her,' said Garibaldi, 'maybe you could—'

Fran turned back. 'I'll mention it, of course I will, but I really can't believe that he, that they, would do this. I can't believe they wouldn't tell me.'

'You'd be amazed at what parents keep from their children,' said Garibaldi, getting up and nodding to Gardner. 'If anything emerges in your conversation . . .'

Garibaldi looked through the high window at the endless sky above Fran's head, before turning and heading for the door.

43

From; NaomiMarsh@lotuspress.com
To; GGarabldi@metpolice.co.uk
Re; Schooled in Murder

Dear Detective Inspector Garibaldi,

As requested, I have dug out (and attached) the insertions Liam made to his MS at proof stage. As I said to you in our conversation, there weren't many – only four of significance as it turns out. You can probably see why I found the changes strange – but Liam was insistent. Please do let me know if I can be of further assistance.

Kind regards,

Naomi Marsh

Proof corrections –
Schooled in Murder

Page 29

Original

He spent much of his time in denial, but in moments of sober lucidity, he realised that if he seriously wanted to beat his addiction he would need professional help.

Insertion

He spent most of his time in denial but there were moments when he realised he had a problem and should face up to the situation and stop his acute addiction – maybe by rehab or something else.

Page 70

Original

He knew he should have stopped it as soon as it had started but he was unable to resist – sometimes he wondered whether it was because the illicit nature of what he was doing made it all that much more thrilling.

Insertion

Though he knew he should stop it he had carried on in the hope that it might remain unknown. Though his personal risk in continuing everything was considerable he simply couldn't stop himself . . .

Original

At the beginning of the autumn term she put her alter ego to bed (the place where she had spent many summer nights) and focused on school. To do otherwise was to take too many risks.

Insertion

        ... The end of the holidays usually meant an end to her escort work. A new term had often meant a stop to her secret activity. It was too difficult on school nights.

Original

Siphoning had always been something she associated with chemistry labs or petrol thieves. She had never considered the way the metaphor was applied to the illicit appropriation of funds but, in her desperation, she now began to do exactly that.

Insertion

        ... She set up an account and redirected money into that. Her action really was a last desperate attempt to ...

Garibaldi reached to the corner of his desk, picked up his copy of *Schooled in Murder*, flicked through it and stuck a pink Post-it on the relevant pages. He then looked at the sheet of corrections he had printed out and read the sections again to remind himself of who was being described in each. The first was a description of Ted Fox, the teacher with a coke addiction; the second described Harry Antrobus, the teacher who had slept with a pupil; the third described Ashley MacDonald, the St Jude's teacher working as an escort and the fourth was a description of Prisha Bedi, the teacher embezzling funds.

Garibaldi looked again at the sheet in front of him. Naomi Marsh was right. These changes seemed both strange and insignificant.

The more he looked at them the less they made sense. And the more he looked at them the more he was struck by how the insertion read so much worse than the original.

He leaned back in his chair, hands behind his head.

He thought again of the code he had discovered in the characters' names. How had he discovered it? The truth was he couldn't remember. He had just looked at the list of names he had written out and looked for a connection. It had been a bit like sitting on the sofa with Rachel shouting answers at the screen as they watched *Only Connect*.

He stared at the sheet in front of him, still baffled as to why Liam had made those corrections at such a late stage. Given that they were saying exactly the same thing as what they had replaced, the only difference being that they were written with far less elegance, what had made him do it?

No wonder Naomi Marsh had been so baffled. The surprise was that she had agreed to them.

Garibaldi picked up the book, opened it at the first pink Post-it on page 29 and read the description of Ted Fox:

He spent most of his time in denial but there were moments when he realised he had a problem and should face up to the situation and stop his acute addiction – maybe by rehab or something else.

He looked at the words through screwed up eyes, thinking again of what Liam had done with the characters, the way he had played around with the letters at the beginning of their names.

Could he have been doing a similar thing here?

He read the description yet again, this time looking not so much at the words as at the letters.

Could it be . . .?

Surely not.

Three hours later Garibaldi stood in DCI Deighton's doorway clutching his copy of *Schooled in Murder* and a pad of paper.

'Have you got a minute, boss?'

Deighton looked at him over her reading glasses.

'I hope you're about to tell me we've made a breakthrough.'

'I'm not sure,' said Garibaldi, 'but I've definitely found something.'

'What is it?'

'It might take some explaining.' Garibaldi pointed at the chair in front of Deighton's desk. 'Can I bring this round to your side? I need to show you something.'

Deighton held out her hands. 'Feel free.'

Garibaldi picked up the chair and carried it to the side of Deighton's desk. He put his copy of *Schooled in Murder* on the desk in front of him, the four pink Post-its protruding from its pages, and set down his pad of paper.

He sat down beside Deighton. 'I hadn't told you anything about this because I didn't think anything would come of it, but when I spoke to Liam Allerton's editor she said he had made some alterations at proof stage that had puzzled her. She sent them through this afternoon and I've gone through them and . . . well, I'm not sure what to make of it. You know that thing Allerton may have done with the names and the letters?'

Deighton nodded.

'Well, I think he might have done something else, something a bit more complex. Can I take you through it?'

Garibaldi reached for the sheet that showed the corrections and the original versions.

'Four changes,' he said. 'They're not changes to the sense of the original, just to the way they're expressed.'

Garibaldi glanced sideways at his boss. Her brow was furrowed in concentration. 'Look at this one,' he said, pointing at the description of Ashley MacDonald on the sheet and opening the book at the relevant page marked by a Post-it. 'Here's the original version.' Garibaldi pointed at the sheet in front of him and started to read, *'At the beginning of the autumn term she put her alter ego to bed (the place where she had spent many summer nights) and focused on school. To do otherwise was to take too many risks . . .'*

He moved the book between them, pointed at the passage on the page. 'And here's the change Allerton made to it. *'The end of the holidays usually meant an end to her escort work. A new term had often meant a stop to her secret activity. It was too difficult on school nights.'*

He turned to Deighton. 'I think you'll agree that the correction isn't much of an improvement. In fact, in terms of prose style, it's considerably worse. So the question is why did he do it? Why did he make that change and why so late, why at proof stage?'

Deighton's eyes were on the sheet of corrections, her face a combination of bafflement and curiosity.

'I had no idea,' said Garibaldi, 'but then I stopped looking at the words on the sheet and started looking at the words as they are on the pages. The words and the letters. And when I did that, I saw something.'

He took a sheet from his pile of notes and placed it between them:

> ... *The end of the holidays usually meant an end to her* **E**scort **W**ork. **A N**ew **T**erm **H**ad **O**ften **M**eant **A S**top *to her secret activity. It was too difficult on school nights.*

Deighton brought her head closer to the sheet, as if she couldn't believe what she was seeing.

'What's going on?' she said, keeping her head close to the sheet.

'It's Liam Allerton playing a game. In what seems to be a description of the character in the novel who works as an escort he's giving us the identity of the St Mark's teacher who is doing that very thing.'

'Ewan Thomas?'

'Exactly. Now look at these.'

Garibaldi took out three more sheets and put them on the table:

> *Though he knew he should stop it he carried on in the hope that it might* **R**emain **U**nknown. *Though* **H**is **P**ersonal **R**isk **I**n **C**ontinuing **E**verything *was considerable he simply couldn't stop himself . . .*

> *He spent most of his time in denial but there were moments when he realised he had a problem and he should face up to the* **S**ituation **A**nd **S**top **H**is **A**cute **A**ddiction – **M**aybe **B**y **R**ehab **O**r **S**omething **E**lse.

> ... *She set up an account* **A**nd **R**edirected **M**oney **I**nto **T**hat. **H**er **A**ction **R**eally **W**as **A L**ast *desperate attempt to . . .*

Deighton kept her head down, looking closely at the sheets in front of her. 'I don't believe it,' she said.

'There's a chance the initials and the names thing might have been a fluke, but there's no way that this is,' said Garibaldi.

Deighton lifted her head and hooked off her reading glasses. 'Let's get this straight,' she said, turning to Garibaldi. 'What, exactly, is Allerton doing here?'

'He's linking the St Mark's teachers to their secrets. Ewan Thomas the escort. Sasha Ambrose the coke addict. Ruth Price having sex with a student. Armit Harwal embezzling.'

'But this doesn't *prove* any of that, does it?'

'No, but it does suggest that Allerton was basing the characters in the novel on those St Mark's teachers. He swapped the genders around and he swapped the secrets, but this is him spelling it out. Literally spelling it out.'

Deighton looked puzzled, as if she were finding the whole thing too difficult to process.

'What I don't get,' she said, 'is how anyone is ever going to work it out. It's so, so *hidden* . . . who the hell is going to see any of it?'

'That's exactly what I thought. I couldn't see how anyone would find those passages, let alone those specific lines. I couldn't see it at all, but then I thought of Liam the Maths teacher. Lover of crosswords, yes, but also lover of numbers. How could he have directed readers to those pages, to those lines?'

'And did you find an answer?'

'Not at first, no. I couldn't see it at all, but I think I've worked it out. It took me a while, but I got there.'

Garibaldi took out another sheet and put it in front of them. He pointed at the top of the page where he had written the letters of the alphabet and below it the numbers 1 to 26.

'A equals 1, B equals 2 et cetera,' he said. 'The code of a thousand quiz shows. And if you apply it to the names of the characters in *Schooled in Murder* you get interesting results.'

'I don't believe this. It's ... I mean, is this getting us anywhere? Is this helping?'

'I don't know,' said Garibaldi. 'All I know is what Allerton was doing.' He pointed at the sheet in front of them, a teacher getting a distracted pupil back on task. 'If you take the four teacher characters in the novel, give a numerical value from 1 to 26 to each of the letters in their name and add up the numbers of the first names this is what you get – '

He pointed at the list.

TED FOX	29
HARRY ANTROBUS	70
ASHLEY MACDONALD	70
PRISHA BEDI	71

'Those numbers,' said Deighton, 'they're the page numbers.'

'Exactly. They're the page numbers where Allerton made the changes.'

'OK, so that directs you to the page, but how do you find the lines?'

'I thought that if you added up the numbers of the second names you might get the line numbers, but when I did that some of the numbers were too large. How many lines on one page of a novel? Thirty? Forty? But when I took the first letter of the surnames and looked at that number I had it.'

'This is incredible, Jim. Absolutely incredible.'

'I couldn't believe it myself when I saw it.'

'But I still don't see where it gets us. What does it prove?'

'It doesn't *prove* anything, but it makes it even more likely that those St Mark's teachers are hiding the secrets of those teachers in the novel.'

'And does it make it more likely that one of them killed him?'

'I'm assuming nothing, but maybe it does.'

'But—' Deighton waved her hand at the book and sheets on her desk. 'It's so obscure. Why would he do this? And who the hell would see what he was doing?'

'All I know is that if you think a writer's put you in their book you look at it pretty closely.'

'Not that closely, surely?'

'You do what we do – you look for clues.'

'This has thrown me completely. I'm baffled.' Deighton leaned closer to the sheet. 'And there's one thing I still don't get. Why did he make these changes so late? Why didn't he put them in at the beginning?'

'I asked myself the same question and I'm pretty sure it's because he needed to know the page numbers and he needed to know the alignment of each page before he knew what he had to do and where to do it.'

Deighton shook her head. 'All that effort,' she said. 'And who would have seen it? What kind of game was he playing?'

Garibaldi gathered up the sheets and picked up his copy of *Schooled in Murder*.

Would now be a good time to share with Deighton his theory about Felicity Allerton being its real author?

Probably not. All that code-cracking had done his head in.

What's more it had made him reconsider the whole idea.

44

'Ollie?'

Garibaldi was on his phone in the passenger seat as Gardner drove them to Felicity Allerton's house in Cambridge Road.

'Speaking.'

'It's Detective Inspector Garibaldi here. I thought I'd catch up with regard to Felicity.'

'Thank God we found her.'

'I think it was more a matter of her turning up,' said Garibaldi.

'The important thing is she's safe. I can't tell you how worried I've been. And poor Fran. God knows what she's been through.'

'Does it seem odd to you that Felicity didn't tell anyone where she was going, not even her daughter?'

'Crazy. Completely crazy. That note must have tipped her over the edge. I mean if whoever sent it wanted to frighten her they certainly managed it.'

'Do you think that's what they intended to do?'

'What else were they doing?'

'I don't know, Ollie. "I know what your husband did – that's why I killed him". Doesn't exactly spell it out, does it?'

'I'd have thought it's pretty obvious. What Liam did was write that fucking novel and I can't tell you the number of times I wish he hadn't!'

'That note could mean anything, though, couldn't it?'

'Like what? What else could it mean? Everything's connected to his fucking book. The way he was killed, the notes in his drawer, the notes sent to those teachers. Even the graffiti on the bookshop window! And then, to top it all, Felicity gets that note – cut-up lettering just like the others. *Schooled in Fucking Murder*. It all comes back to that. Where else are you going to look for Liam's killer?'

'So you think his killer was someone who read his book and took objection?'

'Who else would it be? When was he killed, for fuck's sake? The night after his talk about the book. Who was with him? Who could have spiked his drink? Any one of those teachers from his school, for starters, and why were they there? To hear him talk about his book!'

'They're all part of our investigation. We're looking at them very closely.'

'I blame myself,' said Ollie.

'What do you mean?'

'If I'd been there I might have been able to stop it.'

'How would you have done that?'

'I don't know, but I just wish I'd been there. Liam knew I couldn't make it and he was fine about it, but even so—'

'Look, Ollie, we're on our way to see Felicity again to ask her a few more questions and I just want to check she said nothing more to you about why she went away to Littlehampton.'

'What more could she say? She was terrified and she wanted to get away, to lie low. And do you know what? I can't blame her. After all she's been through. OK, maybe she should have told someone, stopped all the worrying, but, yeah, that's all she said. Nothing more.'

'OK, thanks,' said Garibaldi. 'If anything . . .'

'Of course.'

Garibaldi ended the call and turned to Gardner who had been listening to it on loudspeaker. 'What do you make of that, then?'

'I'm not sure,' said Gardner. 'After your discovery of that second code, I'm not sure what I think about anything.'

Garibaldi grinned. It had been quite a moment when he had stood at the front showing the team what he'd discovered. If they'd thought he was a smart arse before this God knows what they'd call him now.

'I know what you mean,' he said. 'And it's made me change my mind about one thing.'

'What's that?'

'My theory about who wrote *Schooled in Murder*.'

'You're back,' said Felicity, 'I didn't expect—'

'We have a few more questions, Felicity. May we?'

Felicity stepped back, closed the door behind Garibaldi and Gardner and followed them into the living room.

'I think I may owe you an apology,' said Garibaldi.

'What?'

'I no longer think you wrote *Schooled in Murder*.'

Felicity sighed. 'Well, that's good because I didn't. As I've told you already.'

'Certain things have come to light.'

'What things?'

'You had no idea Liam was writing the novel until he presented you with it, is that right?'

'Absolutely. I've told you already it was a complete surprise.'

'And the reason you had copies of it on your laptop is because, once Liam started working on the edits, you wanted to make sure he had back-ups.'

'That's right. I've lost things myself and I didn't want it to happen to him.'

'And you deleted those copies because you wanted, as you put it, a purge.'

Felicity nodded. 'Exactly.'

Garibaldi pulled a folded sheet of paper out of his jacket pocket. 'As I said, things have come to light.' He unfolded the sheet, put it on a table and gestured for Felicity to come over. He pointed at the sheet.

Ted Fox	Ewan Thomas
Ashley MacDonald	Sasha Ambrose
Prishi Bedi	Ruth Price
Harry Antrobus	Armit Harwal

'Do you see what's going on?' said Garibaldi.

'The initials. The letters.'

'Exactly. Liam liked puzzles, didn't he?'

Felicity nodded. 'I had no idea. Those characters in the novel, did they have the same things to hide as . . .' She pointed at the right-hand column.

'No,' said Garibaldi. 'If they did he swapped them around. But—' He reached into his pocket and took out another sheet. 'Have a look at this.'

He flattened the sheet, put it on the table beside the first one and pointed at the first paragraph –

He spent most of his time in denial but there were moments when he realised he had a problem and he should face up to the **Situation And Stop His Acute Addiction – Maybe By Rehab Or Something Else.**

325

Felicity looked at the sheet as Garibaldi took her through the three other paragraphs and explained the code of page numbers and lines.

'I don't believe it,' she said when he had finished. 'So those teachers . . . he's telling us that those teachers had those secrets. He's . . . I had no idea. I didn't see this at all. I mean, who would? It's so . . . hidden, so obscure.'

'We're not sure whether it proves anything,' said Garibaldi, 'but we are turning our attention towards those teachers even more closely.'

'You don't think that Liam was . . . those notes . . . my note?"

'We're still keeping an open mind, Felicity.'

Garibaldi nodded to Gardner and they moved to the door.

He paused, Colombo-like, when his hand touched the handle. 'One other thing,' he said, turning back to Felicity. 'When you got that note that sent you off to Littlehampton, did you tell Ollie about it?'

'Yes, of course I did.'

'You didn't tell him you were going away to be by yourself but you did tell him about the note?'

'That's right.'

'What did you tell him about it?'

'I told him what it said.'

'Did you show it to him?'

'Show it to him? I was on the phone.'

'He didn't come round to look at it.'

'No. I called you and you came round.'

'Tell me, Felicity, did you tell Ollie what the note looked like?'

'What it looked like?'

'The cut-out lettering. The ransom note look.'

Felicity looked confused. 'The ransom note look?'

'The way the letters were cut out of newspapers and stuck down.'

Felicity looked none the wiser.

'It's what the notes looked like in *Schooled in Murder*,' said Garibaldi. 'Like the notes in Liam's drawer. Like the notes those teachers received.'

Felicity's face was still blank.

'You did notice the lettering, Felicity?'

'I didn't take it in . . . I didn't . . . I mean now you mention it, yes, but— I'm sorry, I'm not making much sense, am I?'

'You're making perfect sense,' said Garibaldi, turning for the door. 'Thank you.'

Garibaldi looked out on the Thames as Gardner drove across Chiswick Bridge. 'Did you notice anything odd in what either Ollie or Felicity said?'

'Are you testing me again?' said Gardner.

'Not at all. I'm just curious. Let's start with Felicity.'

'OK. So she had absolutely no idea about those codes. She definitely wasn't faking it.'

'I agree.'

'And she seemed to think it was further evidence that we should be looking at those teachers, though she couldn't believe Liam had actually been blackmailing them.'

'Right again. And what about Ollie? Did you notice anything in our phone conversation?'

Gardner shrugged.

'Do you remember what he said about the note Felicity received?'

'Yeah, he said what it said: "I know what your husband did – that's why I killed him".'

'But he said something else about it. He said it was in cut-up lettering like all the other notes.'

'He's right. It was.'

'Oh yes, he was definitely right, but the thing is we don't know for sure that Felicity told him. From what she says, the chances are she didn't.'

'So you're thinking ... but hang on, even if he hadn't been told, isn't that a reasonable assumption to make?'

'Assume nothing, Milly, assume nothing. The thing is it would have been a reasonable assumption to make if, like the other notes, the ones in Liam's drawer, the ones in the novel, the ones the teachers received – if, like all those notes this was also a blackmail note. But it wasn't. No threat of revelation. No suggestion that the recipient might have to do something like cough up money. This was a different type of note entirely and we have no evidence that Felicity mentioned its appearance to Ollie. She was so fixated on what it said that she barely even registered its appearance when I pointed it out to her.'

'So is that it, then?' said Gardner.

'What do you mean is that it?'

'You're saying Ollie sent that note.'

'I'm saying he could have. We need a record of Felicity Allerton's calls on that Saturday night. And Ollie Masters' car – can we run an APNR check on his car for that Saturday on the route from Winchester to London?'

45

Garibaldi sat on a bench by Barnes Pond, looking through the gap between the reeds towards the island in the middle. It was a still summer evening, and it was quiet. This was the time of year when Barnes was at its best. The loud voices, and all that went with them, had gone away, leaving the place to those who either couldn't afford to jet off for the summer or who chose to stay to enjoy the peace their departure had created.

Two swans glided across the smooth water towards him. Each year Garibaldi welcomed the swans' return to the pond and the appearance of baby swans with a sense of joy and optimism that surprised him. He was as quick as anyone else to stop and stare when the cygnets waddled in line behind their parents.

Seeing them come closer he marvelled at their stately elegance, their sense of beauty and power. He thought of the Yeats poem 'The Wild Swans at Coole'. He'd never felt he really understood it, but he liked the way it made him reflect on these brilliant creatures and the myths associated with them. Could swans really kill you? Or, if not kill you, break your arm? And did they really mate for life?

Looking at them drift towards him between the rich green

foliage he found it difficult to believe that this very place had so recently been a crime scene. This was the bench where Tom Murray had come with his daughter to feed the ducks. This was where Liam Allerton's body had been discovered.

Garibaldi looked at the OSO to his left, remembering Liam's appearance as Ben Joseph, his talk about *Schooled in Murder*. He swept his gaze to the right to the Sun Inn, and imagined Liam and his friends walking from the OSO towards it along the path on the other side of the pond. He saw them, Liam and Felicity, the teachers from St Mark's and Liam's friends, captured on CCTV footage in the pub.

Was it one of that group who had spiked Liam's drink and somehow rolled him into the edge of the pond?

Or was it someone who hadn't been in the pub, who had met Liam when he left?

Trying to imagine how it could have happened, Garibaldi got up from the bench and walked round the path, stopping when he was opposite the Sun. Could someone have met him here and taken him to the pond?

He turned round and walked back in the direction he had come, travelling the route they would have taken. The Day Centre was now to his left and there, in front of it, through a gap in the hedge, was the bench, looking across the pond .

He walked towards the gap, went through, and sat on the bench again.

He looked round. No CCTV on the Day Centre. The cameras on the Sun Inn and on the Church Road houses unable to reach. And nicely hidden by the hedge behind them and the pond's tall foliage. No-one would have seen unless they had walked straight past – possible, but unlikely at that time of night.

He stood up and turned, and as he did he saw a light come on in one of the Day Centre windows. He checked his watch. Nine-thirty in the evening. An unlikely time for anyone to be in the centre.

He moved close to the window, cupped his hands above his brows and tried to peer in. To his surprise, the net curtains opened and he was face-to-face with a woman.

She screamed and Garibaldi jumped back, holding his hands up in apology.

'I'm so sorry,' he said.

'What do you want?' said the woman through the window.

'Nothing. I was just wondering why someone's in the Centre this late.'

'The Centre?'

'The Day Centre,' said Garibaldi, pointing at the building.

'This isn't the Day Centre,' said the woman.

'Really?'

Garibaldi stepped back and looked up at the building, as if he needed confirmation.

'I don't understand,' he said, moving back close to the window. 'You're in the Day Centre, aren't you?'

'Are you snooping?'

'No. I'm—'

'If you don't go away, I'll call the police.'

'No need to do that. I'm only—'

'I know your sort,' said the woman, 'and I've been told what to do. Call the police, and that's what I'm going to do right now.'

Garibaldi reached for his warrant card and held it up to the window as the woman reached for the net curtains.

'I am the police, madam,' he said.

'What's that?' said the woman, peering through the glass at the card. 'Could be anything.'

'Believe me, madam,' said Garibaldi. 'I really am a policeman, a detective and I really was only curious. Look, can we have a word and I can explain?'

'How do I know you're who you say you are? You could be anyone pretending to be a policeman and then I let you in and who knows what might happen?'

'It's difficult talking through a window. Can you maybe open a door and I can explain?'

The woman looked at Garibaldi, as if trying to work out how much of a risk opening a door might be.

'My doors are on a chain,' said the woman. 'Both front and back. That's what I was told to do.'

'OK,' said Garibaldi. 'You keep the chain on and we'll talk at the door. I promise I'll keep my distance.'

The woman looked like she was still risk-evaluating.

'OK,' she said. 'I'll open the back door.'

She pulled the net curtains and walked away from the window. Garibaldi stood back and waited.

A key turned in a door to the right of the window and Garibaldi moved towards it, making sure he was several yards away.

The door opened and the woman looked out over the chain that held it.

Garibaldi could see her more clearly now. The suspicious eyes belonged to an elderly woman, late seventies, early eighties.

Garibaldi held up his card again. 'This is probably too far away for you to read properly, but here it is, and I'm Detective Inspector Garibaldi of the Metropolitan Police. And you are . . .?'

'Why do you need to know my name?'

'OK,' said Garibaldi. 'Maybe I don't, but all I'd like to do is apologise for coming up to your window like that and giving you such a shock. I'm really sorry. As I said, I thought the light was coming from the Day Centre and I was surprised to see someone in there this late.'

'Well, as I told you, this isn't the Day Centre.'

'I see.' Garibaldi stepped back and looked either side of the door and up at the roof. 'So if it's not the Day Centre what is it?'

'It's my home. This is my cottage.'

'Really? I had no idea.'

'It's always been here. Been here for centuries. I've looked up the history. The Day Centre used to be the village school, Barnes National School founded in 1850, and this cottage was the headteacher's house. It all looks like one building but this is a separate house. The front door's round the other side and this is the back door.'

How could Garibaldi have walked past this building so many times and not realised this? Why had he always assumed the cottage-like building was part of the Centre?

'How long have you been living here, Mrs . . .?'

The woman screwed up her eyes as she peered at Garibaldi over the chain. 'I don't think I should give you my name, should I?'

Garibaldi held up his hand. 'That's fine but, out of interest, could you tell me how long you've been living here?'

'I live by myself, you know, that's why . . .'

'I understand.'

'I moved in only a couple of weeks ago. The place had been empty for some time and it's a long story, but, yes, a couple of weeks ago and I'm still trying to sort things out. My children have been very good. They live close, you see, so that's why I've moved here and they've been very good about settling me in and making sure I'm safe. But, you know, I do worry . . .'

'Perfectly natural, and I'm sorry to have given you such a shock.'

'They're getting me cameras,' said the woman, 'but they're taking time. So all I've got at the moment are those doorbell things . . .'

'Doorbell things?'

The woman put her hand under the chain and pointed at the doorpost.

'Camera things in the doorbell. The children said they were good and they'll help until I can have some proper ones. They said I can have them on all the time front and back so that if anything happens, like someone coming up to your window and peering in at night . . .'

Garibaldi wasn't listening. His eyes had followed the woman's finger and were fixed on the doorbell.

A doorbell camera.

Surely not.

He turned away from the door and looked ahead.

He was looking into the gap in the hedge that led to the bench.

46

'What is it, boss?'

Gardner stood in front of Garibaldi's desk.

Garibaldi pointed at his computer screen. 'There's something I want to show you.'

Gardner came round the desk and stood at Garibaldi's shoulder. He pressed a key and an image appeared on the screen.

Gardner leaned closer. 'Where's this?'

'It's a view from the side of Barnes Green Day Centre,' said Garibaldi. 'A night-time view.'

'What's going on?' said Gardner.

'Nothing yet,' said Garibaldi. 'Wait.'

A few seconds later, two figures appeared from the right, walking together towards a gap in the hedge.

Garibaldi pressed pause and pointed at the frozen image. 'Recognise them?'

Gardner peered closer. 'One of them looks like Liam Allerton.'

'Right. And what about the other one?'

'It's not clear. You can't really see.'

'OK. Take a look at this.' Garibaldi pressed play and the

two figures carried on walking. When they reached the gap in the hedge the one with Allerton turned their head directly to the camera.

Garibaldi pressed pause again. 'Now what do you think?'

'Can you make it bigger?'

'Bigger?' Garibaldi's hand hovered uncertainly over the keyboard.

'Let me,' said Gardner, leaning over to press a few keys. The face enlarged.

'Clear enough now?' said Garibaldi.

Gardner nodded. 'Yeah, that's pretty clear.'

Garibaldi pointed at the bottom of the screen. 'Look at the date. The Saturday of his talk. And look at the time.'

'11.08.' said Gardner. 'So after Allerton left the pub.'

'Exactly.'

'Do we see them coming out?'

'No,' said Garibaldi. 'All we have is them going through the gap in the hedge that leads to the bench beside Barnes Pond, right next to where Allerton's body was found the next morning.'

'Is this CCTV?'

'Doorbell camera. Did you know that the Day Centre used to be the village school? At the back of it's what used to be the headteacher's house. Someone lives there.'

'And we missed it? What the f—'

'Exactly.'

'But that's ridiculous. How could they miss it? What were they doing?'

Garibaldi spread his arms. 'Bigger mistakes may have been made in the history of policing, but even so.'

Gardner looked at the screen, scratching her head. 'But this doesn't *prove* anything, does it?'

336

'It doesn't prove anything,' said Garibaldi, 'but it gives us something to work with. And it fits.'

'How does it fit?'

'I've got a theory,' said Garibaldi.

He pointed at a seat. Gardner pulled it up and sat down beside him.

When Garibaldi had finished explaining his theory Gardner said nothing for a few seconds, then pursed her lips and gave a slow nod.

'OK,' she said. 'But you're putting a lot of weight on that image. As I said, it doesn't prove anything.'

'But it's them, isn't it? You can tell.'

'But is it enough to make it stick?'

'It's better than anything else we've got.'

'It still could have been someone else. Just because you see them going through that gap, heading for the bench doesn't mean ... do we see anyone come back through that gap?'

'That's it. Whoever left that place left by a different route. And next morning Allerton's body's found in the pond right next to that spot. It fits. Everything fits.'

They both sat in front of the screen, looking at the enlarged frozen face, saying nothing for a few moments.

'The trouble is ...' Gardner let the thought trail off.

'The trouble is what?'

'No, it's nothing.'

Garibaldi leaned in front of Gardner's line of vision. 'Tell me, Milly. The trouble is what?'

Gardner kept her eyes on the screen. 'That theory you had about Felicity Allerton writing the novel. It all seemed to fit then as well, didn't it?'

It wasn't a criticism. It was a fact, and Garibaldi nodded his agreement. 'You're right,' he said. 'That's the thing about theories. Sometimes you get them wrong, sometimes you get them right. But the important thing is to keep coming up with them.'

'OK,' said Gardner, 'so where do we go next?'

'I think that's pretty clear, don't you?'

47

G aribaldi sat in Interview Room 2, looking across the table at Ollie Masters and his solicitor.

'Perhaps we can begin on the Saturday night, Ollie. You told us that you left your brother's in Winchester at 11.00 pm but your brother seems to remember you leaving earlier than that. ANPR cameras have picked up your car at various stages along the route to London, confirming that you did indeed leave much earlier than you told us. The closest camera to Winchester was near Farnborough and that clocked you at about 9.50 so by our reckoning you must have left your brother's at about 9.00. Two hours' difference.'

'Are you sure I said I left at 11.00 ?' said Ollie.

'Absolutely sure,' said Garibaldi.

'Maybe I made a mistake. Slip of the tongue. Easily done.'

'You were very specific about the time, Ollie, because you were explaining why you couldn't make Liam's talk at the Book Festival.'

'I don't understand. Whether I left at 9.00 or 11.00 makes no difference. Either way I wouldn't have made it back in time for his talk.'

'And you drove straight back to Fulham?'

'That's right.'

'Really? A camera at the junction of the Upper Richmond Road and Rocks Lane picks you up at 10.11 pm. What's strange, though, is that the camera where we would next expect you to be picked up – one on the other side of Putney Bridge – has no record of your car. Which is puzzling.'

'I don't understand,' said Ollie. 'What are you saying?'

'I'm saying that not only do we have proof that you left Winchester considerably earlier than you originally told us, we also have proof that you didn't, as you claim, go back to your home in Fulham. My guess is that when you passed the camera at the junction on the Upper Richmond Road you didn't go straight on but you took a left up Rocks Lane. We don't have anything on the camera at the top of Rocks Lane at the Red Lion junction but that's because you turned off and parked well before that. In fact, you probably parked somewhere near Barnes Common and walked the rest of the way. Is this ringing a bell, Ollie?'

'I've no idea what you're talking about.'

'I reckon you must have arrived in Barnes at about 10.30 pm. That's when you gave Felicity Allerton a call. It's on her mobile phone records and we've checked with Felicity. She says you were ringing on your way back from Winchester to ask how the talk went and I'm sure she's right. You probably did ask how the talk went. But you also used the call to find out where Liam was, didn't you? You wanted to know because of what you intended to do. You didn't want to call Liam himself – you knew that would show up, so you called Felicity instead. You didn't expect her to say she'd gone home before Liam, but that all played into your hands, didn't it? She told you Liam was still at the Sun

Inn drinking with friends. So all you had to do was get to Barnes Pond and wait for your moment.'

'None of this is true,' said Ollie. 'Not a word of it.'

'What is it then? Fiction? A bit like *Schooled in Murder* perhaps?'

Ollie shook his head.

'The truth is it's more than a bit like *Schooled in Murder*, isn't it?' said Garibaldi. 'It's very like it. You had a drink prepared, spiked with Rohypnol. You waited on the other side of the road and then, when Liam came out of the pub you went up to him, said you'd tried to get back to have a drink with him, sorry you were late et cetera. I don't know how you led him round to that side of the pond and how you got him to drink whatever you had. Maybe you offered a toast to his success. You may even have sat on that bench while you drank it. And then when the Rohypnol kicked in you did it. You strangled him and rolled him into the pond.'

Garibaldi raised his eyebrows, inviting Ollie to say something.

Ollie gave a wry smile. 'You're making this up.'

'You may think it's fiction, Ollie, but it's not. You killed Liam Allerton in exactly the same way Alex Ballantyne was killed in *Schooled in Murder*. You gave him a drink spiked with Rohypnol, put on gloves, strangled him and rolled him into the pond.'

Ollie gave a disbelieving laugh and shook his head again.

Garibaldi leaned forward and rested his elbows on the table. 'You wanted it all to look as though Liam was killed because of his book. Those notes you found in Liam's study. You moved them – gloves again – to the back of his bottom drawer, didn't you? To make it look as though he was hiding them, to add to the suspicion that Liam might have been doing the same as the victim in his novel – blackmailing colleagues at St Mark's.'

'This is nonsense.'

'Is it? What about those notes you sent to the teachers? You put a lot of painstaking work into them, didn't you? Must have taken you hours. And you knew exactly who to send them to because Liam told you about his little code. The trouble was, though, that Liam had only told you about one of his little codes. You didn't know he'd swapped the secrets around, did you?'

'I have no idea what you're talking about.'

'Exactly. You had no idea that Liam had played another trick in his book, so you sent notes to the wrong people. But never mind, it kept the focus on the book. The same with the graffiti. You checked out the CCTV for that one, didn't you, and chose your time in the middle of the night very carefully. And just in case anyone drove past or saw you I should think you had a cap and a hoodie. Anyway, nice work. "The Ironic Death of Ben Joseph". Again, it had everyone going back to the book. And then, finally, the note to Felicity. "I know what your husband did – that's why I killed him". You spelled it out this time. What did Liam do? He wrote *Schooled in Murder*. You made it clear that Liam was killed because of his book. But it all went a bit wrong there didn't it, Ollie? You wanted to frighten Felicity but not so much that she would run away to Littlehampton without telling anyone.'

Garibaldi fixed Ollie with a steady gaze.

Ollie turned his head away. 'You've got it wrong,' he said.

'I don't think so. What's strange about that note is that you knew it was in ransom-note lettering just like the other notes. How did you know that, Ollie?'

Ollie looked momentarily confused. 'How did I know? She told me.'

'Did she? She doesn't remember telling you. She didn't even notice the cut-out letters. She was more concerned with what they said. Yet somehow you knew. But there's an easy explanation, isn't there? You knew what that note looked like because you sent it.'

Garibaldi leaned back in his chair and said nothing.

Ollie was the first to break the silence. 'Do you want to hear the truth?'

'I'm all ears.'

'The truth is you can prove none of this. Not one word. It's all speculation, a work of your imagination.'

'That's where you're wrong. You'd decided to kill Liam in the most fitting way – straight out of the pages of that novel. Exactly the same method and exactly the same location. And I'm sure you checked out that location carefully for any cameras that could catch you. None on the Day Centre. None on houses bordering the pond or at least none that would reach. But you missed something, Ollie. The cottage annexed to the Day Centre. No CCTV but something on both the front and back door. A doorbell camera. A lot of them around now and I'm surprised you didn't look for them. Or maybe I'm not surprised, given that our house-to-house inquiries somehow managed to miss it as well. Anyway, the one on the back door to this cottage looks out on that gap in the hedge that leads to that bench, the one where you probably sat with Liam and offered him your spiked drink before strangling him. We haven't got footage of you actually *doing* that but we do have a clear picture of you walking with Liam through the gap in that hedge at 11.08 pm. Would you like to see it?'

Ollie said nothing.

'For the recording the suspect is now being shown

343

doorbell camera footage recorded on the back entrance of Oak Cottage at 11.08 pm.'

Garibaldi looked at Ollie watching the footage. His face had lost its colour, his mouth had tightened in a thin-lipped frown.

'Pretty clear, isn't it?' said Garibaldi when the recording ended. 'As I said, it doesn't show you killing him but it does show that you were there. So the question is what were you doing there, with Liam, right next to the part of the pond where his body was discovered the next morning?'

A long silence followed. Garibaldi tried to catch Ollie's eye but he avoided his gaze. He leaned forward, put his elbows on the table and rested his forehead on clenched fists. Several times he raised his head and opened his mouth as if he were about to say something, but each time no words came and he looked blankly at Garibaldi before returning his head to his fists.

'What were you doing there, Ollie?'

Another long silence.

Ollie raised his head again and this time he spoke. 'I can explain.'

He took a couple of deep breaths to steady himself 'When Marion died . . .'

'Your wife?'

Ollie nodded. 'When she died there was a lot to do, a lot of things to go through. There always is when someone dies. And there was a lot of Marion's stuff. Personal stuff. Some of it I dealt with, but some of it I couldn't face, so I put it away. Difficult, isn't it? You want to be reminded of everything about the one you've lost, of course you do. You don't want to lose those things that will remind you of them. They're precious, but they're also painful. So I kept it all, but I put it away. I knew where it was and I knew it was safe. Then, a couple of months ago, I decided I wanted to go through it all – no, more than that, I felt the *need* to go through it all. I felt strong enough. I felt ready. So I did it.'

He closed his eyes and winced, as if the memory was causing physical pain. 'And then I found them.'

'What did you find?' said Garibaldi.

'Books.'

'What kind of books?'

'Books you write for yourself,' said Ollie. 'Books you write things in that you often don't want others to see.'

'You mean diaries?'

Ollie nodded. 'She had loads of them, going back to before we were married. I didn't know whether to open them or not but I did. They weren't full of intimate feelings and thoughts, nothing like that. They were mainly reminders and records of things. Appointments. Events. Birthdays. Holidays. Things we did. And when I started to read them I was surprised at the comfort they gave. They reminded me of things we'd done together, of happy times. But then I noticed something. I didn't see it at first, but when I did I started going back through them again. And I kept seeing it. A letter. A tiny letter in the corner of certain days. And when I looked at the dates over the years when that letter appeared it didn't take long to work out what it meant. A tiny letter. That's all it was.'

Ollie covered his face with his hands.

'What was it?' said Garibaldi.

'L. That was it. The letter "L". A tiny letter "L".'

'What did it mean?'

Ollie threw back his head and laughed – a loud laugh, close to hysterical. 'What did it mean? Well, it didn't take Bletchley Fucking Park to work that one out did it? L for Liam. I thought I'd never feel pain like the pain I felt when

Marion died but I was wrong. When I saw that letter, when I realised what it meant – that's when the real pain began. The pain of betrayal.'

He said nothing, as if no further explanation were needed. Garibaldi waited.

'And there he was,' said Ollie eventually, 'banging on about his fucking book. That fucking book! He was so full of it, couldn't stop himself talking about it. And he'd told me things about it before it was published. What he'd learned about his colleagues at St Mark's, what he'd done with their names. He even showed me the blackmail notes he'd mocked up. So that's why. I mean, what better cover could there be? Have everyone looking at his fucking crime novel when it had nothing to do with it.'

Garibaldi leaned forward. 'Are you saying—?'

Ollie held up his hand to stop him.

'It went to his head, that book. It changed him, and the more it changed him the more I thought of him and Marion, the more I felt everything I'd ever believed in had gone. There he was, prancing around giving talks about his novel, basking in all that glory and all the time, over the years, he'd been ... I wanted revenge. It was burning me up, consuming me – and suddenly it came to me. What better way to cover it than with his ridiculous book?'

Ollie stopped, gave a little chuckle, and gave Garibaldi a knowing smile.

'Everything had you looking at the book, didn't it? Exactly what I had in mind. It was my cover. My book cover. Who do you think was leaking it to the press? And always with a focus on the book. And that note – do you see what I did there? "I know what he did". Had everyone thinking it was about the book, just like everything else.

But that one came from the heart. "I know what he did". Not write *Schooled in Murder*. No. Something else entirely.'

'OK,' said Garibaldi, 'and that note also said "that's why I killed him". So —'

'If he hadn't written it this might never have happened. I might have done something. I don't know what, but it would have been different. And if I hadn't read her diaries ... dangerous thing reading, isn't it?'

Garibaldi looked at the broken man on the other side of the table, trying to imagine what emotions had driven him to do it. Grief. Betrayal. Envy. Revenge.

Or was it more general than that? A sense that maybe there was nothing more to live for, that whatever game you'd been playing had ended, and that you'd lost?

48

'Cheers!'

Deighton clinked her glass of wine against Garibaldi's.

'And good work.'

Garibaldi took a sip of his wine and glanced round the bar. 'Funny thing, isn't it?' he said. 'Nearly one in five homes has one and most people think their main use is to post footage of Amazon porch thieves on Nextdoor Digest.'

'How the hell did we miss it? Under our noses the whole time and house-to-house doesn't pick it up!'

'It was unoccupied for well over a year and she only moved in a couple of weeks ago.'

Deighton's face showed she was having none of it. 'It's virtually part of the bloody crime scene! The forensics tent almost touched its walls. Unbelievable!'

'I've walked past that place millions of times and I had no idea the back of the building was residential.'

'Are you making excuses for them?'

'No. I—'

'It's not great, is it?'

'No, not great.' Garibaldi took a sip of his wine. 'But the important thing is we've got a result.'

'Yeah, we've got a result.'

'And the funny thing is we were both right, weren't we?'

'In what way?'

'We kept saying we needed to lift our eyes from the pages, look beyond the book. We were being played.'

'Yeah, maybe we were.'

'And talking of playing . . .' Deighton moved her glass to one side and leaned forward, resting her elbows on the table and her chin on her fists. 'Let's talk about you.'

It was as Garibaldi had feared. When he last went out for a drink with Deighton over a year ago – in this same discreet, sophisticated bar – the evening had turned into one of unexpected revelations. He could remember every detail – the way Deighton had spoken of his 'charming eccentricities', citing his habit of quoting writers and his preference for the bicycle, and had pressed him on the real reasons behind his inability to drive. It still amazed Garibaldi that he had revealed the truth – that ever since he lost his parents in a car crash he had been overwhelmed by panic and flashbacks whenever he sat behind a wheel. And it still amazed him that Deighton had chosen that evening to tell him about her partner, Abigail.

'How are you?' said Deighton. 'Still thinking of chucking it all in and going off to university?'

Garibaldi laughed. 'Still thinking of it, but not sure I could afford it. More to the point, I'm not sure how it would work out with Rachel.'

'Ah, yes. Rachel. Funny that we're both living with teachers, isn't it?'

'It is,' said Garibaldi, 'though after reading *Schooled in Murder* I've looked at Rachel sometimes and wondered whether it's such a good idea . . .'

'Really?'

Garibaldi shook his head and laughed. 'I'm joking. Things are good with us.' He paused for a few seconds. 'How are things with Abigail?'

Deighton gave an embarrassed smile. Garibaldi thought he could detect a blush.

'Actually, I've got news on that front.'

'About Abigail?'

'Yes.'

'Is everything OK?'

'We're getting married.'

'Wow!' Garibaldi raised his glass. 'Well, congratulations! That's great news.'

'I haven't told anyone else at work yet, so you're the first.'

'I'm honoured. And I'm delighted.'

'Thanks,' said Deighton, reaching for her glass. 'They can get a bad press, teachers, can't they?'

'They can,' said Garibaldi, trying to shake off a thought that had entered his head and was showing no signs of leaving, 'but it looks like we might have found ourselves a couple of good ones.'

49

A new term was about to begin at St Mark's, and the staff had gathered in school the day before the pupils' return. Harry Reed stood at a lectern at the front of the hall.

'Welcome back everyone. I trust we all had a refreshing summer break and that we're all ready for the challenges of a new academic year. We have much to talk about this morning, not least a spectacular set of GCSE and A Level results. But I'd like to begin by going back to the beginning of the summer holidays when we were all shocked to hear of the murder of Liam Allerton, whom most of you here will remember. He taught Maths at St Mark's for nearly thirty years and then, after he retired, to everyone's surprise, he published a crime novel under the pseudonym of Ben Joseph. There was some speculation at the time over whether he had based the school in his novel on this one and such speculation increased after Liam was murdered in a way that drew everyone's attention back to his book. As you may have read, a man has been charged with Liam's murder. Let's hope justice is served and that it can bring some comfort to Liam's wife and daughter who have been made aware of the school's best wishes and support at every stage of this sorry business. Let us hope the chapter, if I can borrow a literary metaphor, is now closed. And now, as I said, some outstanding exam results . . .'

As Harry Reed spoke his eyes scanned the teaching staff. It came as a huge relief, now that the police investigation was over, to think he would no longer have to concern himself with the secrets they might be hiding.

'We continue to go from strength to strength,' he said, preparing himself for the juiciest part of his address: the drive towards needs-blind access, the opening-up of the school to those of all backgrounds, a return to the vision of the school's founders. 'But as we do, we need to be mindful of the wider world, we need to shift our eyes beyond our own walls, cease congratulating ourselves on what we have achieved, and think of the bigger picture . . .'

Armit Harwal had listened closely when the head was speaking about the police investigation into Liam Allerton's murder but now that he had moved on to exam results he wasn't taking in a word of what he was saying. It was good to be back, comforting to have the chance to immerse himself again in familiar routine. No new school year had ever held for him such a sense of a new beginning and a chance to move on. He glanced round the room to see where Ruth was sitting. There she was. She caught his eye and returned a smile. Nothing flirtatious in it – just a smile. The split, even if it had been more her idea than his, had been a good idea.

He felt his phone vibrate in his pocket. He discreetly edged it out and craned his neck to sneak a look.

A message from DI Garibaldi, saying he needed to talk.

What was going on? The case was closed. They had their man. Why would the detective need to see him again?

*

Ruth Price caught Armit's eye briefly and looked away. Maybe now she could move on from all her mistakes, Armit included, and leave the past behind. Nothing had come of the investigation and although she couldn't be confident that the threat had disappeared, she hoped the arrest of the man charged with Liam's murder might bring that over-used word – closure. Maybe she'd got away with it.

She heard her phone vibrating in her bag on the floor. She bent down, opened it and sneaked a look.

DI Garibaldi.

Ewan Thomas looked round at the assembled staff. He had spent the summer more quietly than he had planned to but he was glad he had. It seemed the storm might have passed and the weeks and months ahead might bring calm. Never again he told himself. He was content with one identity – his other had been put to rest.

His phone vibrated in his pocket.

He waited for a few seconds and then pulled the phone out of his pocket to take a look.

DI Garibaldi wanted to see him again.

Sasha Ambrose listened to Harry Reed praising the staff for their contribution to the school's best ever exam results and resolved never to do it again. The whole thing had been a nightmare and she had, ironically for a teacher, learned her lesson. She would get the help she needed and this time her resolution would stick. She glanced round the room, look- ing for the others – Armit, Ruth and Ewan. Did they know about her in the same way that she knew about them? Even if they hadn't worked out Liam's code, how could they not have some idea of what was going on?

Still, they had got away with it. Liam's killer had been found and the case was closed.

Perhaps they could now forget about *Schooled in Fucking Murder* and get on with their lives.

She felt her phone vibrate in her pocket, but decided not to see who it was.

Whatever they wanted, she was sure they could wait.

50

Garibaldi sat in the Bush Theatre bar with Alfie. It was September, the first home game of the season and the air was fresh with the crazy optimism familiar to all football fans, even those who supported QPR. Maybe this might be their year. Get back into the Premiership. Have a cup run. Rekindle the spirit of 1975–6, or the magic of that Bobby Zamora Wembley moment in 2014. Before a ball had been kicked in earnest anything was possible – it was like clutching a lottery ticket before the balls had dropped.

Garibaldi raised his glass. 'Cheers,' he said. 'To a new season.'

'A new season,' said Alfie.

They sipped their beers and put down their glasses.

'So,' said Garibaldi. 'How's Alicia?'

'Alicia? She's fine. No, she's more than fine. How's Rachel?'

Garibaldi looked out of the window at the crowd heading down the Uxbridge Road and turned back to Alfie.

'Rachel's fine, thanks. In fact, she's more than fine.'

'Thanks again for putting me up like that.'

'No problem. You're welcome any time. You know the score.'

Alfie laughed. 'Yeah, we'll probably lose three – nil.'

'You know what I mean.'

'Yeah, sure. But I know it was a bit crowded. It can't have been easy for either of you.'

'Rachel loved having you there.'

'I see, so you didn't?'

'Of course I did. I'm glad you came. Any word from Putney?'

'I speak to Mum a bit.'

'Good.'

'But nothing from Dom,' said Alfie. 'He's gone strangely silent on all fronts.'

Garibaldi looked round the Bush bar. The few QPR fans who came here before the game, colours hidden to fit in with the theatre matinee crowd, were beginning to leave.

'And the bookshop?' said Garibaldi, finishing his drink. 'How's it working out?'

'I love it,' said Alfie.

'That's great.'

'Yeah. Could be my thing. I'm getting better with the customers, dealing with their questions, making recommendations, that kind of thing.'

'You make recommendations do you?'

'Yeah, someone will come in and say "what do you recommend for a six-year-old girl who likes animals", or "what should I get for someone who's into witches". All kinds of crazy questions, but you get the hang of it.'

'I see,' said Garibaldi, 'so what would you recommend for a detective pushing fifty, into football and country music?'

Alfie laughed. 'I'd ask for a few more details. What kind of stuff does he read?'

'What does he read? Novels mainly.'

'Any kind of novels in particular?'

'He'll read anything so long as it's good.'

'Well, in that case—'

Garibaldi held up his hand.

'When I say anything there is one exception.'

'What's that?'

'Crime. He's not too keen on crime.'

Garibaldi pointed at his watch. They stood up, gulped down their drinks, took their scarves out of their pockets and headed out of the Bush to join the match-bound crowd.

Acknowledgements

Thanks to: Laura Macdougall and Olivia Davies at United Agents, Sarah Beal and Kate Beal at Muswell Press, Venetia Vyvyan and all at the Barnes Bookshop, Fiona Brownlee, Laura McFarlane, Graham Bartlett.

Special thanks, as ever, to Jo, and special thoughts, as ever, of Caitlin.